AVID

READER

PRESS

ALSO BY EMILY GOULD

Friendship

And the Heart Says Whatever

PERFECT TUNES

A NOVEL

EMILY GOULD

AVID READER PRESS

New York London Toronto Sydney New Delhi

AVID READER PRESS
An Imprint of Simon & Schuster, Inc.
1230 Avenue of the Americas
New York, NY 10020

First Avid Reader Press hardcover edition April 2020

AVID READER PRESS and colophon are
trademarks of Simon & Schuster, Inc.

For information about special discounts for bulk purchases,
please contact Simon & Schuster Special Sales at 1-866-506-1949
or business@simonandschuster.com.

The Simon & Schuster Speakers Bureau can bring authors to
your live event. For more information or to book an event, contact
the Simon & Schuster Speakers Bureau at 1-866-248-3049
or visit our website at www.simonspeakers.com.

Interior design by Kyle Kabel

Manufactured in the United States of America

1   3   5   7   9   10   8   6   4   2

Library of Congress Cataloging-in-Publication Data has been applied for.

ISBN 978-1-5011-9749-9
ISBN 978-1-5011-9751-2 (ebook)

For my mother
and her mother

PART I

PART I

1

When Laura was sixteen she wrote a perfect song. It was the first song she'd ever written, so she didn't understand how hard it was to write even an okay song, or how hard it was to make anything new, in general. She still thought, then, that making something was primarily a way to have fun. She didn't know that the song was perfect, just that it was as good as anything on the radio. She played it on her guitar alone in her bedroom, and then for her best friend, Callie, and then for her mother. Her mother made an approving noise and went back to paying attention to one of Laura's brothers. Callie asked where she'd heard it and didn't believe her when she said she'd written it, because it was the kind of song that sounds like it has always existed. Laura started to think that she must have heard it somewhere and remembered it. She hadn't, though. She had written it.

The next day she wrote another song: this one wasn't perfect; it wasn't even okay; it was barely a song. This convinced Laura that the first song hadn't really been hers. She was embarrassed about the whole thing, and so she pretended to herself that it hadn't happened. She didn't think about that first song again for years, and by the time she remembered, it was almost too late.

———

Now, at twenty-two, she stood in line outside a bar on the corner of Lafayette and Grand, sweating through a black dress that was absorbing all the heat of the midday sun. The other women in line were also wearing black, and some of them clutched the page of the *Village Voice* where the help-wanted ad had appeared. Some had printed out their résumés. Laura had never worked in a bar or restaurant. In Columbus, she'd worked selling cheap electric guitars to teenage boys at her family's shop, and then for a while at the Gap in the outlet mall. So she hadn't brought a résumé, but it didn't matter. A man came out and walked down the line of women, assessing each one for an instant, then made his selections.

He looked at Laura and saw the way she smiled and made eye contact with no hint of wariness in her giant dark eyes, the expression on her face constantly saying something mildly incredulous, like, "Wow, really?" He guessed correctly that she was very new here. He walked back a step, pointed to Laura and two others, and told the rest they could go home.

Laura and the other two women stepped inside and blinked as their eyes adjusted from the glaring heat and brightness of the sidewalk to the chilled darkness of the bar. It was painted black, and the banquettes were dark red velvet, meant to give an impression of luxury, but like all bars in the daytime it stank and was sad, like an empty fairground. The guy who'd chosen them started training them immediately, without even asking their names. He had no way of knowing that they even knew English—and, as it turned out, one of them, Yulia, essentially didn't—but it didn't matter, because they weren't being hired as bartenders or even waitresses. The ad had read "front-of-house staff," and their job, as the guy described it, was to greet guests at the door and usher them to a banquette in either the upper or lower section of the bar, depending on how much money they looked likely to spend. Other than that, their job was to walk around in the bar and smile and chat. They were there to provide ambiance, like the chandeliers and the nicer-brand soap in the bathroom's dispensers.

The pay was twelve dollars an hour, he said, plus sometimes the bartenders would tip them out. Twelve dollars an hour, plus (possible) tips—she would only have to work fifty-four hours a month, at most, to pay the $650 rent that her best friend and now roommate, Callie, informed her was an incredible bargain, considering their apartment's perfect location on Third between First and A. Callie had lived in New York for almost five years now, because she'd gone to college there. Callie knew everyone, had regular haunts, and would have told Laura (if she'd asked) not to take the job at Bar Lafitte, might even have been able to hook her up with a better—less gross, more lucrative—bar job, but Laura was determined not to lean too heavily on Callie. She was trying not to just let all Callie's friends become her friends by default.

Laura put her name on the schedule for a shift the next day and walked back out into the daytime, which now seemed even brighter. The blast of warm air carrying the sunbaked smells of piss and pavement felt good on her chilled bare legs and arms. She had shrunk into herself somewhat while inside the bar, and now that she was outside, she could expand fully back into her skin. She tried to ignore how relieved she felt to be out of there, and instead tried to feel happy that she now had a job. Having a job meant she would be able to afford to stay in the apartment she'd just moved into and could start making progress toward her goal: play shows, write more songs, get signed to a label, and make an album. She was going to become a professional musician. She would never go back to Columbus if she didn't want to. The next time she saw her hometown it was going to be because she was on tour.

For the past week, she'd been saying hi to people whom she saw around the neighborhood more than once, thinking maybe those people would become her friends. The rules around saying hi were very different than they had been in Columbus, she had noticed. The man behind the counter at the bodega on her corner, which sold all kinds of Cadbury candy from the UK, had seemed surprised when she'd introduced herself on her second visit. He had been reluctant to reveal his own name, as if no one had ever asked him before.

Laura had broken up with a nice but boring boyfriend in anticipation of moving, one of a series of nice boring boyfriends that had begun when she was fourteen. Chris, Jason, Alex, Jason again, Darrell. She had never been in love. She liked to always have a boyfriend whom she wasn't in love with so that she could have sex whenever she wanted and not have to worry about going on dates or having her heart broken or catching diseases. She had never been in love. She was in love with her music—she really was, and she sometimes told people so. But now she was determined to avoid even having another convenience-boyfriend. She wanted to be single, to know herself as a single person and to focus on writing songs. She listened to the Joni Mitchell album *Hejira* every day on her headphones, using a Discman that predictably skipped during her favorite track, "Song for Sharon," which was about being an adventurer and not worrying about conventional trappings of female life. In that song, someone suggests to the narrator (ostensibly Joni) that she should settle down and have children or do charity work, and Joni responds that the cure for her melancholy is actually to find herself "another lover." Laura loved that line so much.

––––––

It was nice to have the validation of getting a job, even a very easy bar job. Laura hadn't gotten a lot of ego boosts lately, or actually ever. She had never been a great student, but she would often make up the distance between a C and a B by writing poems for extra credit, like the one about the Bill of Rights she'd written in eighth grade that rhymed "probable cause" with "due process clause." Though she had changed in a few crucial ways since then, she still loved doggerel and patter and songs with complicated, weird, funny lyrics. She had gone to Ohio State University and studied English lit and spent a lot of time alone in her room with her acoustic guitar. Occasionally at an open-mic night she would play her songs for other people, who clapped politely and came up to her afterward and thought that she would consider being compared to Weird Al a compliment, which it sort of was, though she would have preferred to be compared to the Moldy Peaches.

In New York, she thought as she walked south down the darkening cavern of Lafayette, people would "get" what she was trying to do with her music, although she had to admit that she didn't always "get" it herself all the time. She described her music's genre as "anti-folk" when she had to call it anything. Her best song, or the one that audiences typically liked best, was a sort of mock ballad about a breakup called "I Want My Tapes Back," in which she rhymed "I hope you know where they are" with "under the seat of your car."

Her father had been a professional musician at one point in his life. He had gone on tour with the Allman Brothers and had played on two of their albums; Laura had cherished a record sleeve that had his name in tiny print in a long list of credits. Then he had come back to Ohio, married her mom and had three kids—two boys and Laura—and opened a guitar store. He had died when Laura was ten, in a car accident that would likely have been survivable if he'd worn a seat belt. Her mother had reacted by becoming extremely—and, Laura felt, perversely—religious. Laura had felt like the whole thing was proof that there was no God. But that wasn't how the rest of her family saw things.

She loved her mom and her two older brothers, but she often felt like she didn't quite speak the same language that they did. Words didn't quite mean, to Laura, what they meant to her mom. Most of Laura's choices—her haircuts, her plans, her friends— were "interesting." The music she liked and the songs she wrote were "funny." Still, as long as she didn't ask anyone for money, the worst her family could do was subtly disapprove. She was an adult and no one could actually prevent her from doing anything, and anyway, no one cared enough about what she was doing to try to change her mind. She was a free adult! She stretched her arms to the heavens as she walked down First Avenue, turning onto her street—her street!—then swung them back to her sides, suddenly self-conscious.

————

The key that Callie had given her didn't quite fit the lock and required delicate pressure and just the right angle. She thought of knocking but didn't want to disturb Callie if she was home. When she finally got the door open, though, Callie was sitting at their small kitchen table, so absorbed in her complicated beauty routine that she hadn't even heard the jangling in the hallway. She had her makeup all over the table and a cigarette burning in an ashtray, a tumbler full of Diet Dr Pepper and vodka next to it. It seemed incredibly bohemian to Laura that Callie smoked inside their apartment. Disgusting, but also bohemian.

Callie looked up at her, taking all of her in for a brief moment. "We're going out," she announced. "You should wear my green dress; don't wear your Ohio clothes."

Laura went into Callie's bedroom, where she extricated the dress (which wasn't exactly clean, but smelled mostly pleasantly of Callie's perfume) from the deep pile on the floor. She'd become aware within minutes of her arrival in New York of her entire wardrobe's humiliating inadequacies. Most crucially, she had the wrong kind of jeans: flared denim with no stretch, so that there was an empty crease underneath her small butt, underscoring its smallness. Callie had jeans that looked like they'd been custom-fitted to her body and that ended just millimeters from her pubic bone. She worked in a boutique and also took photographs and did makeup, and her own makeup, as always, was perfect. Like

Laura, she wanted to perform, but it wasn't clear yet what her talent was exactly. Callie could get up on a stage and everyone would pay attention, but she hadn't figured out what to do to keep that attention going. For as long as Laura had known her, Callie had always taken up to an hour to get ready to go out. When she was done with her makeup she would look like she wasn't wearing much at all; she would just look like the most dewy, ideal version of herself possible.

When Laura came out of the bedroom, Callie gave her an approving once-over. "Perfect. Okay, so we're going to see this band, and then we're going out with the band afterward," she said.

"Anyone I've heard of?"

"Maybe? They're kind of becoming a thing. They're called the Clips—I know, so stupid, but all band names sound stupid."

"So true," said Laura. "Like, Pearl Jam. Can you imagine the moment of thinking that was a good name?"

"Nirvana," said Callie, rolling her eyes.

"Nirvana is actually a good name, though."

"Forget everything you know about Nirvana for a second and then just think about the name. Aren't you expecting something with panpipes that plays in the background at a spa?"

Laura thought about it and decided that Callie, as usual, was right. Laura had gotten in the habit of trusting Callie to point them both in the right direction. Ever since they'd first met, as high school freshmen, she'd happily submitted to being Callie's protégée. True, Callie could be condescending; during that first year of their friendship, she'd coached Laura about what was cool and what wasn't in a way that was sometimes brutal, and often shifted dramatically without warning. One week it was absolutely mandatory that they both wear cutoff jean shorts and peasant blouses, but then the next week Laura showed up to school in a version of the same outfit and Callie found it so unacceptable that she made her change in the bathroom. The next trend was baggy carpenter corduroy pants and Western-wear shirts, and Callie had actually brought spare ones in her backpack to prevent Laura from suffering the humiliation of wearing last week's style one moment longer than necessary. It was mysterious and somewhat magical, the way Callie understood what would make them cool; she seemed to receive messages about it from the ether.

Back then, Laura had wondered what made Callie choose her; she'd thought maybe it had to do with her musical talent. Now that she was older she recognized that Callie had seen that Laura had the potential to be someone whose prettiness and talent burnished Callie's own. She had been the one who had decided what kind of teenager Laura would be: the kind who played guitar and smoked cigarettes in the courtyard when she should have been studying. They had both still been near the top of their class, though; their school was easy, and no one tried too hard at anything besides football. Callie was known then as an "artist," monopolizing the art classroom's darkroom to enlarge giant black-and-white photographs of her own face.

"Your face is fun to put makeup on," she had said one night when they were in Callie's bedroom getting ready to go to a party (upperclassmen, parents out of town). Callie's own face, already anointed with glitter that smelled like vanilla cake, hovered close to Laura's as she dabbed something cool onto Laura's eyelids with a velvety-damp wand. "I can make you look however I want you to look."

Laura wasn't an idiot. She understood, even at fifteen, that this would always be a good friendship exactly to the extent that she wanted to be molded. But also, taking responsibility for her own self-presentation felt, mostly, like work she could happily outsource. And Laura wasn't purely Callie's sidekick, or at least, like most good sidekicks, she could take over as the heroine if the situation demanded it. Once, junior year, they had been driving around aimlessly in Callie's rusted-out old car, talking about nothing and singing along to the radio. Then the car had broken down. They weren't far outside of town, but neither of them recognized their immediate surroundings; it soon became clear that they were really lost, and it was cold out. The joint they'd smoked had not helped. At first it was kind of an adventure. Then as they kept walking, getting colder, talking about how maybe they should flag someone down to help them and deal with the consequences if that person happened to be a serial killer or a molester, it became less of one. It was Laura who spotted the first recognizable landmark. She turned up a side street that led to a gas station and dealt with the details of getting a tow truck and a ride back to her house, where she made Callie a cup of tea and put her to bed in the upper bunk of the bunkbeds in her still-childish bedroom.

The only flaw in Callie's plan for Laura was that it had failed to take Laura's mom's finances into account; though they'd both gotten into NYU, Callie's family was willing and able to pay for it, while Laura's family—reasonably, Laura thought—refused to let her take out enormous loans when she could go to a good school much closer to home. She had feared that they would lose touch once Callie was in the city. But Callie was not the kind of person who would leave a project unfinished. They also both found that it was hard to create the kind of easy intimacy they had with each other with anyone else. They had a legacy of secrets and inside jokes. Combined, they were more powerful than they were apart. So when the roommate who'd been in the second "bedroom" of Callie's apartment moved out to live with her boyfriend, she'd called up Laura and told her there was a spot for her, if she had $650 and wanted to move to New York and claim it. She did.

"So how do you know . . . the Clips?" Laura asked as Callie circled her, tweaking the hem of the dress, smoothing stray pieces of her dark hair into a half-up, half-down situation.

"I had a class with the drummer once, and then I saw them play a few weeks ago at another thing and afterward I went backstage, etcetera."

"Etcetera?"

Callie shrugged and continued. "It seems like musicians are the people you should know, right? Plus, they're all hot."

"I'm looking for people who can help me book shows, not boys to hook up with. And don't ask why can't I do both—you know I'm not good at multitasking."

Callie laughed. "I forgot about your vow of celibacy."

"I'll have plenty of time to slut it up when I'm famous. I mean, when I've accomplished something."

"What are you going to write songs about in the meantime, though, if not love? Or at least sex?"

Callie's desire to basically pimp Laura out had always been a little bit tiresome. Laura tried to distract her. "I wrote a song about egg sandwiches this morning. Want to hear it?"

Without waiting for Callie to respond, Laura put down her drink and grabbed her guitar from the other room. " 'Bacon, egg, and cheese on a roll,' " she sang. " 'Or sometimes just egg and cheese. In a greasy paper sleeve, I eat you on the street.' " She played a few more lines and then noodled around a little bit. "I'm still trying to figure out the chorus," she admitted.

Callie scrunched up her nose. "I don't think that one is going to be climbing the charts." She motioned for Laura to come sit by her near the makeup mirror. Laura put down her guitar and complied.

A few minutes later Callie finished doing Laura's hair and stepped away from her quickly, as though preventing herself from continuing to fiddle with and potentially ruin a perfect creation. They both looked at Laura's reflection in the mirror for a moment with satisfaction.

Something about Laura's looks hadn't made sense in the context of their hometown. To be pretty there, you had to be symmetrical, straight-haired, and small-nosed, ideally white, ideally blond. Within those parameters, you could be pretty or just blandly palatable, like a pat of butter on a squishy dinner roll. Laura's big eyes and off-kilter nose made her look different from different angles, which made figuring out whether she was attractive too confusing for the consumers of the buttered rolls. But with the city as her backdrop, she was starting to make more sense. She didn't have the perfumed, deliberate, and commanding hotness of a Callie. But in their dim apartment, backlit by the lamp Callie kept next to her futon mattress on the floor, she had the look of an ingénue about to step onstage, lit with an anticipatory glow.

———

The band was playing at one of the terrible bars on Bleecker Street unofficially reserved for NYU students and tourists. There were booths and tables, and a waitress in tall black boots who smelled like patchouli came around and sloshed red wine into their glasses from a giant bottle with no label. It tasted like the smell of the industrial-strength cleaner that whoever mopped the hallways of their building used in order to push the ancient dirt around. After a few sips, though, it grew on them. Though the lighting left the musicians in a pool of dimness, Laura stared at them. Specifically, the guitar player. She hoped that he wasn't the one who Callie had etcetera'd. He reminded her of a boy from her hometown who'd played Jesus in a high school production of *Godspell*, skinny and tall with long, pale stringy hair, and he never ever looked up from his guitar. His arm muscles were ropy and hard, and there were holes in his stained white T-shirt. He looked incredibly sad. Suddenly Laura was embarrassed to realize that she was imagining what it would be like to have sex with him. Embarrassed because it was so cliché, and because her imaginings were immediately so vivid and compelling.

The music he was playing, which she almost had to remind herself to notice, was objectively good but not in a way that Laura actually liked. She forced herself to admire his technical skills so that, if she met the guitarist, she could tell him about what she liked in a detailed way and impress him with her musician bona fides. The waitress refilled their wineglasses. Then the band took a break and everyone went outside for cigarettes. Callie put her head close to Laura's as she lit her cigarette, leaning in so far that her hair brushed Laura's face.

"So?" she asked. "You seemed into it."

"I'm not really a fan of this kind of . . . purposely distorted, less-catchy Television-song thing. It's just really heterosexual and derivative," she was saying as the short black-haired drummer came up behind Callie and lifted her into the air by her tiny waist.

"You don't like our music!" he said to Laura with a kind of prideful leer. Clearly, he didn't care at all what she thought of his music.

"Owww, you're hurting me," Callie whined, batting ineffectively at her pseudo attacker.

He turned his leer toward Callie. "Who's this?" he asked.

"This is Laura, she's my new roommate. She's a musician, too."

"Are you coming to our party afterward? I promise it'll be fun, even if you're not into our heterosexual, derivative songs."

She nodded mutely, unable to think of any interesting or clever way of saying yes. Letting Callie be her ticket into social situations made her feel like she was back in high school, both cozily familiar and disappointingly regressive.

The drummer gave Callie a squeeze and put her down. The guitar player was standing under a streetlamp alone, smoking, and Laura let herself stare at him. There was something about how he'd looked playing guitar—his focus and his passion, which he'd seemed to be trying almost to conceal. It wasn't cool to be passionate, but he was, and that made her feel tender toward the part of him that couldn't protect itself from being seen. He glanced up, catching her in the act of staring at his fingers and lips, and he caught her gaze and held it, held it and let his lips curl into a lazy half smile around his cigarette. She felt the blood rise to her face as she dropped her gaze, trying to pretend that she'd been aimlessly staring into space. She'd never felt so powerfully attracted to anyone before. When she looked up again he was talking to the drummer. The whole thing lasted a fraction of a second, but it was still enough to get Laura through the rest of the show.

The party was in a big, weird loft on Ninth between C and D, built out with lots of plywood dividers to make bedrooms for all the roommates, detritus hanging from the ceiling as decor, low light concealing general filth, and a big stand ashtray next to a rotting velour couch whose springs poked Laura in her bony butt as she sat on it, smoking and drinking more than she wanted to because she was both bored and nervous. She tried not to glance at the guitar player too often. He stayed in another corner of the party having an intense one-on-one conversation with the bass player, but she still looked at him often enough that he had to have seen her and sensed her attention. Hadn't he?

As the party wore on, getting louder and later and smokier, she became more and more sure that she had imagined the whole thing, or maybe he just did that to girls at random, testing his eye-contact powers the way you'd press the blade of a knife into whatever was around to see how sharp it was. She hovered on the edge of a conversation that was happening near her, pretending with her head movements to be part of it, but there was no one she wanted to talk to besides him.

A joint kept getting passed to her. She smoked without thinking, then was unpleasantly surprised when she stood up and her head swam. She hadn't eaten since the Juicy Lucy smoothie she'd had for lunch. Of course this was the moment the guitar player chose to begin to make his way toward her, but now Laura's breathing was speeding up and her mouth was watering in an ominous way and her number one priority was to leave the party without throwing up. She said goodbye to Callie, who gave her a puzzled look and quickly turned back to whoever she was talking to. Being full of incipient barf and the threat of humiliation made Laura feel artificially sober; she noticed every detail of the stairwell tile, the uneven texture of the sanded-down stairs under her feet. She ran out to the street, and the stinking breath of the hot summer night hit her straight in the face. She crouched on the curb between two cars, and wine vomit spewed out of her in a torrent, foamy and pink. She stood up shakily and felt immediately better, then gasped as she realized that the guitar player was standing right next to her.

"That was impressive." His speaking voice was deep and smooth, unexpected in a skinny, boyish person.

She shook her head and fished around in her bag for a tissue, but she'd borrowed the purse from Callie, and there wasn't anything inside it that felt familiar. "I'm sorry you had to see that."

He produced a packet of tissues from his pocket. They were clean and new-looking. She must have looked surprised.

"I have allergies," he explained, waving them toward her. "My throat is so sore right now I can barely talk."

"It's brave of you to party in that condition," Laura said, taking a tissue and dabbing at her mouth in what she hoped was a casual yet effective way.

He shrugged. "Davey said we had to. There were supposed to be important industry people here. There's always some reason you have to go to a party, you know? In Davey's mind, anyway."

He paused, and she wobbled slightly on the uneven pavement. "Sorry, are you actually okay?"

"I think so. Just humiliated. I'm Laura, by the way."

"Oh, the musician!"

She looked at him suspiciously; he had to be making fun of her. No one had ever referred to her as a musician before.

"Callie told us about you." He was clearly trying to put her at ease.

"Us?"

"Davey, the rest of the band, my roommates. Callie's a cool girl."

"Oh! Yeah, she's . . . she's cool." The post-puke reprieve from nausea was wearing off, and as much as she wanted to keep talking to this beautiful yet vulnerable (allergies!) guy who thought of her as a musician, she knew she should leave before she threw up again.

"I should go home," she said, backing away so that he didn't get the opportunity to do what it seemed like he wanted to do, which was reach toward her and touch her arm. The possibility that he would touch her was too exciting to deal with at her current level of shaky queasiness. It made her feel like she might explode, and not in a cute way. He shrugged and lit another cigarette as she slunk off down the block, hoping that her instinct was leading her in the right direction, away from the East River and toward her strange, filthy, exciting new home.

———

The next day Laura woke up with a disgusting hangover that made her head feel like a black banana. By 1:00 p.m. she'd managed to ingest a coffee and a chocolate croissant and was feeling much better. She was absolutely sure she would never smoke cigarettes again, until Callie woke up at 2:00 p.m. and started smoking her American Spirits in the kitchen, and without thinking about it Laura lit one, too. Callie was wearing her beautiful teal kimono, deep in the process of removing last night's makeup with almond-oil-soaked cotton balls that she placed in a growing black-and-red pile on the table in front of her, studying her own face in the mirror with infinite fascination.

When Laura walked past the door of Callie's room on her way to the bathroom she noticed that the drummer was lying asleep in Callie's bed. Laura cocked her head toward the bedroom as she reentered the kitchen as if to say, "So?"

Callie looked away from her reflection for a second and smiled. "They're a good band, right? They're going to be famous soon. That's definitely the last time they'll play a venue that small; it's almost for sure that they're going on tour, opening for the Strokes. Did you end up talking to Dylan?"

"His name is *Dylan?*"

Callie smirked. "His parents picked his name, not him. Okay, so . . . let me guess. You either hooked up with him but were too drunk to remember his name—which, since I've met you, I know is unlikely. Or *maybe* you were too shy to even speak to him."

Laura slumped in her chair and ashed into her empty cardboard coffee cup. "Worse. We did meet, but it was right after I threw up in the gutter."

Callie's naked face shone with oil. She was still beautiful without the makeup, but it was weird to see her without it. She looked pink and unfinished. "Well, he'll remember you next time, for sure!"

"As the girl who barfed. Great."

"So you're into him! That's good. We're going to a party tonight that he'll probably be at."

"Except I have to work."

"Come by after."

"It'll be late, though."

"Well, still come, you'll be sober and you'll be able to swoop in for the coup de grâce with all your wits about you."

Laura rolled her eyes. "That's me, swooping in. Always very slick."

———

Laura waded through the crowded darkness at Bar Lafitte, leading people to their tables, smiling and leaving them there, then strolling slowly back to the podium by the door. Whenever she was bored, Laura thought about the album she had been slowly assembling in her mind over the course of the past couple of years. She had a handful of tunes that needed words, and this was why she'd moved to New York—to live the kind of life that she could write songs about, instead of a life in an apartment above a music store that she rented at a discount rate from her mother. Aside from "I Want My Tapes Back," she hadn't mined great material from her utility boyfriends. Inspiration had to come from somewhere else—New York, she hoped. She wanted to be like the artists who'd enshrined her new neighborhood as a place for the dissolute and beautiful and doomed.

But the East Village wasn't turning out to be like the mythic version of itself that existed in her mind. Rents were higher, people died far less often, and there were stores that specialized only in Japanese toys and hookah bars that catered to NYU undergraduates. There were also the internet cafés. There was something about an internet café that could never be glamorous, only grubby and desperate. On Avenue A, across from the park, there was a real café, where everyone languidly sipped their coffees, eyed each other, watched the street outside, chain-smoked at the sidewalk tables, and wrote in little notebooks or pretended to. In the internet café next door everyone just stared at the screens. They had bought their little bit of time, and now they had to use it wisely.

There were still fascinating and glamorous people around, though. The beautiful waitress at the BYOB cheap Italian restaurant on Ninth Street, the one with the giant eyes and acne-scarred cheeks. Yulia, whom Bar Lafitte had hired at the same time as they'd hired Laura, who only ever spoke to say, "Please, your table." The guitarist Dylan. She wanted to write a song about Dylan. She wanted to do all kind of clichéd things, and she was just self-aware enough to know they were clichés but still young enough to think that things would be different for her.

She didn't really like smoking, but there wasn't anything else to do, so she took a cigarette break in the alley behind the bar, where a waitress was also smoking. It was almost sunset and there was a golden light on the stones of the building across the street, and they stood smoking in the fading light, silently finding some kind of comradeship in just standing next to each other. The waitress broke the silence by introducing herself, strategically waiting till both their cigarettes were almost to the filter. "Hey, I'm Alexis, I'm section five tonight."

Laura turned to look at her more closely. The waitresses primarily distinguished themselves from the hostesses by their little black aprons, but there was also something else different about them. The hostesses were softer, newer—they all clearly had ended up there by accident—while the waitresses were professionals. Their eye makeup was dark and deliberate, calibrated to be visible in low light. Their cleavage pushed out of their tight black tank tops, not as if they were shoving their tits in your face but as if they couldn't be bothered to conceal them. Alexis had a short brown ponytail and a dark even tan and perfectly globular breasts. She was intimidating, but there was also something about her that Laura trusted implicitly.

"Do you want to get promoted to server?" she asked as if it were an offhand question, but Laura could tell that she was being evaluated.

"Should I want to?"

Alexis laughed, and her globular boobs jiggled slightly, perfectly. "I'll ask you again after you've had your first shift drink with Stefan."

Stefan was the manager who'd hired Laura. "Oh, because he's a perv?" She could hear herself trying to sound tough, as tough as hard-edged Alexis. "I can shut that down."

"Well, then he'll fire you. Just flirt, string him along a bit. You definitely don't have to do anything, but keep his hopes alive." Alexis pulled out a hot-pink Bic and lit another cigarette, and Laura felt a glow of approval; if she'd been a dud, Alexis would have gone right back to her section, she felt sure.

21

"To answer your question, though, yes you should want to get promoted! You're making shit money considering what you'll have to put up with here, and the bartenders will never tip you out, because you don't do anything for them. The only exception is Max, and he'll just be trying to get you to talk to him, which you shouldn't do if you can avoid it. And you make good money here as a server. Really good."

Laura wished she was a real smoker; her cigarette was out, but she was still feeling slightly too hungover for another one and she wanted an excuse to continue talking to Alexis. "How good?"

Alexis paused, maybe assessing whether she wanted to be honest with Laura, whether Laura merited advice or help. "On a good night you can make three hundred dollars. There's a lot more bullshit, but it's worth it."

———

Even though the party where she might have been able to talk to Dylan was likely already petering out by the time her shift ended at four, a completely deranged part of her wanted to go to the party just in case he was still there. Instead of sprinting out the door and through the streets, though, she made herself sit down at the bar. She needed to ingratiate herself there if she hoped to be promoted to server. She ordered something disgusting from the bartender, rum and Coke, in the hopes that she wouldn't be tempted to drink it too quickly. Alexis sat down beside her and put the contents of her money apron on the counter and began counting the bills. Laura noticed that there was another stack of bills nestled into the lace that cradled her boobs, and she didn't count that one. When Stefan walked over to them she pushed it down out of sight with a subtle movement that might have been involuntary, like smoothing your hair or adjusting the waistband of your jeans.

"Shots!" he said to the bartender as he sat down at the barstool they'd left between them. Wordlessly and expressionlessly the bartender lined up four shot glasses and filled them with top-shelf tequila. Alexis helped herself to a lime from the tray on the bar and sucked it as Stefan asked them how their night had gone.

"Seven hundred and eighty dollars," said Alexis, pushing the stacks of bills she'd made into one pile and shoving it toward the bartender, who took his tequila shot like a sip of water and then started recounting the money.

"Not bad! You reclaim your position as number one. Here's your bonus." Stefan nodded at the bartender, who dealt out a handful of twenties back onto the bar in front of Alexis. Stefan turned to Laura. "Interested in playing? Every night the servers compete for a sales bonus." His eyes were unfocused, and when he touched her arm it seemed less a move than an attempt to keep from swaying. He smelled sickly sweet and powdery. She forced herself not to flinch at his touch.

"I'm not a server," she reminded him.

"Oh, right. What's your name again?"

"Laura." She hadn't told him her name before.

"Well, I should get going," Alexis interrupted, and motioned behind Stefan's head to Laura, who also slid down off her barstool.

"But the night's just getting started! Come on, celebrate your first day," Stefan said, but lightly. "Drink your drink."

Laura watched Alexis's face closely for clues as to what she should do, and when she detected a hint of a headshake she grabbed the rum and Coke and downed the remainder of it in a single gulp, then managed a smile. "Okay! See you tomorrow," she said, aiming for the same light tone that Stefan had used. The trick with men like this, Laura thought, was to behave with complete neutrality so that they could project whatever thoughts or feelings they wanted to imagine you having onto you. She felt good about this realization, like it gave her some power.

"Let me walk you out at least," he said.

Alexis shrugged, and her eyes conveyed "You're on your own" to Laura.

When they reached the door of the bar, he insisted on hugging her goodbye, then delivered a lingering double-cheek kiss. She stood there mutely, disgusted by the sticky redolence of her boss's dead-flowers aura so close to her own skin. He went back into the bar, and she wiped her cheeks.

When she turned toward the street, she saw Callie, Dylan, and Davey were there on the sidewalk, waiting for her.

"We thought we'd pick you up from work, 'cause the party got boring," Callie said. "Want to go back to Dylan and Davey's and smoke a bowl and watch dating shows?"

She wanted nothing more. But when she tried to catch Dylan's eye she found that whatever had passed between them last night was gone, or at least submerged under some resentment or confusion.

"Who was that?" he asked, in a slightly accusatory tone of voice, like he thought she shouldn't have let Stefan cheek-kiss her. That was annoying.

"Ugh, that's my new boss. He's like that with everyone." She stopped just short of actually apologizing.

But then his hand brushed hers, and she forgot to be annoyed immediately. For an awkward, heartbeat-skipping moment she thought he might hold hands with her. Even though he didn't grab her hand it seemed possible that he could, or that he wanted to.

When they got back to Dylan and Davey's apartment everyone smoked weed laced with opium in front of the TV and slumped onto one another in a puppy pile, Callie's legs on Laura's and Laura leaning into Dylan's shoulder. Eventually everyone but Laura fell asleep. Even anesthetized by drugs and exhaustion she was alert to each of Dylan's breaths as he slept and how close she was to him, close enough to hear his heartbeat. She imagined kissing him and felt almost queasy with desire. But after maybe twenty minutes it became clear that he wasn't about to wake up again and she finally passed out, letting her body relax tentatively into the side of his. She had fitful, flashing dreams.

She woke up as it began to get light out, and as she realized where she was and whose flannel shirt she was smelling because it was right up against her nose, her whole body went into a kind of flu-like feverish shock. She had to exert an enormous effort to stay where she was, not wake everyone by suddenly bolting off the couch.

Her breath, though, and her fast heartbeat were outside her control, and Dylan rustled awake. He kept one eye scrunched closed and looked up at her, then reached out an arm and pulled her up off the couch. Callie grunted something disapproving as her legs got rearranged but then rolled over in the empty space and went right back to sleep. Dylan pulled Laura along the hall to his bedroom.

He had a loft bed made out of raw, splintery two-by-fours, with piles of clothes and cables and synths littering the floor underneath. The mattress was so near the ceiling that Laura couldn't help but think about how the only kind of sex they would be able to have would be close together, with nobody sitting up. She was desperate to have sex with Dylan, but she was also nervous. There were so many variables when you hooked up with someone for the first time; would he, after everything she'd imagined, be rushed or lazy or inconsiderate or just not really *there*? She had already experienced more than her share of dull, grabby hands and slimy lolling-open mouths and mistaken ideas from porn.

He saw her staring at the makeshift bed and caught her eye and smiled. "I know, it sucks," he said. "I'll get a real bed one of these days, I promise." She felt a rush of joy at the suggestion that she was going to be around to witness his future bed.

The difference in their heights was thrilling but inconvenient; she had to crane her neck up a lot to reach his mouth. They clambered awkwardly up into the tiny bed and stretched out against each other. He ran his fingertips lightly around the edges of her still-clothed body. She was wearing her unfashionable jeans. There was no graceful way for him to remove them because neither of them could sit up all the way, so he said, "Let's just take off our own clothes," and they each hurriedly did, then lay down next to each other again. He was thin and pale, with only a few wisps of chest hair right in the center and a constellation of freckles in a semicircle near his navel. He'd kept his boxers on——a nice touch, to have taken them off would have been practical but still somehow presumptuous—and his dick strained against the fabric impressively. Without any of the delicacy and finesse he'd displayed in the way he touched her, she reached out and grabbed it. It felt almost improbably thick, and it pulsed in her hand. He made a little involuntary grunting sound as he pushed his waistband down to give her better access, and even though they were still kissing she managed to glance down to assess what she was holding.

Dylan had the most beautiful dick in the world. It was perfectly symmetrical, long, thick, and uncircumcised, and it was even a nice color—not purple or red at all, but the same pale white as the rest of his skin.

She wondered, in the tiny part of her mind that could still think, whether Dylan knew, whether his perfect dick had informed the direction of his life. Probably? If you came to New York with some musical talent and a perfect dick, why wouldn't you take for granted that your band would soon be recording and touring, that you would be able to get by without a day job, that you would be able to get girls to come home with you by, essentially, existing in their presence? But the tiny pang of jealousy that Laura felt in that moment was soon eclipsed by what was happening in front of her. Dylan crouched awkwardly and somewhat perfunctorily between her legs for a moment, then put on a condom and gently, slowly, shoved about a third of his perfect dick in.

He made eye contact with Laura and said, "Is it okay?"

Clearly, this was a thing that he knew he had to do, which should have mildly grossed Laura out, but she was no longer processing this experience from a critical remove. She said, "Unf," in a way that she hoped expressed okayness, so he continued.

It wasn't ultimately satisfying, exactly; Laura was too excited and nervous to let go all the way, and she kept hearing the sounds she was making and getting thrown out of the moment by worrying about the people sleeping in the other room. But she thought that even so, something about this particular morning would end up staying with her, returning to her occasionally over the years in dreams or fantasies or even during sex with other people. There was just something pure about it, something fun and happy that made her feel like anything might be possible. The unavoidable metaphor was that it was her first hit of a drug, and she imagined that she might spend the rest of her life chasing this high and never quite replicating it.

———

A few hours later Laura slipped out of Dylan's apartment into the quiet of what passed for early morning in her neighborhood. The people who had daytime jobs in other parts of the city had left hours earlier, but the people who had nighttime jobs and other kinds of work were still in their apartments, taking long showers, drinking coffee, smoking cigarettes, lighting incense, and reading their tarot card of the day. She splurged on croissants and non-bodega coffee from a bakery on First Avenue, taking a circuitous route toward the shop where Callie worked on Seventh Street. The sign on the door still read Closed, but the door was unlocked and Callie was inside, zipping up a dress that Laura recognized from the window display. It looked even better on Callie than it did on the headless, white-limbed mannequin.

"Oooh," she said when she saw Laura. "So?"

Laura was grinning. "I don't want to diminish the experience by analyzing it or giving you a play-by-play."

"How selfish! Come on, just one detail. Please? I haven't even opened the shop yet and I'm already bored."

"Does anyone even come in here?"

"Oh yeah, it gets busy! I sell lots of dresses. I pick things out for people and make them feel like I'm making them look good." She flipped the sign on the door to Open and then walked toward the mirror-covered pillar in the center of the store, staring herself down, smoothing the sides of the dress. Her mirror face was grim and determined, but satisfied. As usual, her makeup was immaculate, though her hair, never very clean, looked wild and slept-on. Somehow this juxtaposition was, on Callie, glamorous. Looking at her made you want to stop washing your own hair. It was easy to see why she sold lots of dresses; being around her made you want to try to look as good as she did, and also somehow made it seem like it might be possible.

"Do it for me, pick me out something."

"You can't afford any of this, even with my discount."

"I have a job! I could get some new clothes." Having sex had also made her feel pretty. There was no better time to go shopping.

"I get that you're trying to distract me, but I'll weasel some intel out of you before we're done here," said Callie, circling Laura and looking at her from all angles. "This is what I do: I stare at people like I'm computer-analyzing their unique proportions and going through a mental database of our whole inventory. Then I pick the most expensive thing I think I can get away with, or whatever is going on sale next week."

"Well, don't do that with me. Just show me the cutest thing," said Laura.

"For you? It's this." The dress had a halter top that exposed the top of Laura's back. She liked that it was a light color, so she couldn't wear it at work; it was a dress for her actual life, not the dim black-clad half-life of the bar. It was perfect for summer and could even be worn under a cardigan in fall. It showed off Laura's arms and shoulders, where her muscles were well defined from years of both playing and carrying around her guitar. She imagined standing near Dylan and having him reach behind her neck to untie the straps. As soon as she put it on she knew that she would have to buy it, no matter how expensive it turned out to be.

She waited until the flush that rose across her chest subsided and came out of the dressing room to get Callie's reaction, but Callie was paying attention to an actual customer, so instead she walked around the store, pawing the racks. There was a shelf of "vintage" shoes near the back of the store, which the shop's owner had found at thrift stores just outside the city, polished slightly, and marked up several hundred percent. They were good finds, though, pretty eighties pumps and barely worn leather sandals. Laura found a pair of heels in her size and slipped them on. They were lipstick pink, which looked good with the off-white dress and her dark hair. Callie's customer left the store, and she walked back over toward Laura.

"Okay, very nice, but where are you going in that?" she asked. "I mean, how are you going to justify it to yourself?"

"I'm going to wear it onstage," Laura said, without thinking. Callie nodded approvingly. She rang her up with her staff discount and threw the shoes in for free. "They probably cost the owner a dollar, let's not sweat it," she said. "Now, let's figure out where your band is going to play."

"I don't have a band," Laura said. She went back into the dressing room and started putting her dirty clothes from the night before back on. Callie kept talking to her through the door.

"You should get one. You know, I've been thinking about this. No one's going to book a singer-songwriter, that's some open-mic-night shit. I can pretend to be in your band till you find someone better. Then we just need a drummer, and maybe someone who can actually play bass, but that can happen later."

"Pretend to be in my band?" She was still zipping her jeans, but she stuck her head out of the dressing room so that she could see the expression on Callie's face and try to gauge how serious she was.

"Yeah, like a backup-singer type of situation. We've sung together before, remember? In high school."

Laura came out of the dressing room, avoiding the letdown of the mirror. Without the dress on she was returned to her former self, dirty and puffy around the eyes. "If I'm onstage with you, no one will look at me," she said.

"Of course they will, you idiot. You're the one who can actually sing and play. I'm just going to help you get your foot in the door."

The thought of wedging her foot into that door alone was terrifying, which was why Laura hadn't made any attempts to do it yet. "Okay, I'll think about it," she told Callie. "I got you a croissant, by the way." The owner didn't like food in the store, so they ate sitting on the stoop just outside, watching as the sidewalk got more crowded as noon approached and the day properly began.

————————

The Clips were leaving to go on tour in two weeks. Laura had sex with Dylan whenever she could. At 4:00 a.m., after her shift ended, she'd call to see if he was still up or even take the chance that he wasn't and just walk to his apartment and buzz. Most of the time, he answered. Then they would stay in his tiny, uncomfortable bed till the middle of the next day, when he would leave to go rehearse and Laura would be back in the non-Dylan part of her life. She was dreading the tour, already imagining how empty she'd feel on the first day, when this part of her life would be all that was left and she would have to figure out something else to care about. A few times, Callie asked her if she was still thinking about the idea of a band, but she didn't press it. Laura was, of course, but somehow it didn't seem as important as thinking about Dylan.

The day before Dylan left, he invited Laura to meet him at a recording studio in Bushwick where he was supposed to be finishing up some alternate takes of songs the band was going to put on their next album. He told her to bring her guitar so that he could hear her songs for the first time.

The first part of the trip, the walk from her apartment to the J at Delancey, was blissful. Laura loved crossing Houston and looking west at the giant sky over the low buildings, feeling small but fast and purposeful as she marched in a mass of people across the intersection. Her guitar case bumped against her back rhythmically as she walked, reminding her over and over of the purpose of her trip. And the elevated subway journey into Brooklyn was beautiful, too, the same giant sky over the receding city. When she disembarked and walked down the dirty staircase to Broadway, Laura started to feel nervous. She craved contact with Dylan but also felt shy about singing and playing music in front of him. For a moment as she loped down Broadway, attracting stares with her guitar, she found herself unable to quite remember his face, or what his speaking voice sounded like. But, she knew, sex would immediately put everything back in order. If they couldn't have sex at the studio they could at least make out. It had been days, and it would be the last time for a while.

She was passing a Dunkin' Donuts that seemed reassuring in this alien neighborhood, so she went in. Her whole body was buzzing with adrenaline, but it still seemed like a good idea to get a cup of coffee. She got a limp, weird bagel with toothpaste-texture cream cheese, too, because even though she was too nervous to be hungry, she wasn't sure when she was going to get to eat again and she didn't want her stomach to make weird noises in front of Dylan.

The studio was in an old warehouse building with big windows right at the level of the elevated train tracks. A heavyset man buzzed her up and curtly informed her that Dylan hadn't arrived yet, so after looking around at all the expensive gear in the cavelike loft, she just sat and ate her bagel, looking out the window at the trains, waiting. Every train that passed could potentially have him on it, and though waiting and watching like this made it seem like he would never come, Laura felt strangely peaceful sitting there at the window. The sun was beautiful, not scorching, somehow casting more light than usual on the elevated tracks and torn awnings and old dirty-windowed buildings. Summer hadn't really gotten started yet; it was still cool in the early mornings and late at night, and you could still sleep under a blanket.

Laura thought about sharing Dylan's tiny bed, being forced to have some part of her body touching his at all times even as they slept. The first few times she'd thought she would never be able to fall asleep like that, but the long nights had caught up to her, and she'd even dreamed a little and woken up staring into his face, watching his eyelids twitch, free to stare at him for as long as she liked until he woke up.

She got out her notebook and started to write down some of her lovelorn thoughts that could be turned into lyrics later on. Eventually she got bored of that and just started doodling. After half an hour she started to feel slightly angry, then even more angry, then resigned. Then angry again. In the end, he made her wait an hour and a half.

He looked hungover as usual, wincing in the sunlight that streamed through the big windows. He put down his backpack and glanced around the room, taking in Laura, her bagel, and her notebook. "Oh, good, you brought something to do. This might take a minute," he said, and then he went back into the booth to confer with the stern large guy who'd let Laura in. When he came back out he hardly even looked at her again. He sat down with his guitar and tuned it, then nodded to the guy in the booth. The room flooded with the track that Davey and the band had already recorded, another fuzzy banger that wasn't too hard to imagine playing over the PA in a bar or even at a baseball game. Dylan put his head down and played over it with the same detached intensity that he always did. Laura didn't know what she was supposed to do. Stare at him worshipfully? Part of her wanted to, but she was also annoyed that their date seemed to consist of her in a corner with a bagel watching him play. Then again, this was what he'd invited her to do, and she'd said yes. She picked at the bagel.

About half an hour later the guy in the booth gave Dylan a thumbs-up and then, within minutes, had packed his stuff and left. Dylan stood up and shook out all his long limbs, then turned to Laura. "Did you bring any more bagels? I'm starving."

She tamped down a rising surge of annoyance and shook her head. "I brought my guitar, though, I thought you said . . ."

"Oh, right! I still need to hear you play." He made this sound like it was something he'd forgotten to buy at the grocery store, eggs or dish soap.

As she unpacked her small guitar from its dorky soft-sided case and sat tuning it, Dylan kept himself busy by rolling a small joint. By the time she was ready to play he was smoking it as casually as if it were a cigarette. He pushed the window open a crack and ashed on the sill.

She paused before starting to play. It felt like an audition. Or she assumed this is what an audition would feel like; she'd never auditioned for anything before. "Well, what do you want to hear?"

"I don't know, whatever you want to play. Your favorite song? Your best one?"

"People seem to like this one," she said, then played him "I Want My Tapes Back." She didn't know exactly what to do with her face and eyes while she sang, so she mostly looked at the neck of her guitar and out the window. Dylan stayed halfway across the room, smiling inscrutably. He laughed a small knowing laugh—thank God—at the line where the audience was supposed to laugh, the part about "I miss my mix of all Liz Phair / Heavens to Betsy and Huggy Bear."

"That's really cute," he said when she was finished. "I feel like you could make bank if you busked on the subway."

She stayed silent, hoping that he would say something else that would redeem what he'd just said.

"I mean that in a good way. You're a great guitar player."

"Oh! Thanks. No, I'm not." She deflected compliments habitually, as though to accept one might be rude, though it was probably ruder to tell someone they were wrong. She didn't play like someone like Dylan, who could probably do things like improvise a solo. She had mostly taught herself, but she liked how she played.

"So . . . ," he said, stepping toward her. She became more aware of how they were alone in the studio and felt her whole body flush as she imagined fucking Dylan right where they were standing, or possibly, more comfortably, in the booth, in one of the large, cushiony chairs there. He reached past her, toward what was left of the bagel, and stuffed it in his mouth. "Sorry! I'm totally starved. Let's get out of here and find a diner or something." He brushed the crumbs off his mouth and, in the same movement, grabbed her by the hand and pulled her toward him.

" 'I want my tapes back,' " he sang in his dramatic, growling deep voice, nothing like Laura's clear, no-nonsense alto. He spun her around the room in a little waltz. " 'I hope you know where they are.' " She was intoxicated by sheer physical proximity to him, and so flattered that he'd remembered the words to her song.

―――――

Dylan had been gone on tour for two weeks, and Callie and Laura were on their way to alt.coffee to check their email when they passed the magazine store on A and Fifth Street and saw the cover of *NME* with Dylan on it. The other band members were on it, too, but the photo was mostly Dylan, standing in front, looking into the camera like he was sad and annoyed about having his photo taken. They both saw it at the same time and came to such a screeching halt that the man walking behind them bumped into them.

"Fucking morons!" he shouted as he pushed on past. They ignored him and kept staring at the magazine.

"Oh my God, you're dating a rock star," said Callie.

"Dating?" said Laura.

"Oh my God, we're groupies!" said Callie.

"Gross, no. Do you think he's famous now?"

"Yes! If you actually want to be his girlfriend now, good luck. Girls are going to be throwing themselves at him after this."

Callie was always so pragmatic, but she was probably right. The way Laura had felt about Dylan the first time she'd seen him play hadn't just been lust, it had been admiration for his talent; his magic was real. It was inevitable that other people would acknowledge it, too.

She felt both vindicated and frustrated—it was good to have been proven right about Dylan, but she also wanted something like credit for having known him before he became more generally known. Mostly, though, she wanted to actually talk to him.

They hadn't said anything about how they would stay in touch while he was away—it hadn't seemed like a long enough amount of time to justify a plan for keeping in touch—but now Laura wished she'd said something. He didn't have a cell phone, but that was probably for the best. If she'd been able to call him at that moment, she would have asked whether he loved her. Asking someone you've had sex with a handful of times whether they love you, especially if they're turning out to be a famous rock star, is not the right move, she knew. But she also knew that if he called her at this exact moment she wouldn't be able to stop herself. She decided instead to email him. She didn't know whether he would be checking email, but she had his address that he'd scribbled somewhere and she would be able to control herself better if she could revise what she wanted to say to him as much as she liked before sending it.

They went into the café, which was dark and smelled like old couches and cigarettes, and ordered their drinks and their allotments of internet time from the guy at the counter. Laura stalled by going into the bathroom, where a bunch of computer parts sat in a bathtub, some kind of dumb art installation, and while she peed she thought through the decision she had just made to email Dylan. It was such a low-stakes way of reaching out to him. But what would she say?

She sat down at one of the shared monitors, trying to ignore the greasy feel of the keyboard, and began to type. She asked how the tour was going, what the different cities were like. She fished delicately for a response that would indicate that he was looking forward to seeing her when he came back, but she didn't make any dramatic declarations. She tried not to mention her feelings at all. She needed to include at least a sentence about what she'd been up to, but this was tricky because there really wasn't much going on in her life besides working at the bar, hanging out with Callie, and obsessing about him. So she lied a wishful lie about working on her songs and playing a small show that a friend of Callie's had hooked her up with. Callie had mentioned something about introducing her to someone who booked bands at the Sidewalk Café, so it wasn't exactly a lie. Plus, she could even use the lie as motivation to make it true before Dylan got back.

She went through the rest of her in-box unhurriedly, lingering over the details of spam emails she'd gotten instead of immediately deleting them. Really, she was waiting to see whether he would respond. This was crazy; the odds of his even being near a keyboard were so slim. She didn't even know what city or what time zone he was in. Still, when her half hour was up, she went up to the counter for a refill and another passcode to unlock another half hour of internet access.

"Why do you need to stay here longer?" asked Callie, who had finished her coffee and her free issue of *VICE* and was tapping her long nails on the counter.

"I just thought maybe a person I wrote to might write back," Laura admitted.

"A person. Jesus." Callie rolled her eyes and went to wait for Laura in the park across the street.

But then when she got back to the desk, there it was: a response! She felt like the gross shared computer was a slot machine dispensing a flood of coins. He would be home in a week, he wrote, and would be playing a show first thing. He invited her and Callie to meet up after the show at Brownies. He said he missed her.

Laura floated into Tompkins Square Park and found Callie sitting on the patchy grass on the hill. The park was full of people their age with nighttime jobs or no jobs who could treat the park like a beach, lying on blankets with snacks and drinks and joints and cigarettes, getting sun, watching the dogs in the dog run and one another. Callie had bought a large bottle of orange juice, from which she poured out some of the juice and replaced it with the contents of a small bottle of vodka. Laura didn't have to be at the bar until seven; there was still time to get drunk, then nap and shower before work.

This was how they'd been killing all the lengthening summer afternoons lately, but the surge of energy Laura had gotten from her communication with Dylan had made her too hyped up to enjoy lolling around. She told Callie about her email and the response, and the minor lie she'd told.

Callie ashed her cigarette thoughtfully on the patchy grass near the blanket they sat on. "Oh, that's no problem. Let's just go by there right now and see if Alex is working. Well, not *right* now right now. Like in half an hour? Let's finish our drinks at least."

"I have to go grab my guitar and stuff first! And I don't want to get drunk."

"You'll just be relaxed. You need to." Callie took a swig, then offered the bottle. Laura semi-reluctantly accepted. She was suddenly feeling too wound up, almost to the point of panic. Her initial joy at being in touch with Dylan was activating her brain and body in ways that were agitating if she couldn't be around him physically.

An hour later she and Callie were in the dark daytime interior of Sidewalk, in the side of it that was a bar and not a twenty-four-hour diner. Alex, a short, skinny guy with bluish-pale skin who could have been twenty-five or forty, hugged Callie too long and then looked Laura over as frankly as her bar employer had on the day she'd gotten hired.

"So you guys are in a band together?"

"Well, it's mainly Laura, but yeah, it's kind of a band," said Callie, smiling at Alex and doing her "you are the only person who exists in the world" thing.

"Great! Hop up there and do one of your songs real quick."

They conferred quickly and decided to do the song that Laura had started writing at Dylan's studio. For never having techni-cally rehearsed, they weren't as terrible as Laura had assumed they'd be. Callie had heard Laura sing the song so many times that she had memorized it, and she sang almost harmony and shimmied around a little as Laura tried to keep up with Cal-lie's innovations in rhythm. It was uncomfortable to make eye contact with Alex, so instead Laura watched Callie as she sang. She thought again about how anyone watching them onstage together would spend more time looking at Callie shimmying than at Laura playing guitar. But maybe it didn't matter; it was Laura's music, Laura's song.

When she looked out at Alex next, he was grinning. "Come back tonight, I'll put you on at eleven thirty," he told them. "What should I say you're called?"

"I can't tonight, I have to work," Laura said.

"Weird name for a band," said Alex, then laughed at his own joke.

"You can call in sick once. You've been there long enough to get away with it," Callie said.

"Five weeks?"

"I'm sure you're a lifer by the standards of that place." Callie turned back to Alex. "You can call us the Groupies." She wrinkled her nose and laughed like she'd made a hilarious joke. The vodka-OJ was cold and acidic in Laura's stomach.

"You're on the bill," Alex told them. "You get two drink tickets and a cut of the door that you share with all the other bands, so tell your friends to come."

Laura was silent as they walked home, scuffing her Chinatown mesh slippers against the dusty sidewalk, walking like her guitar was heavier than it actually was.

"What?" Callie finally said.

"Well, we're going to make pocket change, for starters. I can't afford to miss my shift or to lose this job."

"But this is what you came to New York to do!"

"Not like this," Laura said.

Callie stopped and turned with her hands on her hips, so close that Laura could smell her breath, orangey and rotten in Laura's face. "Like what?"

"Like . . . the only reason he booked us is because of you."

Callie smiled and turned around, her anger immediately defused. She let Laura walk next to her on the sidewalk again. "That's not true, I'm just training wheels. You're doing it on your own. It's okay to let people help you sometimes!"

"Callie, I'm not blind. When both of us walk into a room, all anyone sees is you."

"Dylan saw you," Callie said almost too quickly, like she'd been planning to say it. And Laura couldn't argue with it, because it was true. Maybe whatever he saw in her would translate now. Maybe things would be different, and Callie was right, and Laura was going to be the one people looked at this time.

It was Callie's idea to both wear the dress Laura had bought from the boutique where she worked, Laura's in white, Callie's in red. Laura wore her dark hair down around her face, so that when she bent her head toward the neck of her guitar it was hard to see her. Callie wore her straight blond hair pushed back. They wore winged eyeliner, applied by Callie's unerring hand. On Callie, it made her light eyes more visible from the audience, but on Laura, it was just another dark thing receding into shadow.

A friend of Davey's was recruited to play drums at the last minute, and to loan them a bass guitar, which Callie pretended to play. The drummer, a sleepy-eyed but highly professional guy named Zach, was actually great to have. They were allowed a little sound check before the show started and he gamely fleshed out Laura's songs, making them sound less folky and more upbeat, like a low-fi version of a sixties girl group. Despite still being slightly disturbed that Callie had hijacked and reshaped her dream, Laura had to admit that the Groupies weren't that bad, especially for being put together in one afternoon. They would have to figure out a different name, though.

They sat in the small audience comprised of the other bands' friends and drank their free vodka tonics till it was their turn, then awkwardly shuffled up onto the stage as the previous band was leaving it.

Laura said, "Hi, we're the Groupies," in a flat quiet monotone into the mic, then pushed into the opening lines of the song she'd written about Dylan. She'd named it "Can I Call You?" It was about not wanting to scare someone off by coming on too strong, but the joke was that of course the narrator of the song, because she was thinking about whether it was okay to call the guy (on the phone) or to call him (her boyfriend), was sort of obsessed. It was supposed to be humorous and pathetic. Callie was so charismatic, though, and so sexy as she tossed her ponytail from side to side, that by chiming in on the choruses she transformed the song into something different. A guy would have to be an idiot not to want to be her boyfriend, she seemed to be saying. She swayed from side to side as Laura played a plinky, cute tune during the song's bridge, her version of a guitar solo. Even though Laura was singing lead and playing guitar, it was somehow Callie who made it work. It was because of Callie that everyone in the bar was clapping with more than the perfunctory politeness they had showed the other bands.

After their set was over and they were back at the bar, Alex came over to congratulate them. "You guys are invited back whenever," he said, looking at Callie, and he gave them their cut of the door: thirty dollars. They ended up giving it to Zach so that he could take the bass home to Williamsburg in a cab.

———

Brownies was unassuming on the outside, just another store-front-size bar on Avenue A, but inside it was a dim, noisy deep cavern, a whole alternate world. The stage lights were sharp and perfect, so bright that they illuminated motes of dust buzzing around them, flecks of sweat bursting from the band as they strutted and thrashed. The floor was packed and writhing, moving in waves pressing closer to the stage. Usually Laura wasn't into close contact with strangers, but this wasn't like being on the subway. It was like being a cell in some larger organism, everyone joining together with the same aim in mind. It was just loud enough so that their bodies were enveloped in sound, just on the edge of discomfort, a vibration rattling up through everyone's shoes, re-regulating their heartbeats and breathing so that everyone exhaled in time. Some people even knew the lyrics of the Clips' songs. A few weeks ago the band had been unknown, playing shows that people came to for the promise of free wine. Now they were galvanizing hundreds of people, maybe thousands before long. Laura was close enough to the stage to see the look on Dylan's face as he played. She thought he seemed happy, but at the same time uncomfortable. There was a twitchiness in his expression she'd never seen before. Maybe he was anxious to see her; she was so anxious to see him that when the show ended, she prayed for no encores. But of course there was an encore; the crowd demanded it. The band waited a desultory minute before strutting back out onstage. Thankfully they played only that one song, though, and then it was finally over.

The basement underneath the venue was a dark cave, too, full of scuffed leather couches and surfaces littered with bottles and half-full ashtrays, bottle caps and empty thin black plastic liquor-store bags. Dylan looked up when Laura entered the room with an expression of pure happiness, almost like he hadn't expected her. When she got closer, though, she saw that the look she'd thought was shocked joy was actually a more abstract kind of euphoria. His pupils were huge, and he had trouble focusing on her face. He smelled sweaty, and she wanted him to close the distance between their bodies immediately, murmur in her ear, and get her out of there. Instead, he just stood there, smiling a goofy smile. She opened her mouth and realized she had no idea what she wanted to say. The two weeks since they'd seen each other seemed like a huge gulf of experience.

Laura had settled further into her new life, carving out patterns of her days, writing lyrics in the non-internet café on Avenue A, riding the subway, eating egg sandwiches in the morning and pizza at night, drinking dozens of cups of sweet light bodega coffee, getting incrementally better at being a cocktail waitress at night, making friends with Alexis on their smoke breaks, teaching Callie the new songs she was writing to prepare for their little shows. They had played twice more, once at Sidewalk again and once at a terrible NYU bar on Bleeker, which had gone less well. Part of her still felt Ohioan and alien. No matter what clothes she borrowed from Callie or how much makeup she wore, she didn't quite look right. She still smiled too much at people on the street and at patrons at the bar. She didn't know how to act in this loud smoky basement full of strangers. She wished that she and Dylan were alone and naked. She looked over at Callie, who was drinking from a tallboy can of malt liquor and letting Davey drape his arm around her.

Laura moved closer to Dylan so that he would put his arm around her, too. She relaxed into him. He handed her the beer he was drinking, and she took a long sip and thanked him.

"You were great," she said, trying to look into his eyes so that he could tell she really meant it, wasn't just saying it by default because it was the thing to say. For a second, his face lost its vague look and he really seemed to appreciate the compliment. He even seemed hungry for it, like he wasn't already sure of himself. He led Laura to a low velvet couch with a coffee table in front of it and introduced her to the band's manager, who was already sitting there, wearing a green army jacket with deep pockets. As she watched, he pulled handfuls of drugs out of them: cubes of perfectly intact marijuana buds with shimmering crystals on each folded leaf catching the light, bottles of pills, a small pile of plastic bags full of powder.

"It's the world tour of drugs," said Davey, diving toward the table and scooping up a handful of bags. Laura laughed; it was ridiculous, a caricature of rock-star behavior. Dylan didn't laugh. He started dissecting a cigar, removing the tobacco to refill it with weed. He licked the paper, and she felt a shiver of desire at the sight of his tongue. He reached for pills from the pile and ate a couple of them like Tic Tacs.

"It's just Adderall; we're exhausted," he explained, but he also shook some of the powder out of one of the bags on top of the weed before rolling up the blunt.

"So are you back here for a while?" she asked.

"No, they're sending us back out again soon. We just have a couple of weeks, but we can hang out the whole time I'm here."

Laura fought back the urge, again, to tell him that she loved him, to claim him officially somehow. The thought of him with random girls in different cities made her want to peel off her skin. She wished that they were married. She wanted everyone he met to know they were together. There was no possible way to express any of this to him.

He lit the blunt and took a deep, desperate drag on it, then passed it to her and lit a cigarette. She wanted to ask what the powder was but was worried about seeming naive. She tried to take a small hit, but the flavor of the smoke was delicious, and she could feel it relaxing her into the couch, making the situation seem normal much faster than the beer could. She smiled at him through half-lidded eyes.

"Are you good?" he asked. "I'm sorry we're not alone. I have to stay here, but you should go home and get some rest. Tomorrow we'll hang out, just us."

He was swaying and slightly slurring as he said this. Laura understood, without wanting to, that Dylan was much more interested in getting fucked up than he was in having sex with her. She still couldn't make herself give up and leave. After he finished smoking the blunt, he started walking around the room playing air guitar, dancing unsteadily. Laura got up and followed behind him, unsure what she should do next. Callie extracted herself from underneath Davey's armpit and reached over and pulled Laura toward her.

"We're getting out of here," she hissed in Laura's ear.

"I'm just going to stay another twenty minutes, I'll see you at home," Laura whispered back.

"No, you're coming home with me. It isn't happening tonight, and you look stupid. Let's just go; you'll see him again when he's more sober."

She waved at Dylan as Callie forcefully grabbed her arm and moved in the direction of the door. He waved, smiling in her direction, then turned his attention back to the world tour of drugs.

———

When Laura came over to his apartment the next afternoon, as he'd asked her to, Dylan still wasn't alone. The whole band was there, and there were some girls who looked vaguely familiar from the night before, and everyone seemed to be wearing the same clothes and not to have slept. It was the hottest, sunniest part of the afternoon, and the apartment had one window air-conditioning unit that wasn't doing anything to cut the fug of smoke and bodies and sickly sweet spilled booze. Cigarette butts marinated in the dregs at the bottom of beer bottles. Laura almost turned around and walked back down the stairs and out onto the relatively less gross street. She didn't even see Dylan at first. But he was there, on the couch, slumped over and holding his head. She rushed over to him.

"Are you okay? Can I bring you anything?" she asked, realizing as she said it that she was acting like she was at work.

He looked up at her, pale and grateful, annoyingly still beautiful. He stood up, and she thought he was going to greet her with a kiss or a hug, but instead he grimaced and went into the bathroom, and a minute later she heard him vomiting.

She was repulsed, of course, but then quickly remembered that he'd watched her puke on the night they met, and also there was nothing he could do, by that point, that would have truly turned her off. "I'm going to the deli, back in a minute," she shouted through the door.

At Sunny & Annie's she bought a liter of ginger ale, a handful of Advil in little foil packets, and three bacon-egg-and-cheese sandwiches. The store had a friendly smell of bacon, burnt coffee, disinfectant, and cut-up fruit sitting on ice. She felt cheerful and competent, like a nurse in a starched white uniform taking brisk care of a bunch of invalids.

Dylan and Davey looked at her with pathetic gratitude when they saw her come in the door with the supplies. They consumed them sitting on the couch in front of the TV, passing another joint, watching a movie. The girls sat on the floor for a while and then got bored and left. For a moment Laura thought she might go with them. There wouldn't be an infinite amount of summer sunshine, and she had to work later in the dank velvet gloom of Bar Lafitte for hours. She wanted to walk around in the daylight as much as possible, to let it sink into her skin and bleach away the residue of the time she'd spent in this smoky, filthy apartment. But she also wanted Dylan, even if all he was up for was some light cuddling and aimless conversation. She wondered if he would think it was dorky or weird if she cooked him a meal. The movie was something only stoners would watch, an experimental Italian horror film that had lots of tomato-saucy blood, and Laura realized that she was hungry. She hadn't eaten any of the egg sandwiches herself. She got up to look at the kitchen and determine whether cooking in it was even possible.

The counter was stacked with empty bottles of malt liquor, and there was a crusty George Foreman grill, but the fridge wasn't disgusting because it seemed never to have been used to store food, only beer, and there were no dishes in the sink. She found a saucepan and a frying pan, a spatula and some forks. She could work with this. She made another trip to the deli and came back with the ingredients for a soup she'd perfected in college, consisting of one can of cream-of-potato soup and one can of creamed corn, plus milk, salt and pepper, and red pepper flakes.

"Dylan, your wife is the best," said Davey as he ate, stoned and ravenous. Laura felt offended, a little ashamed of herself, and also thrilled. She looked down at her bowl so she wouldn't see Dylan's reaction.

That night after work she told Callie about the day and what she'd done, cringing preemptively in preparation for her judgment.

"So you were supposed to go on a date, and instead you sat around with him and his friends, and then you cooked for them?"

Laura couldn't see Callie's face—she was at the kitchen counter, mixing bran cereal into nonfat yogurt for dinner—but she could imagine her look of lightly amused pity and contempt.

Laura nodded.

"What was the date supposed to be, even?"

"I don't know, he just said we'd be alone."

"So it was a booty call, and then you didn't even have sex." Callie sat down at the table to eat her gross meal directly across from Laura, so that Laura couldn't evade her eye contact.

"It wasn't to have sex—well, not *just* to have sex. I had thought we would . . . go to a museum or something." As she said it out loud, Laura realized how laughably improbable the idea of going to a museum with Dylan actually was. She tried to picture them holding hands and walking through a gallery, Laura maybe explaining or criticizing some aspect of the artwork on display. It was so patently a fantasy that she might as well have been imagining them riding bareback on unicorns through an alpine field of wildflowers.

Callie nodded like she could read the realization on Laura's face. "Yeah, I see where you're at with him. You're thinking, *Maybe someday. I'll teach him. I'll train him. When we've been together longer.*"

Laura was embarrassed, but she had to laugh. Those had been her exact thoughts.

Callie didn't laugh. Her brow creased, and despite her perfect makeup, she looked older. "There's no evolution for guys like him. You can be with them, but the version of him you're seeing right now is who you're going to be with. If you're okay with that, by all means."

"But I . . ."

"But I luuuuhv him," Callie mimicked. It was what Laura had been about to say. Callie was right. But what was Laura supposed to do, stop?

———

Laura was checking her email at alt.coffee again when she got an unexpected message: her sophomore-year roommate, Amanda, had found out she was living in New York from one of their mutual acquaintances and she wanted to hang out. They'd had very little in common then, but maybe they had more now? And they had lived together for a year, so there was an automatic semi-intimacy; Laura could remember how Amanda had smelled and what noises she'd made in her sleep, though she was hard-pressed to remember what her major had been. Via email, Laura made a plan to go over to "check out" Amanda's apartment that night.

Amanda lived in one of the strange brand-new apartment buildings on Houston below Avenue C. Laura walked down beautiful First Street and then cut over onto the charmless blank concrete stretch and past a gas station to arrive in the lobby of the gray square building. To get upstairs, she had to tell the doorman where she was headed, and then he actually called Amanda to let her know Laura had arrived. She had never been in a doorman building before.

Amanda greeted her at the door and ushered her in with a hug. She still smelled the same, like Secret antiperspirant and gum and onions. She looked basically the same as she had in college, except that she'd traded her ironed-straight brown hair for a studiously stylish angled bob. Her makeup was perfect and even and thick, like a layer of fondant icing on a fancy cake. The apartment was big, and Laura knew she was supposed to be impressed, but it was deeply charmless and seemed not to belong in New York. One of the things that Laura liked about the apartment she shared with Callie was that it was a dark little warren of tiny rooms, basically a tunnel with space to turn around every so often. You could imagine the people who'd lived there a hundred years earlier; starving garment workers squinting over their piecework by lamplight. That *appealed* to Laura.

This place was carpeted. You walked in and you were immediately in the entire kitchen/living room. It was of a piece with the large prefab houses outside of Columbus where she'd hung out when her richer high school classmates' parents were out of town. Amanda pulled her toward a coffee table and poured her a glass of red wine in a real wineglass, then one for herself in a wineglass that matched. She set the glass down on a coaster. Laura remembered suddenly that Amanda's major had been communications.

"So how long have you been here? What are you doing? Isn't it great? Tell me everything!"

Laura smiled and sipped the wine, which tasted salty and sweet, almost like food, not like sugared gasoline, as the jug wine she drank with Callie did. "This place is great," she said because she knew she was supposed to. "Do you live here alone?"

Amanda cackled. "Oh my *God*, no; I have two roommates! It's just like college, basically, we have to put a sock on the door when one of us is sexiled, but it's worth it to be in a doorman building. I just feel safer. And I'm never here, anyway, I work all the time."

"Where do you work?"

"I'm the assistant to the editor in chief of *SPIN*, it's literally the hardest job ever. I have to be at my desk by eight, but I also have to go to all these shows. I never sleep. And my boss is such a slave driver."

"Oh yeah, I know *SPIN*," Laura said. It was a music magazine that covered mostly stupid arena-filling bands and was just starting to pay attention to bands that Laura knew and cared about. Maybe she and Amanda had something in common after all, apart from their hometown.

"Do you still do music at all?"

Laura summoned all the self-confidence she could. "Yeah, I've been playing a few shows. And I'm working on an album. I'm still writing the songs, but I'm hoping to have enough finished to start recording them soon." This latter part was a lie, but like the one she'd emailed Dylan, it was the hopeful kind of lie. "I'm kind of in a band called the Groupies with my roommate, Callie. I'll let you know when the next show is; you should totally come see me. And also . . ."

She paused. She both did and didn't want to tell Amanda about Dylan. It was still thrilling to tell other people about him; talking about him conjured him and made it almost like he was there. In some ways it was better than actually being around him. For the past week he'd been so stressed out that when he wasn't practicing or in the studio or gone, he only wanted to sit inside and smoke blunts and watch movies. Eventually they would crawl into his tiny bed, or she would have to leave for work. It seemed like whatever he was going through was a natural reaction to the sudden onslaught of attention and pressure, and therefore, she hoped, temporary. When she went to watch band practice—which made her feel gross, like she was a cheerleader watching her quarterback boyfriend—she still saw him radiating joy in his skill, magnetizing something in her that wanted to, simultaneously, fuck and be him.

All of this raced through her head as she tried to figure out how to describe him to Amanda. "The guy I'm seeing is in a band, too. But, like, a real band. A successful band."

Amanda drank the remainder of her glass in a single gulp and made a wincing face as though she was about to do something difficult or brave.

"Okay, I have a confession. I heard you were dating him. That's part of the reason I wanted to see you." She gave a cute little shrug, then refilled both their glasses. "I wondered whether you might be able to get me an interview with him. If I could do a profile timed to the release of the new album, it would be my first long article for the magazine. They'd have to promote me! Or at least get me off my boss's desk. I'm so sick of answering his phone. If this is too awkward of a request, don't worry about it. But I just thought, if it was easy, you could introduce us, and then I'd convince him it was a good idea."

Laura tried to figure out what she was supposed to do. "I think stuff like that has to go through their label or their manager or whatever." She wasn't inclined to do favors for someone who had just admitted to using her.

Amanda shrugged. "I figured. I mean, I'll try that, too, but they haven't been doing much press, and . . . okay, well, just think about it."

Laura had an impulse to make the ensuing silence less awkward but squashed it. Let Amanda feel awkward. She deserved to. Laura wished she'd stayed home, maybe finally picking up her guitar and working on new songs. It probably wasn't too late, though she'd absently already drunk too much wine to get anything done well.

"I'd love to hear your songs sometime," said Amanda as she walked Laura to the door.

Before she could stop herself, somehow, Laura found herself telling another hopeful lie. "Well, we're opening for the Clips soon, so maybe you'll hear them then."

———

Laura decided to ask Dylan if she and Callie could open for the Clips the next time he was in the right mood, which was tricky. She rarely saw him during daytime, conscious, sober hours. Even in the noonish times they spent together after waking up late he was often preoccupied, smoking joints with his headphones on as he fussed with the piles of electronics that lined his cavelike bedroom.

She knew that if she waited for the perfect moment, it would never come, and of course part of her didn't want it to. The thought of playing for a large crowd that had come to hear the Clips and would likely hate her music was terrifying. But she didn't want to look like an idiot to Amanda, and she also wanted to give herself a chance to be serious. If nothing else, Dylan would have to take her seriously after seeing her perform on a real stage. He would finally understand that she wasn't a subway busker. He would start to see her as an equal, a partner.

They woke up the morning after a late night, hungover as usual. There was a cool breeze blowing in through Dylan's open window from the direction of the East River, bringing with it a briny smell that cut through the dirty laundry and ashtray fug of his bedroom. Laura rested her head on Dylan's chest and traced his bicep tattoo, an outline of an anchor.

"What are you doing today?" she asked.

"Practice, write songs, meet up with everyone at Joe's later," he told her.

"What if we went to the beach instead?"

"What beach?"

"I don't know, Coney Island? We could just get on the F and be at the beach in an hour. Summer's almost over, and I haven't been to the beach."

"Is this a date?"

"Yes, this is an extremely romantic date," Laura said, rolling her eyes at him. Being opposed to "dating" was one of Dylan's things; he had drunkenly rambled something once about how the construct was artificial and oppressive. But he was malleable today for some reason and smoked a cigarette instead of a joint as she hurried around his apartment, throwing things into a tote bag: towels from the floor of the bathroom, a soda bottle refilled with water from the tap, an opened bag of pretzels. They were both pasty and would need sunscreen, but she could buy it on the way. Her black underwear would be fine as a bathing suit. She hustled them down the sidewalk toward the F so that Dylan wouldn't have time to think better of the plan. They ate the pretzels on the way and looked out the window, sharing headphones attached to Dylan's Discman, listening to Belle and Sebastian with their shoulders and hips pressed together. Her hand brushed his accidentally, and he reached out and grabbed it, which made Laura feel a stunning burst of happiness.

It was a perfect beach day, with a high, blindingly blue sky. Neither of them had brought sunglasses, so they bought novelty pairs with neon pink rims from a boardwalk vendor. When they passed a photo booth Dylan wordlessly grabbed her hand and pulled her into the darkness inside it, put money into the slot, and then ducked down out of the camera's frame so that it would catch only her expression as he knelt between her legs for a few insane and unexpected seconds, then, grinning, stopped when their time in the booth was up and pulled her back out into the sunlight, reeling and dully aching with unsatisfied desire. They didn't wait for the photos to come out. The beach was crowded and filthy, littered with trash and suntan-oil-glistening bodies of all kinds, from very large older people to impossibly wasp-waisted teenagers in tiny bright-colored swimsuits. Laura ran down the wide expanse of sand, dodging bodies on blankets all the way to the edge of the water, then stripped down to her bra and underwear. She coaxed Dylan into taking off his shirt, and they stood in the knee-deep surf where the waves were breaking. She reached down into the water and grabbed handfuls of it, using her hands as paddles to splash him so that he'd have to go in all the way.

The waves were wild and huge, and the water was a thick, soupy beer-bottle green. They dove and then floated, trying to ignore whatever brushed against them and hope that it was seaweed. Laura was a good swimmer; she'd always loved the water. "I'll race you to that soda bottle that's floating over there," she said breathlessly after dipping down and then hurling her wet hair back away from her face.

"No, I can't," said Dylan. His deep voice wavered in a way she hadn't heard before.

"Yeah, you can, come on, it'll be fun. I'll give you a head start."

"I really can't. I mean, I can't swim," he said quietly. He was tall enough that his feet touched the bottom where they were standing, even though Laura was treading water.

"Oh! Well, if you start to drown, I'll save you. I'm very strong."

Laura paddled over to where Dylan was standing and rubbed her mostly naked body against him. He felt so warm against the cool water. She ran her hands down the length of his long pale back, loving how it tapered down from his shoulders. He had the kind of body that would always look good, no matter what he did to it; beauty inhered in his proportions, his graceful slender hips, angled perfectly to press into her exactly where she wanted to be pressed. She lifted her face up so that he could lean down and kiss her, but he was shivering.

"I'm gonna get out, okay? I'm too afraid of losing my balance," he said, and headed for the shore, leaving her no choice but to trail after him, awkwardly bodysurfing the small wave that carried her all the way in.

They dried off with the gross towels Laura had packed, then put their clothes on and headed back to the boardwalk because Dylan wanted to get a beer and go on a ride. Laura got an ice-cream cone and licked it pensively while Dylan chugged his entire first beer, then bought another one right away. They walked down the boardwalk toward the Cyclone, and Dylan reached for Laura's hand again. Laura thought about whether anyone they passed would recognize Dylan and wonder who his girlfriend was.

They rode home as the sun was setting, watching the last of the day wash over the exotic faraway neighborhoods as the elevated train passed avenues far into the alphabet, beautiful and ugly streets alike rendered cinematic by the golden light. Dylan smelled objectively bad, because he was unshowered and sweaty and had alcohol oozing from his pores, and though Laura was a little bit self-conscious about what their fellow passengers thought, to her he smelled good.

The train was full of smells of its own, and raucous noises of sunburned families coming home laden with inflatable toys and buckets and chairs, shouting at one another. Dylan swayed and nodded. She had to ask him now. The worst he could say was no. It would be humiliating to admit to Amanda that she'd lied. She could always say it had been canceled or called off for some reason beyond her control, but Amanda had barely believed her to start with and would definitely not believe any excuse she proffered. On the other hand, who even cared what Amanda thought? She had just given Laura an excuse to do something she'd wanted to do anyway.

She didn't want to seem pathetic. She wanted to seem triumphant, like she was conquering her new New York life and beginning her real musical career. And she also, despite her fears, wanted to play for a big audience. Some of them might like her music, and those people would become her fans. Then her band would be real, and playing in a band could become the focus of her life, the way it was the focus of Dylan's. She wouldn't have to feel like she was waiting to fail definitively so that she could give up and get back to real life, the way her father had. That was the version of her future that her mother and brothers probably envisioned, if they even bothered to envision her future. But Laura now had access to a different vision: given the chance, she now knew she could be like Dylan, or better. If Dylan could manage to be Dylan even though he barely bothered to make an effort at anything in his offstage life, then she should be able to do as well as he did. She tried so much harder than he did all the time.

She thought about explaining all of this to Dylan, but he would probably fall asleep before she got to the point. So instead she just asked, point-blank, whether he thought her band was good enough to open for his.

He was breathing with his mouth open, head on her shoulder, almost dozing, but he perked up for a moment. "Of course you're good, baby. I love your little songs."

"Okay, well, do you think you could talk to someone about putting us on the bill before your next show?"

He shook himself more awake. "It's in DC, next Tuesday. You work Tuesdays, right?"

"I can get someone to cover for me," she said, trying to keep her tone casual as the thrill of terror and joy vibrated through her entire body. Dylan probably wouldn't have noticed anyway. He curled up and dozed off for real just as the stations began to be more recognizable, and then the train dove back underground for the final time. Soon she was shaking him awake at Second Avenue, wiping at the spot of his drool that had pooled on her shoulder, composing a triumphant email to Amanda in her mind. She couldn't wait to tell Callie. They would have to practice with Zach, but there was a whole weekend to prepare. They could become professionals by then.

———

Sound check was a train wreck. At first Laura couldn't hear Callie or Zach, only herself, and they played half a song before the guy in the booth's agonized shouts overpowered Laura's nervous determination to just muscle through. They must have all been playing at completely different speeds; she heard a moment of Callie's amplified voice and registered how bad it sounded, how clearly she was improvising some unrelated tune rather than actually singing harmony. But then they got the levels adjusted and somehow all managed to chug through "Can I Call You?"— even beginning to have fun by the end of it, getting excited by the sound of their voices so loud and clear in the enormous empty room and prancing like horses from end to end of the enormous stage.

"It feels like we're getting away with something. Like, is this all a joke?" Callie asked as they packed their gear away again at the end of their allotted fourteen minutes. "How is it possible that we're playing a venue this big with no album, no single, and a set that's five songs long?"

"We can write more songs—I mean, I'm already writing more songs," said Laura. "This is how we get to record an album. Someone will see us tonight and make it happen."

They clambered clumsily down off the stage, into the darkness of the cavernous empty room. There were several hours to kill before the show, too long to spend backstage, and it would have been a perfect time to get dinner if Laura hadn't been too nervous to eat. Instead, she sat at a diner with Zach and Callie and watched them eat pancakes and burgers, listlessly sipping a Coke and nibbling the hard edge of one of Zach's fries. The Clips had traveled separately, in a giant black van with their expensive guitars and amps. She wanted to at least see Dylan before she played. She didn't think he would give her a pep talk or anything, but she knew that touching him for a minute would ease her fear and replace it temporarily with brainless lust. They were probably there now, unloading, sitting backstage and passing one of the ludicrously oversize blunts that Dylan rolled. It seemed almost possible that he'd forgotten that he'd arranged for the Groupies to open.

But when they got back to the dressing room, no one from the Clips was anywhere she could see. The sound guy told them with bored, irritated indifference to hurry up and get onstage, so they did. Laura looked out at a sea of studiously indifferent faces. Clearly, the crowd was just holding their places near the stage so that they wouldn't have to push through and fight for them when the Clips came on. The music from the PA died, but the crowd didn't stop talking. Callie and Laura stood there waiting for them to stop for a few minutes, but they still didn't. Laura made eye contact with Callie and smiled, but Callie looked pissed-off and scared. Laura had just had a weird flash of inspiration. If they were going to be completely ignored, then this was a chance to do whatever they wanted, without trying to please anyone. She put down her guitar and picked up the toy piano that she used to plink out a solo on "I Want My Tapes Back," and began to play that song's opening lines on it. Callie walked over and whispered in her ear, "Um, what the fuck are you doing?"

"Who cares? It doesn't matter, they don't care what we do. Isn't that kind of great?"

"No, it's humiliating!" Callie hissed.

"Or it's great! Let's just sing the song and see what happens, okay?"

Callie gave her a freaked-out stare, but she sauntered back over to behind her own microphone. They started to sing "I Want My Tapes Back," accompanied only by the *plink plink* of the little piano. Laura sang slower than usual, making sure every word was crisp and audible, and for once Callie was actually able to harmonize, so that they sounded funny and sweet but a little bit eerie, like a pair of creepy baby ghosts in a horror movie, singing about a high school breakup.

The chatting, indifferent audience was still louder than they were, but some people in front, at least, were turning their attention toward the stage. Laura could see them looking up at her—the lights in this room were focused on the stage, but there were scattered spots on the audience, too, and she could see individual faces. They looked befuddled, but some of them—girls, mostly—were smiling. One girl, standing in front of her taller boyfriend who had his arms wrapped around her from behind, was beaming up at the stage. The dude behind her looked off to the side, too cool to even deign to notice whatever was going on.

Laura put down the toy piano at the end of the verse and picked up her guitar, letting the crowd noise rise into her silence. Callie looked over at her again, and without exchanging words both of them understood themselves to be on the same page. They launched into the chorus of the song with gusto, amplified louder than they ever had been before, shout-screaming over the pounding of Zach's drums. They sang the chorus through again and again, getting faster every time. It sounded unhinged, but every time they did it they got a little bit better. By the fifth and final time, a few people were singing along. When they stopped playing there was a smattering of applause, and some laughter.

Were they laughing because the Groupies were ridiculous? Or were they just laughing at the spectacle of girls having fun, doing whatever they wanted in front of a huge crowd that wasn't there to see them and couldn't care less? It didn't matter, Laura realized as she started playing "Can I Call You?" The point was for her to have fun, and for Callie to have fun, playing, and for the rest of their set that's what they did. They marched all over the giant stage, told jokes, danced with each other, theatrically tossed their hair and leaped in the air like they were in a metal band from the eighties. The crowd never completely stopped ignoring them; near the bar, out in the room, the low hum of conversation still competed with their music. But that girl in her indifferent boyfriend's arms in the front row eventually broke free of his grasp and stood a foot in front of him, eyes closed and dancing like she was in her own private universe.

2

At nine the night had barely begun at Bar Lafitte. There was only one table in Laura's section: tourists drinking light beers who seemed lost and likely wouldn't stay. A new hostess had seated them, correctly, at a table deep in shadow. Laura was glad she wasn't a hostess anymore, even though it had been easier than being a waitress. The patrons could be disgusting, and she still avoided being alone even momentarily with Stefan. But she had begun to develop patterns of speech and thought that made her job easier and protected her real self inside a persona. Besides, she made much better money, which was useful since she was working fewer shifts, scheduling them around nights when the Groupies could play or practice. Being in a band made it easier to be a waitress, too. She could remind herself, in unpleasant moments, of her moment of triumph onstage in DC. That was the true Laura, the one who'd fearlessly converted a crowd; the Laura who had to laugh at a table of NYU seniors' sexist jokes was earning money so that the real Laura could book studio time and finish her album.

She was standing by the service bar when her cell phone rang. She hurried to silence it—they weren't supposed to carry phones, but everyone did—and surreptitiously checked to see the caller ID. Amanda. Out of curiosity, she dumped her table's round of Bud Lights and then went out into the back alley to smoke a cigarette and return the call.

Amanda picked up on the first ring. "Oh, good! I caught you. Is this a good time to talk?"

"Not really, I'm at work. But I could talk later? Well, much later. Or tomorrow."

"Are you sure? I have big news. You work at Bar Lafitte, right? I could come by and tell you in person."

"I don't know—it gets kind of busy."

"Trust me, you're going to be excited. I'm near there, I'll see in you in twenty." She hung up the phone before Laura could protest any more.

True to her word, Amanda came through the door about twenty minutes later, sailing past the hostess stand to sit down at the bar, where she made herself at home, ordering a cosmo and striking up a conversation with the bartender, who was early enough in his shift that he still could be bothered to have social interactions. Laura had a few more tables by then—luckily, she'd thought as she'd waited for Amanda to arrive, because it gave her something to do while she waited besides speculate nervously about what the news might be.

She scanned the room to see whether Stefan was anywhere nearby and then motioned Amanda to follow her through the dark hallway stacked with spare chairs and out into the alley. Amanda took her ridiculous pink drink with her, managing, waitress-like, not to spill a drop from the precarious triangular glass. She balanced it on a ledge and took out her cigarette pack.

Of course, hers were Marlboro Lights. There was a manic gleam in her eyes.

"I loved the show you guys did in DC, and I pitched a story about you to my editor. He said yes! I'm going to get a byline, and soon I won't have to answer his phone anymore!"

Laura smiled. "Well, that's great news for you. And I guess it's good news for me."

"We'll do a photo shoot and everything. Are you opening for the Clips on the rest of their tour? The idea is to interview you and Dylan together—talk about how you influence each other, how your bands are coming up at the same time, that kind of thing."

Laura paused. That didn't sound like something Dylan would appreciate at all. Maybe she could convince him to at least show up to the interview, though she cringed inwardly imagining how high he'd probably get beforehand and how unintelligible he might be. Still, it was a music magazine; that was probably par for the course. Callie would lose her mind over this; being in a magazine was exactly what she'd always dreamed of. She would plan their outfits with such meticulous care. And it was what Laura had dreamed of, too, in a way. If it led to more moments on the stage like the one she'd experienced a week ago, it would be worth whatever she had to do to get there.

"I'll think about it, okay? I'll ask Dylan, anyway," she finally told Amanda as they walked back to the bar so Amanda could drop off her empty glass and make a big show of leaving Max a two-dollar tip, winking as she left.

———

The next day, Laura didn't have to work, so she invited Dylan over. Callie was out somewhere. The stage was set, she felt, for romance—actual romance, not just sex. (Though of course they would have sex.) She thought about sex all the time with a physical intensity that sometimes felt almost sickening, it was so exciting. Alone, at night, she would shiver remembering the details of the last time he'd been in close proximity. Lying next to him in bed, sometimes, after he'd fallen asleep, she would be so possessed with desire—even after they'd just done it!—that she felt feverish. It wasn't an easily scratchable itch, either—when she was alone, she thought it might be possible to masturbate and then calm down, but that wasn't the answer, somehow. Her thoughts of Dylan were too complexly real. It was distracting, and she actually had to force herself to think about something more abstract in order to come.

He was supposed to be there at seven, but it ended up being more like seven thirty, which for him was like being on time. She'd thought too late of making dinner, but there was no food around except eggs, bread, milk, and coffee. They bought four slices of pizza from Two Boots and took them up to Laura's roof. The streets looked beautiful from there, miniaturized and shining all the way to the water.

They drank vodka straight from a bottle that had been in the freezer, with Laura matching Dylan sip for sip for no good reason. Then he rolled a joint and put two black blobs of opium in it, and they smoked it on Laura's bed-couch, watching the walls as the room got darker and darker around them. She reached for him first, and he deflected her gently. She watched his lips and mouth as he sucked the last drops out of the vodka bottle, which was warm now, sickly tasting. He wanted to go out for more, but she was already feeling woozy. She just wanted to be lying down and getting slowly, endlessly fucked.

Instead, she watched as Dylan canvassed the apartment for more alcohol, eventually finding a dusty bottle of red wine between the piles of clothes on the floor of Callie's room. "It's fine, we'll get her a new one tomorrow; she would never even notice anyway," Laura told him, just wanting him to get whatever he wanted so that he would want her.

He poured himself a coffee mug full of wine and put it down on the floor, then got out Laura's guitar. He played one of her songs. She felt loose and careless.

"There's this girl Amanda who's been pestering me about doing an interview, and it would be good for the Groupies to get press. But she wants you to be there, too."

"Of course, baby, that's so exciting. Wow, you guys are like a real band now," he said, and she thought fleetingly that he would likely not remember the conversation. He segued into a Clips song, extending a riff endlessly, looping it around, making it more and more boring. He'd made Laura's song sound boring, too. She had a weird brief flash of wanting to grab her guitar away from him and show him how to play it better, but his hands moving on the guitar's body distracted her. She wanted him to touch her so badly. It had been a couple of days, maybe three days, since the last time they'd fucked. In the close, dark, small room she could smell him, sweat and nicotine and the cheap detergent they used at the wash-and-fold Laundromat unless you specifically asked for Tide and paid a dollar extra. She waited as long as she could and then reached out to stop his hand as he strummed.

They were too fucked up. He could still get hard, but neither of them came. They moved gently against each other for what seemed like hours. The hot room smelled like a body, like their bodies, sweating onto each other and rolling over to find a new cool patch of sheet to press each other into until it started to get light and they both finally fell asleep. They slept late, and when they woke up, everything had changed.

3

Laura met Dylan's mom for the first time on September 13, when she drove down in the doggy-smelling family mini-van from Concord to pick up Dylan and whoever else wanted to come home with him. Davey and Callie came, too. It felt wrong to leave, but it also felt dangerous to stay. Being around a mom, anyone's mom, seemed like a good idea. Deep underneath the more panicked and pressing concerns, it occurred to Laura that these were strange circumstances in which to meet her boyfriend's (he was her boyfriend, right?) parents for the first time, but there were nothing but strange circumstances to choose from.

At first glance, Daisy seemed like momness personified: short, practical gray hair framing a pretty face; a soft, sweatered body, helping them load their bags into the trunk and offering them all long, sincere hugs, with an especially long hug for Dylan, who winced.

They stopped for lunch at a Chili's in Connecticut. At the table, looking at the long, laminated menu, Laura felt as though she were in a dream, a terrible one. In the car she had felt oddly soothed by novelty and motion. But going to a chain restaurant with a boyfriend's mother felt familiar, except under the circumstances bizarre, and also thousands of people had just died horribly blocks away from what was now her home, and it seemed not only possible but also likely that something just as bad or worse was going to happen next. She felt grief and terror and, most pressingly, the absolute dry-eyeballed gut-clenched agony of being sober for the first time in three days. She decided to order a beer.

But when the server came to take their order, he asked for her ID, which in her hungover haste she'd left in a different purse back in New York. "Sorry, miss, I can't serve you," the waiter said with a condescending smile. It was humiliating that he assumed she was underage, though of course very recently she had been.

She smiled back like it was no big deal and ordered some kind of pasta with chicken. Dylan's mom ordered an iced tea, and everyone else also ordered water or soda. When the waiter left, Daisy turned to Laura with her eyes very wide and bright.

"I can see why you'd want a drink!"

Laura tried to smile.

"I don't drink, myself. I'm in recovery."

"Mom," said Dylan, in a warning tone.

She turned to Laura and looked straight into her eyes and grabbed one of her hands. Laura's own family were not big touchers. Laura prevented herself from recoiling.

"I didn't mean to imply anything about your drinking, dear. We all have our own ways of coping, right?"

Laura nodded mutely and sipped her water. She tried to think of something to say that would erase the awkwardness and enable

Daisy to see that she was a sane, stable person and a great match for her son. But what was the right thing to say? She wished Dylan would step in here and give her a clue.

Davey jumped into the breach, ultimately. "So, Ms. P., it was so nice of you to come and get us, and to let us all come crash at your house." He made it sound like they were all in high school.

"Oh, please, call me Daisy," said Dylan's mom. She smiled. "I'm just so happy you all can come stay with us. I'm so happy you're safe."

Dylan's childhood home was a red farmhouse, surrounded by tall, thick-trunked maples whose green leaves were just beginning to yellow. There was a black Lab on the porch and a curlicue of smoke coming from the chimney like in a child's drawing. The dog made a beeline for Laura and rose up ecstatically as she petted her, pushing her back into Laura's hand and circling her with polite barks of welcome. Laura felt loved and trusted immediately by the dog, and when Dylan saw this he smiled a genuine smile, a smile Laura had never seen before. She felt a surge of hope and gratitude, and she continued petting the dog as the rest of them went into the house and put their things in bedrooms, Daisy chattering happily the whole time.

Later, after a long dinner accompanied by glasses of soda, Dylan's quiet, bearded dad and Daisy went to bed, and Dylan and Callie and Davey and Laura headed out into the dark woods behind the house with a flashlight. They walked a short path till they got to a clearing with stumps in a small circle, and Dylan took a small blown-glass pipe out of his pocket and packed a bowl.

"We have to ration this because it has to last us till we get back to the city," he said very seriously.

"That's soon, right?" Laura didn't want to seem eager to leave, but she was. Something about Dylan's family and the eerie quiet of their rural home was the opposite of calming. No matter how disturbing and dangerous things were in New York, at least she felt at home there. She wanted to be with Dylan, but for reasons she couldn't quite pinpoint, she didn't want to be with his mother.

"We were supposed to leave for LA on Tuesday," said Davey. "I mean, we are. Are we still going on tour?"

"Is anything that was supposed to happen still happening?" said Callie. "My boss at the store hasn't even returned my calls." Laura realized that it hadn't occurred to her to call in to Bar Lafitte, but it was possible they were open; people needed bars.

"I don't know. Do you want to go back, Laura? It feels sort of . . . safer here," Dylan said.

She watched him as he drew smoke into his lungs with a desperate pull. He didn't seem like he felt safe. She didn't really feel safe, either.

"I want to go home," she said.

The next day was pleasant, or as pleasant as it could be. At least the disaster had moved to the periphery of their focus, only coming to the forefront when they turned on the radio or looked at the newspaper. During the day, they took a long walk in the woods with the dog and then piled into the minivan and drove to a café. For whole long stretches of time, up to ten or twenty minutes, Laura even forgot why they were there.

After lunch they walked up and down the two blocks of stores, and Callie pulled them into a wine store. They got a few bottles, just the kind of thing that, if you were a guest in someone's house for a couple of days, would be normal to bring. Though when they got home, around 4:00 p.m., they divided the bottles and the boys went down to the basement, where Dylan still kept a drum set and some guitars, and Callie and Laura sat on the front porch with coffee mugs full of wine. It started getting cold, and the sun turned the browning lawn copper.

Laura and Callie exchanged glances when they heard Daisy's car in the gravel drive. The bottle of wine, mostly empty, stood between their mugs. As she approached, Daisy smiled at them until she saw the mugs.

"Girls, I'm sorry, but it's very hard for me to be around any kind of drinking or drugs or addictive behavior. Can you please keep your drinking out of my house?" Her voice wasn't chilly and commanding, it was wheedling and sad, a little-girl voice. She went inside, letting the door slam behind her. They heard the dog greeting her, then the sound of Dylan's parents talking in his dad's office in voices that started out hushed and then became louder.

Laura felt ashamed but also angry at Daisy for making her feel that way. She felt bad for Daisy, of course, but also it was an international crisis, a time of intense worldwide mourning and panic, and people who drank wine should be allowed to drink wine at such a time.

"Asking people around you not to drink because you have a problem seems really selfish and inconsiderate," she whispered to Callie.

Callie finished her mug in one long chug. "Totally. I mean, we're also being inconsiderate, but she's being cuckoo."

In the kitchen, Dylan and Davey were standing at the kitchen counter chopping vegetables badly and laughing. A boom box with a cassette deck was playing Led Zeppelin, a welcome change from the nonstop disaster coverage on NPR. Whatever they were cooking seemed far from completion. Laura walked up behind Dylan and put her arms around him, sniffed and got a lungful of weed's buttery-popcorn smell. If she and Callie had been inconsiderate, Davey and Dylan had been worse.

Just then, Daisy burst into the kitchen and stomped over to the fridge. She swung it open with some force, assessed its contents, then slammed it shut, as though it wasn't her own fridge but some impostor's fridge put there purely to annoy her.

"What's for dinner?" she asked the boys.

Davey smiled. "Old family recipe."

"I didn't know you could cook," said Laura.

"He can't! We just thought it would be fun," said Dylan. "We're making a stew, Mom. I got the meat out of the deep freeze in the basement."

"That'll take ages to defrost!" Daisy's voice was high, panicky.

Dylan shrugged. "Well, it'll defrost eventually. We can put it in the microwave. Right?"

Daisy was rummaging through the fridge. She pulled out a block of cheddar cheese and, peeling back an edge of the plastic packaging, took a bite out of it.

"I happen to be very hungry right now. What people who drink don't realize is that alcohol has calories that make you feel full. Other people need to eat food."

Davey had his back to the confrontation, still determinedly chopping carrots. Laura and Callie exchanged glances and tried to move toward the far corner of the room as invisibly as possible. The dog stayed in the kitchen, staring at Dylan and Daisy with her head cocked expectantly.

"Chill out, Mom," Dylan said, and sighed. He had a resigned air, as though he was used to having this conversation, or conversations like it.

"We're making dinner. I thought you'd be happy not to have to cook. We can order takeout and have the stew tomorrow if you're really worried about how long it'll take."

"Takeout! Do you think you're in New York City?"

Laura felt herself suppressing nervous laughter. The whole situation was ridiculous. Daisy and Dylan had to know that on some level. She waited for one of them to burst out laughing.

Instead, Dylan walked over to Daisy with his arms outstretched as if to hug her, but the knife he'd been using to cut vegetables was still in his hand and Daisy backed away quickly. Behind her glasses Laura could see a big expanse of the whites of her eyes. The next moments registered mostly as a blur of color: greens and oranges of the cut vegetables, the white tile kitchen, Daisy's pastel-purple sweater, Dylan's black shirt and silver knife.

"Are you trying to murder me?" Daisy screeched.

"No, Mom, Jesus Christ, I'm trying to hug you. What the *fuck*?" he shouted.

Daisy collapsed in high-pitched, keening sobs. She sounded, again, like a child, not an adult. Dylan embraced her, he had to, but Laura saw his face over her shoulder, stony and artificially aged-looking. She caught his eye momentarily, but he shook off the contact, staring up at the ceiling.

Dinner was very late, and no one talked much. Daisy didn't eat with them; Dylan's dad said she'd gone to bed early.

Dylan and Laura were supposed to sleep in separate rooms, but of course she snuck in to see him after she figured everyone else would be asleep. She crawled into his childhood single bed with its nubby flannel sheets and pressed her body against his, but he stayed on his side of the bed, looking away from her.

"Is that how she always is?"

"Could I make it any more clear that I don't want to talk about it?"

"Okay, sorry, I thought it might help to be able to talk about it."

"You don't understand. That's my *mother*."

"I also have a mother. I know what it's like to fight with your parents. You've never even asked me—"

"Well, we don't know each other that well," he said, and rolled away from her.

As angry as she was, she was still powerfully attracted to that turned back. He was so muscular and warm. She wanted to wrap her arms and legs around him and take long breaths of the smell of his neck and slightly greasy hair. So she did, but he just lay there, even as she brushed the sides of his body with her hands, dipping her fingertips below his waistband, gently testing the waters. When he finally rolled toward her, she felt overwhelmed with relief; she'd won. But there was no warmth in his face as he yanked up her T-shirt, pulled down her underwear, and without any indication that he enjoyed what he was doing, pressed into her. He kept his head turned to the side, his shoulder pressed into her face. When she made a sound, he pressed his shoulder down harder, so she stopped making noise.

In the bathroom afterward, after she peed to prevent herself from getting a UTI, she looked down at the swirls of snotty goop in the bowl. She walked back to bed, to the bedroom with Callie in it instead of the one with Dylan, and after assessing the depth of Callie's slumber, she turned over on her stomach and rubbed out a quick orgasm.

4

aura slipped into Bar Lafitte as quietly as she could at the beginning of her afternoon shift. The door was open, but she didn't see anyone around, so she started doing the side work she and the other waitresses sometimes occupied themselves with so that they wouldn't get too bored, stacking drink menus and wiping down tables and chairs with a damp bar rag. She allowed herself to zone out, polishing one tabletop till she could see her blurry reflection in its surface. It was a shock when Stefan's voice called out her name from the top of the staircase where he typically sat at the table he called his "office." Laura tensed, preparing for a lecture. After all, she hadn't been at work for more than a week and hadn't even bothered to call. For all she knew, she was about to get fired.

Instead, she found herself wrapped in a lingering and, thankfully, very platonic-feeling bear hug.

"I'm so happy to see you! I knew you were likely fine, but one couldn't help but worry." Stefan seemed almost to be on the verge of tears.

Alexis was just walking in the door at that moment, and she ran over to both of them and joined the hug. "Oh, Laura! Thank God you're okay!"

This welcome was the opposite of what she'd anticipated, but it made sense. She was also thrilled to see her coworkers. It was a gross, sort of exploitative job, but the bartenders and waitresses there were the constants of her life. She hugged Stefan back and told them she'd missed him, sincerely.

The rest of the shift was manic and blissful because there was no time to think. She was becoming better at waiting tables. She felt the pleasure akin to that of learning how to speak a new language, making small mistakes and learning from them. She slapped down her tickets with a smile or a joke so that the bartenders would prioritize her orders and she could deliver drinks more quickly and endear herself to her customers. She got faster at making change, and her muscles learned the wrist-flick that eased credit cards through the slot in the machine on the first try, the exact pace to walk at so that the tray of drinks in her hand would sail and not wobble or slosh. Everyone she served said yes to another round. People were determined to eke out fun wherever and however it might be found. The men hit on her, of course, but there was something in their eyes, even among the drunker ones, that made the most lecherous things they said tolerable. Everyone had to acknowledge one another's shared humanity, or something. Everyone was just so glad not to be dead.

Even after tipping out the bartenders, she'd made more than she usually did in a week in that one night. For the first time, she allowed herself to hail a cab to get home, even though it wasn't a long walk. She tipped the cabbie 100 percent of the tiny fare and danced up the stairs to the apartment, feeling only a little bit ashamed of how euphoric she felt. It was unseemly, at a time when so many people were mourning, to feel so happy, especially because it was their misery that had, indirectly, caused Laura to be able to feel accepted and useful. But she couldn't help the way she felt.

Callie was sitting at the kitchen table in her beautiful kimono, chain-smoking. Laura couldn't keep the joy out of her voice as she greeted her; she was excited to tell her how much money she'd made. Maybe they could look for a bigger apartment soon, one that actually had a separate room for Laura to sleep in. Callie looked up at her, and Laura saw that her usually immaculate makeup was smudged, black mascara leaving streaks down her cheeks.

"Something terrible happened," she said.

"Oh my God. Where was it this time?" Laura hadn't heard anything or smelled anything different, and she hadn't heard sirens. The streets were still somewhat deserted, but that was normal now. They were under attack.

"They found Dylan. They were staying in a hotel with a pool. He can't swim, I guess? He didn't know how to swim, but he was in the pool. Everyone was fucked up, I mean, I'm sure they were. I don't think he meant to. Oh God." Callie started crying too hard to keep talking.

"He's in the hospital?"

Callie's face was down, her shoulders were shaking. "He's dead, Laura. By the time they found him he'd been underwater too long. They couldn't bring him back."

Her first thought was of the incredibly unsatisfying way they'd said goodbye. Or really, the way they hadn't; she and Callie had left the house in the chilly early morning, before even Dylan's parents were awake; they'd had to continually keep feeding and shushing the dog as they waited for the cab to take them to the bus station. It had seemed important to be secretive, mostly so as not to offend Daisy, who might feel that her heroic drive down to the city to get them and keep them safe had been in vain. But Laura had also wanted to avoid a conversation with Dylan about why she didn't want to stay there any longer. Even so, she hadn't been able to resist going in at the last minute to kiss his sleeping face. His dirty-blond hair had been greasy and spilling across the pillow like a girl's. He'd stirred and half woken, tried to pull her back into bed with him, and she'd even thought about letting him, missing the train, staying. But what then? He was going to LA soon anyway; what difference did another day together make? He'd kissed her one last time before slipping back into a doze. She'd had the uncomfortable feeling that he'd been about to say her name but hadn't quite trusted himself to remember what it was.

She decided to wait for the pain on their building's roof. She gathered a few supplies—some cigarettes, the Pyrex measuring cup they used for coffee that she filled with water, a warm hooded OSU sweatshirt. Still in her black work clothes, she climbed the small, filthy final flight of stairs to the rooftop and picked a corner facing southeast, then just sat there, waiting.

The sky was beginning to glow purple; the sun was preparing to rise. The noise from the street below picked up a few notches in intensity as the city, which had been oddly still, began to come to life for the day. It had to, despite everything that had happened. It had no other choice. Laura lit another cigarette, more for something to do than because she really wanted it, and smoked it as slowly as she could as the sun breached the lower corner of the horizon, sending neon orange streaks sizzling up between all the still-standing buildings. She became aware that she was crying, and had been crying for a while. The crying was for Dylan at first, but as it continued, it became for everyone dead, for everyone who'd lost someone, and for herself, for how empty the rest of her life would be.

———

She spent that day in bed. She wasn't hungry or thirsty, and she wasn't even bored, she just lay there and stared at the ceiling, feeling pinned to the bed by an ache in her chest that radiated outward, weighing down all her limbs and keeping her immobilized. She didn't know where Callie was. It had been dark for a long time when Laura heard her stumbling into the apartment in her tall chunky boots, and then she also heard a male voice—not Davey's—mumbling something drunk and inaudible before the door to Callie's room closed firmly. Laura got up and went to the kitchen. Her stomach felt painfully empty, like its dry walls were clenched together in a knot. She got a packet of ramen out of the cupboard and ate it dry, with the seasoning packet sprinkled on top, and drank a glass of tap water standing up by the sink. Then she went back to bed and lay down and fell fast asleep. When she woke up it was 9:00 a.m., a normal time to get up and start the day, so she did.

Third Street was empty, but that wasn't so unusual for this hour. The Hells Angels had strung an American flag between their building and the one across the street somehow; it hung down toward the center of the street, drooping rather than blowing in the wind. Laura bought an egg sandwich and a light and sweet bodega coffee on her way to the F train as though she were a commuter on her way to work somewhere. She had no idea where she was going, but it seemed important to be going somewhere.

The subway stopped in the tunnel between Fourth Street and Fourteenth Street for a blood-chilling minute and then started again. People chatted with each other and read the *Post* over each other's shoulders and talked about the headlines. The sudden familiarity was horrible but wonderful, and Laura almost wished she could participate in it. She felt tears threatening the Wet n Wild pencil she'd stupidly applied, and a woman sitting across the aisle caught her gaze and said, "You okay, dear?"

It felt fraudulent to get this sympathy; no terrorists had robbed her of her boyfriend. He'd done it himself, by being drunk and high and stupid, or worse, wanting to die. He'd put her in the terrible position of feeling like she didn't deserve this stranger's kindness and resenting it because of how guilty it made her feel to be getting it anyway. And she could never tell him how angry she was; he would never have to pay for his crime against himself. She hated him and ached to be near him. She tried to distract herself by looking at the subway map above the woman's head and found herself devising a plan.

In the months she had lived in New York City she had not yet once been to a cultural institution, unless she counted Brownies. No operas, no public lectures at Cooper Union, no museums. She had never been to the Metropolitan Museum of Art in her life, only read about it in *From the Mixed-Up Files of Mrs. Basil E. Frankweiler* in grade school. That book had left an indelible impression, though. Now, in the echoing lobby full of kids and families, Laura looked at a paper map and tried to find the French king's bed those fictional kids had slept in. They had spent a lot of time looking at ancient Egyptian things, too, and had swum in a fountain where they also collected change to pay for their next meal. The museum smelled like cool clean marble and burnt coffee and soup; she was hungry again, probably from not eating all day yesterday. She followed the smell of the food to the ground floor, where there was a crowded, fluorescent-lit cafeteria, serving all kinds of gross food for outlandish tourist prices. She picked out a flaccid bagel stuffed with an inch of cream cheese, paid for it, and took her tray to a corner of the room. The bagel's skin was pliant, not crunchy, and her teeth slid through the giant disk of cheese with a pleasantly disgusting ease. She finished it and still felt ravenous, so she went and bought another and ate it with the same speed and gusto. Her body, at least, seemed determined to live.

She took an elevator to a random floor and exited into a mostly deserted gallery of eighteenth-century Spanish paintings in which dark figures rolled their eyes upward in various ecstasies and agonies. She tried to stare at them until she felt something, but it wasn't happening, so instead she decided to just walk through each room of the museum as fast as she could, stopping only if something arrested her gaze and made her feel compelled to stare. She was desperate to feel anything from an external source; she wanted to be forced to feel some other way besides how she already felt. The music that was typically in her head all the time had gone silent, she realized. There were no random jingles and half-remembered melodies trickling through her brain, trying to distract her, forming themselves into new songs if she paused long enough to listen. This pleasant static had always formed the backdrop to her thoughts, and now it was gone as though it had never existed.

Ancient Egypt was the last place she tried, and at the entrance to the Temple of Dendur something finally happened; she felt angry. The people who had built this temple had built it to guide someone into a supposed afterlife; how fucking stupid was that, was all of this? Death was final, she was sure. She thought of the kids in the *Mixed-Up Files* and how magical they had found this place. To Laura, at this moment, it seemed to embody false hope that you could be reunited with someone you loved in another realm, if you followed the right protocols, built the right shrine. That kind of thinking was dumb and dangerous. But how could kids have understood that? She herself had not understood it until just now. She wished she could go back to not understanding.

5

Laura was sitting on the stoop outside her apartment building and she couldn't figure out how she was going to stand up and walk. Callie stood next to her, leaning on a parked car. Laura had made it down the steep flights of stairs but then felt woozy and blacked out slightly. Now she was clutching the filthy pavement where thousands of trash bags had sat and thousands of dogs had pissed because she felt the world turning too fast, trying to tip her over, too.

She kept thinking of Dylan's body. It had been such a perfect body, and then via some process she didn't understand, it had now been transformed into something that his parents had transported, in some kind of small container, so that his friends could gather and say goodbye to what had been Dylan and then do something with the container's contents, together. Did no one else realize how bizarre this was, how completely disgusting and surreal?

"I can't go. I'm not going. I can't move," she explained to Callie.

Callie winced and tugged on the sleeve of Laura's black hooded sweatshirt. "You don't have to go, but you'll regret it if you don't. And I really don't want to go without you. Come on, get up."

She hoisted Laura up by the arm in a businesslike way. Blackness swarmed behind Laura's eyes for a second but then dissipated. She counted her breaths and tried not to think of anyone's body as they walked south toward Joe's Bar, where the memorial was being held. It was midafternoon but felt later because the days were getting shorter. It was too cold to be outside in just a sweatshirt. Callie had put on her makeup for her, painting her eyelids and her lashes with layers of waterproof liner and mascara, dabbing concealer onto her puffy, tear-chafed cheeks. Still, she knew she looked bad. She had a momentary pang about not wanting Dylan to see her looking like this, then realized she'd never have to worry about that again.

There it was, on the bar, visible as soon as they walked in: a generic-looking black urn no bigger than a beer stein, flanked by vases of what looked like cheap bodega flowers and what must have been Dylan's senior photo from high school. He looked so different in it from the Dylan she'd known: awkward and skinny, with a bad droopy wave of bangs covering part of his zitty forehead, and a blankness in the eyes that negated the effect of his forced smile.

Callie left her side and moved toward Davey. The bar was full but not packed, and there was a stage area set up with instruments and amps and a mic, as if for a concert. She wondered who was going to speak and what on earth they could possibly say. No one had told her anything about what to expect from this event, or made it seem like she was responsible for doing anything, and it occurred to her now to be insulted by this. Shouldn't she say something? She had been his girlfriend. Did that matter now at all? There were lots of other women in the bar, and they all looked just as sad and stricken as she did. How was anyone supposed to know that she was different from the rest of these women, more entitled to grieve? Or maybe they'd all slept with Dylan. Maybe they felt the same way she did. She hadn't even known him well enough to know if his relationship with her was the kind of thing he got into all the time. She had to believe that she'd been special, because otherwise the pain she felt now was so, so extraordinarily stupid and pointless.

Callie came back over to where she was standing and handed her a vodka tonic. It was heavy on the vodka, and the first sip made her feel like she was sinking through the floor of the bar. "Davey's saying they're going to play soon, but they need someone to sing. I told him we would do it since we know the words to at least a few of their songs."

"They didn't think of this beforehand?"

"They thought they would just play and let the absence of Dylan's voice be, like, a poetic statement about his loss or some shit. But I told him that was stupid. We'll sound good with their band, it'll be a nice way for you to feel close to him, and it will be nice for everyone to see you as part of, you know, his legacy or whatever."

"I'm freaking out right now, Callie. I don't want to get up onstage," Laura said, but as she said it she looked around at the girls in the room. One tall one with a perfect fashion-mullet haircut had a blue leather jacket and pointy matching boots. She was crying streaks of mascara-smeared tears in a beautiful, photogenic way, and someone else with a fancy digital camera was taking pictures that she wasn't quite posing for, but also wasn't exactly shying away from. Looking at her, Laura realized that if she didn't stake a claim to Dylan today, she would relinquish any right to it in the future. It was the last thing she wanted to do, but for future Laura, she had to.

"People are going to get up and say things first, right?"

"His parents are going to speak. I haven't seen them yet, though. Oh, and your friend Amanda is here. Ryan from the management company tried to make this no-press, but she got in."

Laura looked around but didn't see Amanda. Davey and the other members of the Clips were clustered by the bar smoking cigarettes. It was oddly like an ordinary night at Joe's except that it was happening during the daytime. The buzz of chatter was punctuated by an occasional laugh, and every time that happened, Laura was pierced with a sharp twinge of anger. Dylan's fucking cremated ashes were sitting on the bar! She shuddered and drained the glass and went to the other end of the bar, far from the creepy photographer, but before she could get the overtaxed bartender's attention she felt a firm tap, almost a poke, on her shoulder.

Laura turned around to face Daisy, who was wearing a shapeless black dress that had some dog hair clinging to it.

"He cared about you," Daisy announced, without any preamble. She looked at the empty glass in Laura's hand and her glassy expression became focused; her eyebrows lowered, and her quivering voice turned hissy. "Yes, by all means, drink up. Lucky you, you have a way of feeling better. That is, if you feel bad. You probably think you feel pretty bad, don't you?"

Laura tried to figure out what she was supposed to say. They were, after all, at a bar. "I do feel bad," she managed. The bartender pushed another drink toward her, and without thinking she picked it up.

"Shove it in my face, why don't you!" The hissing was turning into screaming. Dylan's father came up behind her and put a soothing hand on her forearm.

"I'm fine! I'm fine! Don't touch me!" she shrieked at him.

"It's almost time for us to address everyone," he said evenly to Daisy. Laura, grateful for his interruption, murmured that she was sorry for his loss.

He nodded and smiled wryly at her, seeming anesthetized, very far away. Still, because it seemed important to have said it, Laura tried to stammer something about how much she had loved Dylan.

Without warning, Daisy grabbed Laura by the shoulders and shook her. "Loved! *Loved!* You don't know what love is, you little whore! You think you *loved* my son? He came from my body. My *body*! I *made* him! And now he's *dead*! You have no idea! No idea!"

Warm flecks of Daisy's spit were on Laura's cheeks. She turned away, shaking. Dylan's father made eye contact with Laura—briefly, maybe apologetically—and led Daisy away. Laura wiped her face with a bar napkin and drank the second vodka tonic even more quickly than she had the first.

A couple of minutes later, they were on the small stage. The microphone shrieked as Dylan's father began to speak. He thanked everyone for coming and said some things in a monotone about how Dylan had been talented and special. That his band had been important to him, and that he had been proud of his son for pursuing his dream, even though he didn't always understand his choices. That what had happened was tragic, and an accident, and that accidents happen all the time, and no one knows why but that we have to be comfortable not knowing, and it's just part of the great mystery of life. He didn't mention God. Laura had a flash of something like envy; she thought of how her own family would have responded to a death like this, how they would have twisted things around until they could convince themselves that it had been the Lord's will. Dylan's dad seemed like a smart, reasonable guy.

She looked over at Daisy, standing beside him. Her eyes were wide and bloodshot and her wet mouth hung open like a frenzied dog's. As scary as Daisy was, Laura sympathized with her, too. She also wanted someone to blame for Dylan's death, because of how uncomfortable it was to blame Dylan. But the thing was, it *had* been Dylan's fault. He'd been cavalier with everything—the feelings of people who cared about him, his possessions, his career, and ultimately, his life. Laura wished more than anything that she could see him again, smell his cigarette-sweat rankness as he bent down toward her to embrace her. But she also knew that he had been kind of an asshole. If he'd lived, he would have found another way to leave her that would have been just as final as this one. Of course she still loved him, though. How could she not?

Dylan's father embraced each member of the Clips as they traded places on the stage, but Daisy pointedly did not. Callie materialized near Laura and pulled her gently by the arm as they, too, climbed onstage. They huddled with Davey, who handed Laura Dylan's guitar. "I know you don't want to play, but do it for him. It would mean a lot," Davey said.

"What song are we even going to play?" Laura whispered. "It's going to be a disaster, I've never sung any of these before,"

"Whatever you want. What's the first song you ever heard him sing?"

It was the one she'd heard on the night they'd met, the one that had initially put her under his spell. She flashed on the memory of making eye contact with him outside, of the feeling she'd had of wanting to touch the skin that showed through the holes in his shirt. The skin that was now incinerated. Laura's stomach lurched. Those drinks had been much too strong; she hadn't eaten breakfast.

Still, she and Callie stood in front of the band as they played the opening notes. Callie started singing the doleful verse, and Laura began to harmonize with her, making the song sound less bombastic and more sad than its original version. For a minute, it seemed like everything was going to go okay, but then Laura's stomach roiled again and she felt sweaty all over. She made eye contact with Callie, whispered "Sorry," then ran offstage.

Outside the bar, she puked watery spatter against the side of the building, feeling like she might not be able to stand up for much longer. She could hear, from inside, the band's moment of indecision and then its resolution: they continued to play, and Callie kept singing. Laura wobbled, thinking of going back in, but then decided against it. She needed to lie down and rest; she had to go to work at the bar in a few hours.

———

When Laura woke up, it was dark out and Callie was just getting home. The apartment was cold; the radiators hadn't clanked on yet for some reason, and Laura burrowed into the pile of blankets, curling against the back of the couch, willing herself back into unconsciousness. Then she had the disturbing thought that she might have actually slept past the start of her shift; she hadn't bothered to set an alarm because it had seemed impossible that she'd sleep longer than a few hours. She rushed to stand up and immediately felt dizzy again. Slowly, she made her way down the hall to the kitchen and collapsed into a chair at the kitchen table. The wall clock said it was nine; she was due at the bar an hour ago.

Callie was standing by the sink, filling the Pyrex measuring cup with water and chugging it. She barely glanced up at Laura; she was drunk and seemed distracted.

"What happened to you? Are you okay? I wanted to come check on you earlier, but by the time we finished playing you were long gone, and then there were so many people there who wanted to talk. . . . Someone said they saw you throwing up outside?"

"I think I'm really sick," said Laura. She put her head in her hands.

"You just haven't been taking care of yourself. You'll start to feel better soon; you just need some food." She was probably planning to go back out later; it was early for her to call it a night, and Laura was sure that Davey and the rest of the band would be celebrating Dylan's life till well into the next day. She felt disgusted by all of them. Dylan's death was just another excuse for them to party.

"Callie, are you even sad?"

Callie was spreading butter on a piece of toast with her back to Laura. She put the toast down in front of her and took out her makeup bag and started redoing her eyeliner at the table. It had smudged, but it didn't look like she'd been crying.

"Of course I'm sad; I liked Dylan a lot. But it's complicated. I can't imagine how you feel, but it's a sad time in the world, too, and Dylan's just one person. . . ."

"I feel really bad. I don't know if this is normal for when someone dies. I feel dizzy and nauseous, and I'm worried something's really wrong with me." Laura picked up the toast and took a bite. She could feel it crunch under her teeth, taste the butter and salt, but then she couldn't figure out how to make her throat muscles work to swallow. She kept chewing it, hoping she could find a way to make her face and stomach work properly before it became necessary to spit it out.

Callie put down her hand mirror and scrutinized Laura.

"Are you pregnant?"

She reminded Callie that she was on the pill, then thought back to the last time she'd had sex, in Concord. The missed days. Laura felt sweat pool under her arms and immediately become clammy in their cold apartment. She hugged her knees up to her chest on the chair and shivered. Callie had already moved on.

"I told the Clips we'd play the rest of their tour with them. Like, as part of the band, like we did today."

She watched Laura for a reaction—waiting for permission, it seemed, to unveil her own smile.

It wasn't forthcoming. "Wait—so the Groupies? My songs? We're going to abandon our thing to replace Dylan?"

"Not abandon our thing. It's just to finish out the tour— they've already sold the tickets, somebody has to sing. It may as well be us, right? And then we'll see where it goes from there. If nothing else, it'll make it so much easier for us to get a recording contract—to actually put out an album of your songs. This is going to be how you become a star, Laura!"

Laura couldn't process what was happening. Callie was sitting there beaming, like she was delivering good news. But the piece of toast was still sitting in her mouth, saliva pooling around it. Callie was waiting for a response, though, so Laura had to speak in spite of it, sort of around it.

"If you want to do it, go ahead. But I can't. There's no way. I'm sorry." She grabbed Callie's water and took a gulp.

Callie returned to her makeup. "You just need more time to think about it. You won't pass up this chance, I know you won't. What are you going to do, stay here and work at the bar while I go on tour? I'm not even the one who wanted to be a musician!"

"Well, congratulations on getting to be one anyway," said Laura, then went back to bed so that she wouldn't have to talk about it anymore.

———

The days got even shorter, blurred together. Laura added leg warmers to her work uniform of black skirt and black tights. She woke every morning full of a heart-racing panic that dissipated gradually as she tried to bury herself in distracting activity. She took as many shifts at Bar Lafitte as she could, hoarding the money in a shoebox under her couch-bed. The initial mood of mania dissipated quickly, but the bar stayed busy; the customers drank harder and harder.

She passed fading posters on lampposts that people had put up looking for their lost relatives and friends, with blurry color-photocopied photographs, as though the people were dogs and cats who might turn up in a vacant lot or in someone else's home. She wished that she could mourn with all the other mourners. Maybe then her burden wouldn't feel so huge. Dylan had been the love of her life, but he was also just a guy she'd been dating for a few weeks. She had never even mentioned him to her family. No one knew to treat her carefully. And when she caught herself weeping silent tears while walking down the street, she knew that people assumed that she was crying for one of the other dead people, and again she felt like a liar.

———

When she finally got around to taking a pregnancy test, it confirmed what she already knew. A secret feeling, buried deep and almost beneath the level of conscious thought, was a tiny glowing ball of happiness and even excitement when she'd seen the second line appear. Part of it was just relief; the physical and emotional strangeness she'd felt lately had a concrete cause that could be resolved. But another part of it was a feeling of escape from the finality of Dylan's death. He was still alive, in some illusory but also real way. She remembered how he'd felt and smelled, but when she tried to imagine his face, the version she called to mind was the version she'd memorized, not his true face. A baby would not be vague. A baby would keep some part of him tethered to this world, and she had the power to make that happen.

PART II

6

Laura woke up with a panicky start. Someone in her dream had been crying. Was Marie crying, or just making impatient *babab* noises in her crib? Was the hour morning-like enough that she should feel obligated to retrieve her, open the blinds, and begin the day, or should she try to lie silently and fake sleep so that Marie might learn to sleep a little longer? She wasn't going to be able to go back to sleep because she'd remembered that it was the first of the month; rent was due, and she was going to be late with it again unless she asked for someone's help, but she was running out of people to ask.

Marie's *bababa*s were turning into shouts. Laura rolled out of bed and crossed the room almost at a jog. She was still in the habit of rushing, even though now that Marie was almost ten months old, there wasn't the same risk there had been when she was newborn and her cries would escalate into raspy, full-throated wailing if Laura didn't appear within seconds. Back then, Laura would run to her as though to a bomb that required immediate, steady-handed defusing.

Marie was sitting up in her crib, and when she saw Laura, she made eye contact and smiled as though all her most cherished dreams were all coming true at once. The black muck circulating all through Laura's body and around her brain dissipated immediately, and she smiled back at Marie with equal radiance. They beamed at each other for a moment, and then Laura picked up Marie and Marie smacked her happily in the face and yanked her hair while sucking a tiny circular bitemark into the flesh of her upper arm while making delighted, gleeful gurgles.

"Gentle," Laura said, as though Marie could understand or care, and "Look! Outside!" as they approached the window. She pulled the cord and sunshine streamed into their small room. "Look, there's the Laundromat. And the pizza place, and the Chinese place, and the bodega."

Marie interrupted her pinching exploration of Laura's tattered T-shirt and upper chest to wave to these businesses. All their graffitied shutters were still down; it was six thirty and even the Laundromat didn't open till eight. But there were streaks of light making the dingy storefronts look somewhat appealing, at least, and soon there would be leaves on the spindly trees instead of just plastic bags flapping in the wind. The winter would be over soon. As long as she didn't have to wake up while it was still dark out, Laura thought, she could withstand almost anything. She would never have to live Marie's terrifyingly helpless first few months on earth again; that alone was cause enough for celebration.

Laura nursed Marie in the chair by the window instead of lying down in bed so that she wouldn't be tempted to fall back asleep. The last time she'd done that, she'd been jarred out of her lazy drowse by a moment of cold-blooded horror as she saw Marie scuttling with lightning speed toward the edge of the bed. At first Marie focused so hard on nursing that she was almost cross-eyed, but once her initial desperate hunger was sated, she looked up at Laura as she sucked and gently whapped her chest with an open palm. Laura grabbed her hand and absently toyed with her fingers, which Marie found so funny that she stopped nursing to laugh. She laughed all the time now, usually at things that Laura didn't see the humor in, like the face she involuntarily made when Marie pulled her hair, or at a particular page of the frankly idiotic book about penguins. But it was so good to hear her laugh that Laura offered up her hair and read the stupid penguin book every day. She was more smitten with Marie than she had ever been with anyone in her life. Her feelings for Marie made her feelings for Dylan seem even more like a distant memory. She had never glimpsed his likeness in her baby's face, which had seemed from her first moments like a wholly original face, nothing to do with how either of her parents looked at all.

She had worked at Bar Lafitte far into her pregnancy, wearing low-cut empire-waist dresses in an attempt to focus patrons' attention on her growing breasts and not on the bulge below. After Marie's birth she'd tried to work nights again but had to quit after a week; she'd spent every minute at the bar in a state of barely concealed panic, imagining the ineptitude of the teenage neighbor whom she was paying to sit on her couch while she tried to smile at the tables of men who just had no idea, no possible idea, of what it was costing her mentally to make small talk with them while her daughter was probably crying for her a full half-hour subway ride away. And then she'd had to pay the teenager almost all of what she'd managed to make. It made no sense.

So she had set out to combine all her interests—making money, playing music, and being in the same room as her baby—

by teaching baby music classes. This brain wave, when it had first occurred to her, had seemed like the solution to all her problems. She quickly learned a repertoire of classics about ducks and buses and monkeys jumping on the bed, wrote a couple of originals whose loopiness belied their late-night origins, put up some brightly colored flyers in the nicer neighborhoods immediately adjacent to her less nice new neighborhood—a liminal zone that included warehouses and a toxic ribbon of sludge called the Gowanus Canal—and soon she had booked a few regular gigs at toy stores and yoga studios. One of the women who ran children's programming at a local yoga mini-chain had even heard of the Groupies, which made Laura feel fleetingly cool, linked to her old self in a way she hadn't felt for a while. The first few months of this new career were pure bliss. Marie was still a little butterfly who could be distracted for ages by dust motes or a rattle attached to her wrist, and sometimes she would even fall asleep—just like that, with no preamble or coaxing, leaving Laura free to march around the room interacting energetically with other people's children, hamming it up as much as possible in order to cement herself in their tiny minds so that her class might become an important part of their routine, important enough that they'd sign up for a five-class or ten-class package and enable Laura to buy another week's worth of groceries.

But as Marie's personality had asserted itself and her mobility increased, it was becoming much harder to both wrangle her and amuse ten other babies and their respective handlers. Instead of sitting mesmerized and clap-flapping her hands like the other babies did as Laura strummed hard and bounced around, Marie would crawl around the perimeter of the room, inevitably finding the one non-hidden cord or uncovered socket. She would open other people's diaper bags and upend their contents onto the floor, or steal her compatriots' bottles and drink some stranger's breast milk from them.

She did not intend these actions to be aggressive or evil, of course. She was a little baby! Still, it was hard not to interpret her antics as a form of sabotage, especially because it was working. Attendance was down, and reenrollment was getting rarer. Laura was beginning to suspect that she would have to find another new line of work, something lucrative enough to justify the amount of babysitting it would require, but she was already treading water every day trying to fulfill her existing obligations, and it was impossible to imagine how she would find time to seek out new ones. She worried about money every waking moment, her brain ticking through a litany of options one by one and finding each mental door closed. Her mother, though delighted to have another grandchild, was so cash-strapped that Laura could not imagine asking her for anything; the $50 gift card she had sent when Marie was born had, Laura knew, required her to cut a corner somewhere else in the budget. When she would inevitably reach the end of the mental hallway, Daisy was always there. Dylan's family clearly had money in a way that Laura's did not. In Laura's imagination Daisy was always wearing the same shapeless black dress she'd worn to Dylan's memorial, but she was sitting at a table piled high with stacks of cash, like a waitress at Bar Lafitte at the end of the world's most successful shift. It was tempting. But Daisy was awful, and she hated Laura. Laura didn't want someone like that in her and Marie's new life.

Marie popped off Laura's nipple and began thrashing around, begging to be put on the floor. Laura obliged and dressed as quickly as possible, finding her last pair of acceptably clean jeans and her second-to-last pair of underpants, all with one eye on Marie, who was grunting as she fished around between the uneven floorboards in the hopes of finding another delicious nail like the one Laura had prized out of her mouth a few days earlier. After Laura managed to clothe herself she set about the miniature wrestling match that was dressing and diapering Marie, finishing with just enough time to feed Marie a banana and make herself a cup of instant coffee before it was nonnegotiably time to strap the baby onto her front and her guitar to her back and hustle the five long and ten short blocks to her first class of the day.

Laura sailed through the class undisturbed by Marie, who seemed uncharacteristically subdued. As the other babies clapped and flailed along to Laura's original composition about an octopus who needs to buy—but cannot afford—eight new shoes (semiautobiographical in origin), Marie sat at the periphery of the circle, chewing listlessly on someone else's expensive rubber giraffe. Laura imagined that Marie was attaining some new milestone of maturity and could now intuit when her mother needed her to be calm. They were going to work together as a team now, Laura thought, and her heart swelled. The true cause of Marie's newfound mature attitude revealed itself, though, as class was ending, when she simultaneously puked and shat herself so profoundly that Laura had to rush off to the bathroom to change her clothes. The moms and nannies of the other students looked on in horror as Laura hustled a wailing, drippy Marie into the yoga studio's pristine, lavender-scented bathroom. Three of those bitches had arrived late and had not yet paid. "We'll get you next time, Laura!" one of them had the grace to shout through the door on her way out; the other two didn't even mention it. Even though thirty dollars wasn't the difference between what Laura had and what she owed her landlord—three hundred was more like it—it was still enough to make her feel a flush of rage as she stuffed Marie's sodden, reeking onesie and leggings into a plastic bag, resisting the temptation to just throw them away. She finished wiping Marie down as best she could despite her vehement protests, then sat on the toilet to comfort her with a boob so that she would chill out enough to be put into the carrier. Marie's fluffy head was damp with sweat. How had she become so sick so quickly? Laura bent down and kissed her poor little baby's clammy brow while dialing the only phone number she knew by heart.

On the third try, Callie finally answered, and Laura hastily begged her to come to Brooklyn and take care of Marie while she taught the rest of her classes.

She heard Callie shifting around and making bleary thumping sounds. "Are you trying to figure out what time it is? It's ten thirty a.m.," said Laura. Laura always knew what time it was, now.

"Can you not be a bitch for a second? I'm just waking up. How long do you need me to take her for? We've got band practice later. I mean, I do."

"I just need you until my last class of the day gets out; it's near the apartment, so I should be home by four fifteen. You could be back in Manhattan by five, probably. The other thing is, the reason I need you to take her is that she's sick, but you won't need to do anything except keep an eye on her fever. She'll probably just snooze for most of the day," Laura said, hoping she was telling the truth. "Oh, and the apartment is a bit of a mess, I apologize in advance."

Callie sighed. "So, wait, I'm going to be exposed to some super-toxic baby germs? I can't get sick right now, dude. And you know I'm not a baby expert."

This was true. Laura avoided asking Callie for help except in cases like this one, when she absolutely could not avoid it. Everyone else she knew in New York was either a late-night acquaintance, like Alexis, or a fellow new mom with her own shit to deal with. Callie was still her closest friend, and as underqualified as she was as a babysitter, she at least would show up, however late, and do it. She meant well, and didn't hate kids by any means. It wasn't her fault that she didn't operate on a momlike frequency. She didn't understand those little semi-intuitive things, like how to figure out that Marie needed to nap and put her down before she became punch-drunk, overtired, and inconsolable. Once, after Callie had been called in to emergency-babysit, Laura had discovered Marie's onesie fastened underneath her diaper.

Laura sighed. "Callie, I am really sorry about this, but I wouldn't ask if I wasn't in a total bind. I can't afford to miss my classes, and if I pay a sitter, it'll cost just as much as missing them. Can you please try to get to my place before noon? I really think she'll just sleep, and I will totally owe you one."

"One what? Redeemable when?" Callie said, in a way that seemed like she mostly was kidding, but almost not.

Laura snapped. "If anyone owes anyone anything, Callie, it's you! I could be waking up at noon and doing what you're doing, if it wasn't for . . ."

"Well, that was your choice!"

Laura thought she could hear tears in Callie's voice. She always had been an easy cry. It was always how she'd won fights; it was impossible to yell at a crying person.

"What am I supposed to do, sit out everything good in life until you're ready to rejoin me?"

"I'm sorry. I didn't mean to be harsh, I'm just running on so little sleep here and I . . . look, you'll come, right?"

"I don't know." Callie sniffed and paused, but Laura knew she would help. She would be late and resentful, and she would put in the bare minimum, but she would come.

Laura managed to get most of the way home before Marie puked again, warm liquid squishing against her chest and immediately turning cold in the early-spring air. They entered the apartment building with Marie wailing, but in a subdued way that conveyed her extreme dissatisfaction with the state of affairs in the carrier as well as her weakened condition. As repulsed as part of Laura felt by her barf-covered baby and self, the other part of her—the animal that had not existed before Marie was born—wanted nothing more than to comfort Marie and hold her close, no matter what vile substances covered her. She ran up the four flights of stairs to minimize her neighbors' exposure to the sound, shucked the guitar, carrier, and diaper bag as soon as she entered the apartment, then stripped both herself and Marie naked just inside the front door and walked straight into the shower. She would throw all their wet clothes into a plastic bag later, she told herself. Marie was not a fan of this experience, but by the time they were rinsed clean, her hoarse protest cries had begun to taper into resigned, sustained whining. As quickly as she could, Laura got the limp-limbed baby into a diaper and set her in her crib, where she ratcheted up to sob screams again for the twenty-five seconds it took Laura to put on underpants and the T-shirt she'd slept in. Finally she scooped up Marie and lay down with her in the unmade bed, where Marie lunged for a boob and fell asleep within seconds. Laura shifted around, getting as comfortable as possible in the odd side-lying position that Marie's presence next to her necessitated, and made a mental note to wake up before Callie arrived and try to get the apartment looking baseline livable, then fell asleep and didn't wake up again until she heard the buzzer. She looked at the clock. It was twelve thirty; her class was half an hour away at a toy store in Fort Greene.

Complaining about Callie's lateness was probably not the best way to greet her, but Laura's panic had to rest somewhere. Callie shrugged and waved her hand in front of her face to indicate that the apartment smelled bad. She was wearing a suede miniskirt, long dangly earrings, and hot-pink lipstick. Had she spent an extra half hour making herself cute?! It was an impulse that Laura could no longer relate to on any level. She handed Callie a seminude Marie, who at least was not crying, and hurriedly shoved the barf clothes pile into a trash bag.

"I'm sorry about the smell. I'll open a window. I didn't have time to make a bottle, but there are bags of pumped milk in the freezer—you know how to defrost them, right?—and she probably won't be hungry anyway. Do you know how to take her temperature? It would be great if you can keep an eye on it. And there's baby Tylenol around here somewhere that you can give her. Oh, and can you put clothes on her?"

Marie was, mercifully, not seeming all that sick at the moment; her nap had renewed her and she was happily *bababa*ing and playing with Callie's long earrings.

"Watch out," Laura warned. "She'll yank those right through your earlobe."

Callie put Marie down on the floor so that she could remove her jewelry, and Marie immediately scuttled over to a puke-soaked sock that Laura had missed and began happily waving it around. Puke droplets spattered onto the grimy floorboards. Marie grinned up at Laura and Callie with total trust and joy.

"Oh my God, she's so gross," Callie said quietly.

Laura had an almost uncontrollable impulse to scoop Marie up into her arms and tell Callie never mind, that she would skip her classes and stay with her baby. But, she reminded herself, there was an outside chance, if attendance was good, that she would be able to make enough money today to at least give her landlord the impression that she was trying very, very hard and would be able to pay the remainder of her rent within the week. Callie might not be Mary Poppins, but she would keep Marie alive, and being able to keep living in their own apartment was worth one less-than-stellar afternoon of Marie's life.

Laura ran to the bedroom part of the studio and threw on leggings, a bra and an oversize, not-too-stained cardigan in a bright color that the babies in her classes seemed to like, grabbed her guitar, and snuck out of the apartment as quickly as possible; long goodbyes only made Marie more unhappy. With a final apology to Callie, who was picking up the wet clothes on the floor with the very tips of her painted fingernails, Laura ran down the stairs, filled with the feeling of having forgotten something vital. She had her keys, wallet, phone, and guitar, though; the feeling that nagged at her was the absence of Marie's soft weight against her chest. For the first block of her sprint northward she fought back a dumb lump of tears that threatened to emerge from her throat, but soon she began to feel light and even a little bit free. It was extremely rare for her to be without Marie, and even though it was strange and sad, she couldn't help but also feel that it was nice, for a moment, to be out in the world alone.

The first of the afternoon's classes passed without incident and with a decent number of babies enrolled, and Laura decided to treat herself by going to the diner across the street to get a cup of soup to go. She even had a small break to eat it, about ten minutes. She thought about calling Callie to check in but decided that fewer distractions were probably better.

But as she opened the lid of the paper container full of soup and the warm, brothy smell rose to her nostrils, Laura was assailed by a wave of nausea. "Fuuuuuck," she murmured aloud, and the toy store clerk, seated at the register a few feet away from the bench where Laura was crouching, gave her a schoolmarmish "There are children present" look, even though currently there were none. Laura sat very still, willing the feeling to subside, but there was no getting around it: she had been puked on, and she would not escape unscathed.

"I have to cancel the rest of the day's classes," she told the officious toy store lady. "I'm feeling sick, and I shouldn't be around the babies."

"I understand, Laura, but we really need someone reliable teaching these classes," said the lady, who was quickly becoming

Laura's mortal enemy. "If you can't teach, you know that it's your responsibility to find a sub."

"Of course. I'll give it a shot. I'm just going to use the restroom first," said Laura, hustling the words out as quickly as possible with the certain, doomy foreknowledge that there was vomit hot on their heels.

In the brief, illusory period of feeling shaky but okay that followed immediately after she'd emptied her stomach into the receptacle labeled "Tiddle-Tidy the big-kid potty," Laura called Johannes, the only other children's musician whose number was in her phone. Once she'd managed to ascertain that her afternoon classes would be covered, she pressed her hot forehead to the cool rim of Tiddle-Tidy for a moment before gathering her strength and wobbling back out into the store.

"Johannes is coming," she said as she walked past the desk. "Thanks for understanding; see you on Tuesday."

"You'll definitely make it?"

Laura was too sick and enervated to even expend the emotional energy being annoyed. "Of course," she said, and hurried to leave before she had to throw up again.

———

When she got back to the apartment, Marie was practicing pulling herself up on the coffee table and banging on it with a wooden spoon, and Callie was lying on the couch, looking as exhausted as Laura felt even though it had been only an hour and a half since she'd left.

"Looks like someone's feeling better!"

"Oh my God, Laura, she's relentless! If she isn't trying to crawl into the bathroom to play in the toilet, she's yelling nonsense at the top of her lungs and insisting that I try a bite of her toys. I have no idea how you manage to handle this twenty-four/seven. Hey, aren't you home early?"

Laura sank to her knees next to Marie and felt her forehead, then kept sinking till she was lying on the ground. Marie crawled on top of her, pulled herself up, and started biting her shoulder, grunting with excitement. "Yeah, I had to bail. I think I'm coming down with Marie's stomach flu. I really hope you don't get it."

"No worries. I made sure not to touch her."

"You what?"

"I just shooed her away from places she shouldn't be with my foot."

Laura paused for a moment, willing herself not to be annoyed at Callie. "She probably needs a diaper change . . ." She paused and sniffed Marie's butt. "Wow. Yeah, she definitely—ugh, fuck."

Disengaging herself from Marie's clutching hands as quickly as possible, Laura lurched into the bathroom, just managing to shut the door so that Marie wouldn't follow her. As she heaved, she heard Callie through the door.

"I'm gonna go, but just call me if you need anything, okay? Oh, and also your landlord came by—did you know your rent is overdue? He said he'd be back again later to pick it up."

Laura rested, dizzy, then vomited again. "I don't have it," she said, not sure if she was talking loudly enough for Callie to hear.

When she emerged, she was surprised to see that Callie was still there, and that her vintage pink plastic purse was open on the coffee table. "How much are you short?"

"A lot. You really don't have to . . . I wasn't asking."

"Is two hundred fifty enough? That's all the cash I have on me."

"That's amazing. I'll get you back next week." Laura smiled weakly, too sick to feel humiliated, just relieved. "You're a life-saver, Callie, seriously. Thank you so much for this."

"You're welcome, and next time, just ask me, okay? Do *not* hug me. I'll check in with you guys later. Bye, little monster," she said, giving Marie a parting nudge with her heel.

Laura sank back down to the floor. It wasn't even three yet, but all she wanted was for the rest of the day to be canceled, stricken from the calendar. Her immediate problem was solved, but a new one had presented itself: How was she supposed to take care of Marie while the only activity that she could really see herself doing for the next twenty-four hours was lying in bed shivering, occasionally getting up to vomit?

She wanted someone to bring her saltines and ginger ale, change the sheets, press a cold washcloth to her forehead. There was no one in her life like that, though. She was the person who brought saltines.

She picked Marie up off the floor and went to change her diaper. The poop was slightly more solid than it had been the last time she'd done so, but it still wasn't a great sign that it was happening so often. Marie was, mercifully, much less fazed by being sick than Laura was. She smiled up at her mother as she changed her diaper and laughed uproariously as Laura bent forward to blow kisses on her warm little belly. Marie was so beautiful, Laura thought helplessly. They happened, these per-fect moments, glittering brilliantly between the horrors. The afternoon stretched ahead of them, and Laura had no idea how she'd fill the four hours before bedtime. She was too sick to leave the apartment, and just the thought of the maneuvers necessary to get Marie back into outdoor clothes and strapped into the carrier made Laura feel like sandbags were pressing down on all her limbs. She put Marie down in the kitchen while she washed her hands at the sink, and when she turned around Marie was holding a butter knife she'd found somewhere, thoughtfully sawing it back and forth between her toothless gums. She just needed to stay occupied long enough that Laura could do some dishes, so that she wouldn't be completely ashamed for their landlord to see the state of the apartment.

She shoved a threadbare VHS tape into the combination TV/VCR she'd found on a nearby curb and set Marie, who was still clutching the butter knife, down in front of it. To Laura's chagrin, Marie was still too young to really care about TV but would usually get sucked in after a few minutes of the *Sesame Street* compilation's brightly colored singing and talking. Laura pulled out her wallet in order to add what was in it to the cash that Callie had given—lent? Ugh, let's hope given—her, hoping that her mental math was off and that she'd be at or possibly even over $750, the magic number.

"BA!" Marie shouted at the TV, gesturing with the knife, then turned her back on it to crawl over to where Laura was sitting. She pulled herself up on the edge of the coffee table and grabbed for the stack of twenty- and ten-dollar bills.

"Baby, Mommy is counting. Can you just watch TV, please? Look, Grover!" Laura's head was pounding.

Marie, undeterred, stayed at the table's edge, bouncing her big diapered butt happily up and down.

"Okay, you can help me count. Twenty, forty, sixty, eighty, one hundred!" She put the bills into neat piles. Marie watched, mesmerized. Laura tried to keep the disappointment out of her voice as she announced, "Seven hundred and ten!" at the end of the last sheaf of bills. She hurriedly shoved them back into her purse before Marie could grab them.

As if on cue, there was a knock at the door. Laura shivered with a combination of feverishness and dread. Even when she hadn't done anything wrong, she still hated interacting with Sean, her landlord, who had the mien of a feudal lord visiting his serf's hovel. The smell of his mentholated cologne would linger for hours, even if she didn't let him sit down and get it on any of her furniture. This building, like most of the ones on her block, belonged to his family; this one was "his" to manage and maintain. He was blond with no eyebrows and always wore a Yankees cap, even in winter. Even though he couldn't have been that much older than Laura, he oozed smug superiority, the contempt that city people feel for tourists. She wished that she'd had time to look harder for a place when she was pregnant, but it had become clear to her a little bit late in the game that having a baby and continuing to live in Callie's East Village living room was a terrible idea, and she'd taken the first livable, theoretically affordable Brooklyn apartment that she'd seen. She'd been thinking of space for Marie and proximity to other people who had babies, even if she didn't know them yet. She hadn't thought about having to deal with someone like Sean. On Third

Street, she and Callie had paid their rent by mailing checks to a PO box, which was only stressful because they had to remember to do it on time or else risk a sternly worded form letter and a fifteen-dollar fine. She had never paid Sean late or been short on the rent before, but he'd always counted it in front of her while leering at her milk-swollen boobs in a way that dared her to say something. In the context of Bar Lafitte, she would have laughed off a skinny, obviously powerless goon. In the context of the interior of her own apartment, it was less easy to do so.

"I'm forty dollars short, but I'll get it to you tomorrow," she said as she handed him the cash. "Also, Marie and I have the stomach flu, so . . ." She made a shooing gesture with her hands. "We're super contagious, I'm pretty sure."

Sean seemed unfazed. "I have a great immune system. You really can't be late with the rent, Laura, I don't recommend doing that around here."

Laura shrugged. "Sorry. Tomorrow. Okay, see you then!" She waited for him to move toward the door. Instead, he counted the handful of bills she'd given him, arriving at the same number she just had but much more slowly and not out loud. Marie peered curiously up at him and flapped a hand, waving and smiling.

"Hey, kiddo," he said to her, and as Marie laughed and smiled, Sean bent down as if to pick her up or touch her. Laura's entire body clenched with hatred that, for the moment, overpowered her flu-ish weakness. She couldn't stop herself from bending to snatch Marie and move away from Sean.

"Chill out, sweetheart, I'm just trying to be nice here," he said.

"I just really wouldn't want you getting sick," said Laura through clenched teeth. They stared each other down for a long beat, and Laura felt her face twitch with the effort of maintaining her strained mirthless smile. Then Sean turned and walked out the door, and Laura shut it behind him. She exhaled slowly as she heard him knocking on the next door down the hall.

This surge of adrenaline carried Laura through till the end of Marie's day, keeping her upright as she dosed an increasingly cranky baby with bright pink liquid Tylenol, fed her some applesauce and yogurt that she managed to keep down, and gave her a more thorough bath than the slapdash emergency shower she'd taken midday. They lay in bed together, and Laura read the stupid penguin book and nursed Marie to sleep and put her down in her crib. Almost as soon as Marie was sound asleep, Laura's body realized it was allowed to collapse and she found herself hovering over the toilet again, vomiting even though she hadn't had anything but water in hours. The sheer force of her heaves reminded her of what it had been like to give birth.

After she was done purging every ounce of fluid in her body, Laura lay in bed shivering, feverish, drifting between thoughts and dreams. She wondered repeatedly whether she should get up and take Advil to attempt to break her fever and risk vomiting it up, deciding each time that staying supine and shivering was the best and, for now, only viable course of action. She wished someone would bring her Advil and maybe a handful of freshly fallen snow to wash it down with. She thought about her own mother, when she'd been sick as a child, getting up in the night to bring her medicine and staying with her, rubbing her back until she found sleep again. It was hard to reconcile this memory with the current version of her mother, who never seemed attuned to or curious about the specifics of her continued existence. They talked on the phone once a month or so, and Laura was never exactly honest about anything; her mother still didn't understand why she was living in New York or how, exactly, she'd ended up with a baby, and this had created a gulf between them that made real communication impossible, so instead they said nonsense things about the minutiae of their days, TV shows that were terrible, her brothers' kids doing well or badly in school.

Despite all that, Laura still wished for her mother to come and rub her back. When she was little, at least, her mother must have loved her—maybe even loved her as much as Laura now loved Marie. How else could it be possible to take care of someone who needed so much, all the time? The scariest thing was the idea that a similar gulf could someday exist between Laura and Marie. She wanted to cry just thinking about this possibility, but she was too exhausted and dehydrated to even summon tears. It was impossible, anyway. Laura and Marie were always going to be a dyad, united against the oppressive world, as close as they were now, even in an impossible-to-imagine future when Marie did not sleep five feet from Laura and get much of her nourishment from Laura's body.

As Laura thought this, Marie woke and rustled, as if to determine whether she was unhappy enough to cry. Ultimately she must have decided that yes, she was. With an enormous effort Laura pulled herself out of bed and went to the crib, lifted Marie back into bed with her, and pulled up her shirt to give her a boob. Marie closed her eyes again and kicked both feet against Laura's leg happily as she soothed herself back into slumber, one hand draped languidly across Laura's chest and the other gently tugging on a tuft of her own hair.

7

In the spring of 2005, Callie texted Laura and asked her if she could get a drink later in the week, and because it had been probably a month since she'd had any recreational social contact Laura texted back "YES!!" without even checking first to see whether she could get either of Marie's two favorite sitters.

Luckily, Caroline was free. Marie was obsessed with Caroline. She had actually told Laura that she preferred Caroline's company to Laura's, which did sting a bit. "If I got paid sixteen dollars an hour to hang out with you, I'd be much more fun to be around," Laura felt like telling her, but it wasn't really the kind of thing you should say to an almost-three-year-old.

In the week leading up to their date, whenever her brain was in an idle mode—doing dishes, picking toys up off the floor, teaching rich ten-year-olds how to play folk songs their grandparents liked—Laura found herself wondering why Callie had gotten back in touch. Their lives and schedules were so different these days that they often went a month or two without seeing each other. The primary way Laura kept tabs on her friends who did things in the world was now via the internet. Callie's iteration of the Clips had made two albums, played midsize venues all over the country and the world, and had even opened for the Shins on a few dates where they'd played arenas.

They had arranged to meet on the early side, in deference to Laura's schedule, at a bar in her new neighborhood. As usual, Callie was running almost half an hour late, but Laura didn't really mind; half an hour to herself, just to be alone with her thoughts, was almost better than having a drink with a friend. Okay, it *was* better. But any longer than thirty minutes and she would relax too fully, get too luxuriously wrapped up in her solitude, and Callie's eventual arrival would be as jarring as an early-morning alarm clock intruding on a pleasant dream.

She ordered a grilled cheese sandwich and a pint of IPA, then claimed a seat close to the front windows of the dimly lit Pencil Factory bar so that she could read. She had forgotten to bring a book, so she had to read the daily free newspaper that she found on a barstool. Any text that wasn't about Busytown was a balm to Laura's brain.

When Callie finally arrived, the grilled cheese was long gone and Laura was well into her second IPA, a decision she would likely regret at five forty-five the next morning. The sun was setting, and the bar was fully transitioning from late-afternoon sleepiness to its more bustling nighttime mode. Callie had done her eyeliner in the same way that she'd worn it in the music video where Callie and Davey, who were no longer romantically involved, made out in a field of poppies that turned into dripping hearts as they slid hypnotically down the screen toward a puddle of what looked like blood on the floor. That particular song wasn't like the rest of the Clips' second album; it sounded more like one of Laura's songs, with a simple structure and a basic, hooky chord progression. That was because Laura had written it. The songwriting credit, especially since it had gotten licensed to a commercial, had provided enough cash to pay off one of her credit cards, and it continued to provide a small but much-needed cushion of what now felt like checks for nothing. Whenever Laura heard it, which was rarely because she never really sought out new music these days, she felt like she could hear something missing in it. Possibly her voice.

Callie seemed, on the surface, not to notice that people were looking at her, but Laura had known her long enough that she could see the emboldening effect a little bit of attention had on her. She straightened up and became more poised and pretty. Looking at Callie was like looking at an image of Callie: her edges were so crisp. Laura had taken some pains with her own appearance, but she was very conscious of her own blurriness—the halo of frizz across the surface of her air-dried, split-ended hair, the pills of fuzz on her years-old black acrylic cardigan. Laura wasn't unattractive, she knew, by anyone's standards—she was young, and thin because she barely had time to eat, and her face was still open and inviting. But Callie was an idea that people were already familiar with. They looked at her and saw their memory of her superimposed on her actual self. That was being famous.

"You have a little something . . . here, let me," she said as she reached over to dislodge the tiny piece of burnt grilled cheese crumb from the corner of Laura's mouth. It was a disorienting moment of humiliation mixed with pleasure; she was a slob, but also, how nice to be gently touched. It had been a while since anyone had touched her.

"I'm just going to grab a drink. You need a refill?" Callie pointed to Laura's glass as she walked to the bar. Her glass still had a few sips left in it. Laura hesitated, knowing that if she did, Callie would decide for her. The drinks she ordered came quickly, even though there had been several people waiting before her, and she set another beer down in front of Laura, and a vodka soda in front of herself. She clinked the rim of her glass against Laura's and started politely asking her about her life and politely listening to her answers, or at least pretending to.

Laura had long since stopped trying to fill Callie in on specifics. Spinning the latest events of Marie's life into a funny anecdote for someone who didn't have any points of reference for what little kids were like just made her feel gross, like a bad stand-up comedian, and like she was selling out Marie's intimate little details in a way that was disrespectful to her. With a fellow parent—someone from Marie's day care or one of her coworkers—she would not have hesitated to share the week's big events, which had included Marie shouting to a full coffee shop that she had just pooped. But with Callie, it was different. She wanted her life to seem cozy, not shit-smeared.

"I've been really busy!"

"Busy how?"

"Well, I'm doing all these different jobs—teaching private music lessons, working in a school part-time. I work all the time that I'm not with Marie so I can afford her childcare, basically."

"But when she's in day care you get some time to think about your own music again, right?"

Laura took a larger sip. "I haven't really been doing that at all. It's just not coming. Like, there's no idle time for ideas for songs to just float in my direction."

"Not even in the shower?"

"In the shower I'm thinking about my schedule for the week, making grocery lists, keeping track of money—my brain won't let that boring shit drop for long enough to let anything more interesting in."

"That's disappointing."

It was a strange thing for Callie to say.

"Like, you personally are disappointed in me?"

Callie paused, and Laura could tell that she was trying to act casual about something that was actually a big deal. She had always been so transparent when she wanted something. Now she shot Laura her winningest smile, all teeth visible. Had she had them whitened?

"I had been hoping . . . We, I mean, the band was hoping you would write more songs for our next album. Maybe even play some dates on the tour, even just the East Coast shows, if that's all you have time for, but if you can, we'd love it. I've been feeling like we need more of your kind of songs."

Callie's charm wasn't working; it was having the opposite of its intended effect. Did she really think she could use Laura as needed, forgetting about her in between times when she came in handy? Laura felt her breathing speeding up, and struggled to keep her tone light. "I'm so surprised to hear you say that!"

"Why?"

"I just thought I was this totally ancillary part of your success. I just happened to be there at the beginning of your story."

"Well, that's not what happened." Callie clinked her ice cubes and looked directly into Laura's eyes. Her beautiful, seamless makeup crinkled softly in the center of her forehead, where she was making a wrinkle appear to express her concern.

"It's just hard to think about without getting mad. But I'm not mad at you, exactly."

She was, though. The combination of the low-grade irritation of having to wait for Callie plus the beers and the attendant worry about how unpleasant tomorrow morning would be had unlocked some capacity to feel truly angry that had lain dormant in her until this exact moment. But there was another feeling running in a channel parallel to it in Laura's body. It was, maybe, excitement. She'd had slightly too much to drink.

Callie moved closer to her, like when she'd brushed the crumb away, but this time she held Laura's face cupped in her hand. It was like when she used to do Laura's makeup, when she'd wielded control of Laura's face, how people saw her. From the corner of her eye, Laura saw several men at the bar trying to be subtle about the fact that they were openly staring at them. From an outsider's perspective, it did seem like they might be about to kiss. But what was between them was more complicated than sex.

"Don't take your anger out on me. Channel it into your music, make something out of it. You still can," Callie said, intoning the corny words with total seriousness, like a fortune-teller or a self-help guru. Laura nodded, mesmerized by Callie's closeness, her perfume, her beauty, the beers.

"So you're in?"

"I'm in," Laura heard herself saying, without quite believing it.

8

The initial moment of leaving Marie to go to Philly to play a show went much worse than Laura had imagined. She should have left Marie overnight much earlier in their life together, before Marie had the ability to describe her feelings with words. That would have been so much easier for both of them, or at least for Laura. But there had never been a reason to leave her until now, and so they were both unrehearsed for the moment of their separation.

She had wangled an invitation for Marie to spend the weekend with Kayla, her best friend from day care, whose dad, Matt, was one of the more relaxed-seeming fellow parents. He had sleepy eyes and a potbelly, and had done a credible job of not seeming scandalized by Laura's age when he'd first met her. No one in her bougie neighborhood believed that an English-speaking white woman under thirty could be a toddler's mother, not her babysitter.

All week long, whenever she'd been able to work the upcoming trip into conversation, Laura had told Marie about how much fun she was going to have at Kayla's house and what a big-girl treat it would be to sleep in an unfamiliar bed and to eat breakfast from unfamiliar dishes, to the point where she worried that no possible slumber party could ever live up to how wildly exotic she'd made it seem. Marie had, after much deliberation, picked out a select, top-flight crew of toys to bring with her, and Laura had watched with heart-mangling pride as she explained to these toys, using some of the same enticing vocabulary Laura had used with Marie, how much they were going to enjoy their adventure. The whole time, Laura thought about how, if this went well or even okay, they were going to do it again, and again. She both did and didn't want it to go well. She had no idea what she wanted.

On the morning of the show, Laura managed not to cry in front of Marie as she dropped her off with Matt and Kayla. She hugged her tightly once but didn't linger. She could hear Marie crying the entire time she was racing for the door, taking the stairs so quickly she worried about tripping over her own feet and falling. It seemed to take forever to get out of their building. When she got out to the sidewalk she allowed herself one gasping full-body sob and then a fast-paced block of silent tears. She texted Matt, asking him to tell her when Marie chilled out, and hoped that he wasn't lying when he texted back to say that the girls were already busy investigating the little suitcase full of toys Marie had brought. By the time she met up with Callie a half an hour later in Manhattan, Laura was feeling almost normal.

———

They were staying in a group house that often hosted touring musicians, which Laura had expected to be gross but turned out to be less gross than her own apartment. It benefited a lot from having high ceilings and the vaguely healthy ambiance created wherever you see a lot of bikes.

Laura didn't get a good look when they were arriving, because it was much later than her usual ten-thirty bedtime and she crashed immediately on the couch provided for her, but in the morning, when she woke up hours earlier than anyone else, she had the entire place to herself and realized it was gorgeous—light blazing through the windows' thick old glass, well-established houseplants sending a green smell into the air to mingle with the vinegary whiff of the clean countertops. It was so nice just to be somewhere besides home. Even though she and Marie had been in the new place for only a couple of months, there was already a patina of toddler grime on everything: Goldfish crackers fossilizing in the little divots where the radiator met the floor, greasy handprints visible on the walls when the light hit them at the right angle. It was exotic for Laura to wake up somewhere where cleaning up was someone else's responsibility. The people who lived here probably had a chore wheel. A vestigial part of her brain made a note to ask if they were looking for new housemates, but then she remembered that she didn't live in Philly and also that she already had a roommate: her tiny child. It had happened: for a fraction of a second, Laura had inhabited the version of herself who would have existed if her daughter had never been born, and it felt good.

The utopian group house began to seem less so when its residents began to stir, their noises emanating from behind old, thin walls. Laura washed her face hurriedly in the small downstairs bathroom and left a note for her bandmates before venturing into the world outside.

She'd never spent much time in Philly, but something about its modest architectural ambitions felt immediately homey and comfortable to her; there was something of Columbus here, for sure. But there was also NYC-style beauty here, of both humans and buildings. When it happened, it was even more striking amid the disrepair and kitsch. She walked through the Italian Market, dawdling over a choice of breakfast pastry in a way she hadn't in years (three). The whole day opened up to her, dazzling with possibility. Then she remembered that she was going to play music onstage tonight, and her happiness evaporated instantly.

She had never had stage fright before—even when the Groupies had opened for the Clips, she'd been too besotted with Dylan to register the situation as anxiety-inducing. Tonight would be the most people she'd played for since then, and she'd rehearsed with the band only a couple of times. She tried to summon the first few words of the new song she'd written with them and drew a blank. Her stomach clenched, and she threw the remainder of her churro in the nearest trash can.

Luckily she was saved from spinning out into panic by a text from Callie, who gave the day shape by telling her where to meet up to "rehearse and chill." It was far enough away that it justified taking SEPTA, which would be a fun challenge and would remind her of her own city's relatively sparkling, efficient, and democratic subway system. But she had so much time to kill that she decided to walk there anyway.

She was just beginning to regret this decision—it was getting hotter, and though she knew she was heading in the right direction, she was slightly lost—when she got a call from

Matt. She answered on the first ring, breathless. "Is everything okay?"

"Sorry! I didn't mean to freak you out. Everything is totally, totally fine." Something about his voice, which was unmistakably the voice of a grown-up, reassured her. Every part of Laura that had clenched up as soon as she saw Matt's name on her screen released somewhat.

"I am so sorry I'm even bothering you with this. It really is no big deal, but Marie is saying that she isn't hungry and will wait till Mommy comes home so she can make the food 'the way Mommy makes it.' Is there some strategy you use to get her to eat? Like, what does she mean by that?"

"Oh, this trick. She's pulled this on babysitters before. What a little dissident."

Matt gently laughed, like they were in this together. Parental solidarity was new and very welcome.

"She'll break her hunger strike eventually, but if you want to be on the safe side, put out some Goldfish crackers or something and don't specifically say they're for her or that she should eat them. She'll sneak them when she thinks you're not looking. It's better than nothing. See if you can get her to drink water, though, it's hot out." She paused. "Sorry, I know you're not an idiot."

"I'm not *not* an idiot. Once I sent Kayla to her mom's for a weekend when I was going out of town with no underwear and they'd just sent their laundry to the drop-off place and K had to wear a bathing suit till I came over with a pair. They told her it was special superhero outfit for big girls."

Laura indulged him with a mild laugh. "Okay, we're definitely both idiots. Hey, what are they doing right now?"

She could hear him walking into the other room, the girls' piping voices becoming just audible. Laura's heart leaped unexpectedly.

"It looks like they're at it with the Barbies again. Or whatever these dolls are. The healthy-body-image Barbies. They seem to be going on a trip."

"They're trying to find their mommies," she heard Marie say. Matt was silent on the other end.

"I should go," she told him, keeping her voice light and level.

"Sure you don't want to talk to her?"

"I don't have time right now, but definitely later, before bed. I'll talk to you soon, okay? Thank you for letting me know about the food. And, Matt, thank you so much again for taking care of her. I owe you guys one."

"We will most assuredly take you up on that, sooner rather than later. Break a leg!"

"Thank you! I will! I mean, thanks."

As she hung up, Laura realized that she'd wandered mindlessly while on the phone, and now she definitely didn't know where she was. The neighborhood she was in now had blocks of undifferentiated vinyl-sided two-story houses, uglier even than the ones on similarly ugly blocks of her North Brooklyn neighborhood. It was midafternoon, but the people she passed seemed as menacing as they might if it had been nighttime.

She was wearing cheap Urban Outfitters jeans that had been through the washing machine too many times and a shapeless gray T-shirt. Sweaty curls stuck to her forehead. She was grateful, in a way, that she looked so shabby; she didn't look like someone who had anything worth stealing, plus, she didn't. Her guitar had traveled in the van straight to the practice space, she had $20 in cash, and her credit card was within a hundred dollars of its limit. Cataloging this stuff made her feel less vulnerable, but also depressed.

When she asked for directions she found that the studio was much closer than she'd assumed. Soon she was entering the echoey stairwell of a converted industrial building where she could already hear the dull thump of drums. At the end of the hallway Callie drew back a beaded curtain and enveloped her in a hug that smelled like cigarettes and the same perfume she'd worn since high school, Tommy Girl, the smell of candy and tea. She was holding a beer, which she handed to Laura. It was icy-cold, a shock to Laura's sweaty hand. She drank it and started on another.

They ran through the new songs Laura had written, and it felt effortless, even though a few minutes earlier she hadn't been able to remember any of the words. She and Callie grinned at each other and danced around the way they had in her bedroom as teenagers. After another beer Laura realized that she wasn't going to have energy left for the show if she didn't take a nap, so she curled up in a corner of the loft on a pile of foam sound insulation and fell into a deep sleep. When she woke up it was eight. She frantically dialed Matt as soon as she'd opened her eyes.

"Oh my God, I'm so sorry. Was she okay going to sleep? Did she ask about me?"

"I thought of calling you, but I know you're in the middle of stuff. Like, being a rock star." His tone was kind, gentle, appeasing. He was clearly willing her not to freak out. "She's still really high on the big-girl factor of being with Kayla. I mean, she asked where you were, and I told her, and I said you were coming home tomorrow, and she wasn't thrilled about it but she didn't cry or anything. I'll keep you posted, of course."

Laura was silent, willing herself not to cry twice in one day in front of this guy she barely knew except from a year's worth of generic wry playground/pickup interactions. He seemed to notice the tension in her silence, though, and stayed on the phone with her a little longer. After a minute of just letting her breathe through her stifled tears, he seemed to figure out what to say.

"I remember when Demetria and I first split and we were just figuring out divvying up time with Kayla—she was too little to understand what was going on, but she still *knew*, you know? And it's so hard, not just missing them, but thinking of them feeling bad even for a second. I always tell myself that it helps them figure out how to be independent, and maybe that's bullshit—or maybe it's not. Who knows? Who knows whether anything we do with them, good or bad, even matters. All we can do is try our best. But you also have to do what's best for you. I'm sorry to lecture you, I mean it as a pep talk. It's the one I give myself, like I said."

"It's the one I give myself, too, but it's nice to hear it from someone else for a change," Laura said. She felt outsize gratitude toward Matt. If they'd been in the same room, she would have hugged him.

She hung up feeling shitty, but not totally gutted. It was almost time to head back to the house, where she would let Callie doll her up, and then to the venue, where she would walk onstage and sing a love song that no one in the room would understand was actually about a child. And back in Brooklyn, in a toddler bed in Matt's small apartment, Marie would sleep peacefully till morning, or so she hoped.

———————

Onstage, the bright lights blinded Laura at first, but then she began to make out the shape of the crowd. There were men in the front row and women behind them, as there were at every show. She heard a tremble in her voice when she began to sing. Callie heard it, too, and shot her a warning look. To kill her nerves, she started making eye contact with the dudes in the front row, giving one of them fuck-me vibes and then icing him completely, ignoring him and moving on to the next one. She started to have fun, and then she started to feel downright euphoric. By the end of the set, she felt like she was at the dawn of a new era in her life, one where she could do this every night that someone would let her get up on a stage.

She was so adrenalized after the show that there was no way she was about to sleep. Fortunately the after-party took over the entire group house afterward, so she couldn't have slept if she'd wanted to. She had been determined to get up early, get on the Chinatown bus, and get back to see Marie as soon as possible, but before she realized exactly what was happening she'd had several beers and no dinner and even a bump off a key held by a sweetly solicitous group-house resident named Jeremy who couldn't have been much older than eighteen. He seemed to think there was a chance that he could hook up with Laura, which meant that he somehow didn't realize that she, though temporally twenty-six, was in fact dozens of light-years older than he was. The attention was flattering, though, and Laura let herself be led into his bedroom. On a lumpy mattress she allowed herself to be pawed at while experiencing no real feelings except bemusement, and even a little bit of purely physical happiness. She let him kiss and suck her boobs, suppressing a laugh when she thought about how the last person to have done so was Marie. But she kindly but firmly cut things off when he tried to venture toward her belt buckle. Then she went to go see if the party had died down enough that she could get her couch back.

Callie intercepted her with a red SOLO cup full of mostly vodka, and said she had to come up to the roof with them now. The hot day had dissipated into a sparkling night, now nearing dawn, and the dimmer lights of the smaller city allowed several stars to peek through. She and Callie lay down next to each other and looked up at them.

"I'm so excited we're back together," Callie said. "This feels so right. It's what we always dreamed of, and it's finally coming true." It was clear that she was drunk. Sincerity was not her usual mode.

Laura thought about her actual dreams, which she had almost forgotten existed, and which did not include Callie. In them, Laura was the only one onstage, playing and singing her own songs, traveling around free of all encumbrances.

She shook her head to dispel this fantasy. She had only committed to this one show; she still wasn't sure whether she had it in her to do more. It was both gratifying and irritating to know that for the past three years, every time she had tried to dismiss the feeling that there was something she was missing out on, she had been right. She had missed a lot of nights on roofs, meaningless kisses, red SOLO cups, and flickers of hardworking transcendence in a sweaty spotlight. What she had done instead seemed distant at this moment. She wanted to pine for the weight of Marie's little body automatically cuddling into hers as they watched TV or read stories, but she couldn't quite summon it. It had taken only twenty-four hours to forget. The moon shone down on the rooftop like a spotlight.

———

The Chinatown bus ride was excruciating; every bump (there were many) reverberated all the way up her spine to the crown of her head. She tentatively sipped a Vitaminwater, but her mouth remained dry. It was exotic to be so hungover. She had almost forgotten what it felt like. The novelty wore off quickly.

Still, she felt a surge of excitement as the bus emerged from the tunnel and the bustle of Canal Street was suddenly visible through the windows; she was home, where she belonged, and in less than an hour she would be reunited with Marie.

She wolfed an eggy pastry and a supersweet tea at a Chinese bakery, then took the Q to Union Square, transferred to the L, and waited an annoyingly long midday wait for the G. She felt too tired and sick and nervous to read the magazine she'd brought, so she played a game where she looked at her fellow passengers and tried to guess whether they had children. Something about their faces, she imagined, would always give it away, regardless of age or race. Some harrowed, ennobled thing. But she found that she often couldn't guess, and she wondered what anyone would guess about her: a woman in her midtwenties, a girl, really, with smeared remnants of last night's eyeliner and hair that smelled like cigarettes and the tar of a roof where she'd slept.

Last night's drunken feeling of having severed the invisible cord that tethered her to Marie was now completely gone. She would have run alongside the subway if doing so could have gotten her home any faster. And even so, simultaneously, a contrary part of her still wanted to linger in this moment of being separate and plausibly childless, young again and free.

Matt answered the door in a shirt stained with some kind of pink juice, looking as tired as Laura felt but also genuinely happy to see her. "You look like you had fun last night. How was the show?"

Laura grimaced. "Way too much fun, but it was worth it. Where are the girls?"

"Hiding in Kayla's room. They've been up since five thirty playing some game they invented that involves yelling really loud."

Again Laura felt the impulse to give Matt a hug. They were like soldiers meeting in a wartime hospital and comparing notes about the battles they'd been injured in. She wondered whether raising a child with someone else felt like that all the time.

She opened the door to Kayla's room tentatively. The girls were both sitting on Kayla's bed in a nest of blankets and pillows and stuffed animals and various bits of plastic-toy flotsam and jetsam, and both of them looked perfectly calm and happy. But as soon as Marie saw her mother she ran to her legs and began to cry hysterically.

Laura bent down and embraced Marie, who clung to her with almost bruising force as she continued to cry.

"Mommy, Mommy, why did you leave me?"

"Baby, it was just one night, we talked about this. I had to go play music in another city, but I came right back for you. And you got to have a slumber party with Kayla! Didn't you have fun?"

Hot tears soaked through Laura's T-shirt. A towering wave of exhaustion washed over her, almost immobilizing her. Marie's warm little body was so heavy in her arms.

Marie was crying so hard that it was hard to understand what she was saying. "I didn't know if you would come back," it sounded like. "I missed you. I was scared." She said the word so that it sounded like "scowed."

"Did you tell Matt you were scared?"

"Mommy, don't do that again. I promise, I won't be bad."

"Honey, you weren't bad. I had to leave you, but it wasn't because I didn't want to be with you. I always want to be with you."

"*Then why?*" screamed Marie. Kayla dropped a nude doll over the edge of the bed as she watched them with impassive curiosity.

"Baby, sometimes I need to leave, because . . ."

Marie cried harder and Laura decided to abandon this line of conversation. Anyway, what could she say? That she needed to go to work and make money to support Marie? It was true, but that wasn't why she'd gone. Was she supposed to explain how it had felt to sing onstage, that it was like one of her limbs had been severed and then reattached and now blood was flowing through it again? Marie would never understand why her mother would choose anything over being with her. "Something else is more important to me than you are" would be what she would hear, no matter what Laura said.

Between her racking sobs, Marie was saying the same thing over and over again, and again it took Laura a second to decipher it; her enunciation was still toddlery and garbled. But when she realized what it was, she felt like her heart and lungs were being scooped out with a dull trowel.

"Mommy, I'm sorry. I'm sorry. I'm sorry!"

Three days later, Laura dropped Marie off at day care and then went to meet Callie at Oslo to talk about the rest of the tour. She got there early so that she could order a coffee and sit by herself at a table and try to clear her mind and make a decision, but her mind remained stubbornly clouded over. She got up to get a refill and took it back to her table and nursed it.

Ever since Laura's trip Marie had been acting maddeningly clingy and babyish, which Laura hated except in the moments when she secretly enjoyed it. A part of her liked the sick-day feeling of sitting up late at night after Marie claimed to have had a nightmare, reading *Madeline* in a purposely boring monotone until Marie finally passed out, lips cutely parted and drooling slightly on Laura's arm. Less cute were her uncharacteristic lapses in potty-trained-ness, which both of them found jarring and humiliating, though Laura did her best not to act ruffled. Her day care wasn't the greatest, just a group of kids and their caretakers hanging out in an older Polish lady's fluorescent-lit basement, and Laura worried that they were probably snappish when kids wet their pants. But she couldn't afford anything better. It was only thanks to the work she'd done on the album that she could afford day care right now at all. She couldn't let herself dwell on it.

The patrons of Oslo at ten thirty in the morning on a weekday ran a predictable gamut. There were the neighborhood's rich-hippie moms (in Laura's imagination, in her darker moments, everyone with children except her was rich). These women all seemed to be friends with one another; their older kids ran around in the park together while the younger siblings relaxed in their strollers. When Laura was with Marie, she could socialize with them a little bit, in a superficial way, but when she wasn't she became invisible to them again. It was fine, she got it; they had to stick together with their own tribe. They somehow had correctly intuited that she wasn't one of them.

And then there were the young people, who were, confusingly, probably Laura's exact age. But she could tell in an instant, just from their clothes and the women's makeup, that they didn't have kids. They talked with enormous gravity about a TV show they'd watched, which wasn't as good this season as it had been in previous seasons, then segued into a conversation about a guy one of them was dating. As if it made any difference who you dated or what TV shows you watched!

There was also a woman, sitting by herself near the entrance of the coffee shop with a large iced coffee at the big square communal table, with a tiny baby in a woven wrap. It was probably one of her first times venturing out of the house with the baby, whose livid-pink head was barely visible within the wrap. She had been one of the young people a couple of weeks ago—pregnant, but still able to care about trivialities deeply, unable to imagine not being able to care. Now she wasn't a member of any of the coffee shop's constituencies. Her baby cried, that steely newborn wail, and she soothed it inefficiently with bouncing when really the only thing that was going to work, Laura knew, was feeding it. Laura tried to force herself not to pay attention, to focus on her own life, what she was going to tell Callie, how she was going to make it make sense.

No matter how she put it, though, Callie wouldn't understand, because she was a young person like the ones in the corner, the ones wearing recently purchased clothes without stains or holes except ones they chose or intended. To Callie, eschewing months' worth of nights like the one they'd had in Philly because you had to take care of your daughter didn't make sense. To childless people, children were a logistical problem to be solved: find a way to pay for and arrange childcare, and you were free. They didn't understand that even when you weren't with your child, the child continued to exist in a part of your brain that you had to consciously work to silence, or as a low hum of anxiety that colored everything. Either way, you were fucked. Either way, pleasure and creativity were sacrificed entirely, or only permitted in small doses.

She would tell Callie that it wouldn't always be like this, that soon Marie would be older and wouldn't need her as much and they could try again. She didn't know whether that was true. She hoped that it was.

———

Later that day, Laura ran into Matt at day care pickup, and when he asked if she and Marie wanted to go to the park with him and Kayla, she said sure. On the way to McCarren, Matt motioned them into a bodega, where he bought cups of Italian ice for the girls and, without asking, brown-bagged cans of beer for Laura and himself.

They sat on a bench and drank while the girls ran back and forth on the dusty path in front of them, playing some variation of tag that required a lot of screeching. Matt didn't try to get Laura to talk, so they just sat there in silence, watching the girls. Halfway through her beer Laura burst into silent tears.

"You want to talk about it?" Matt moved tentatively closer to her on the bench, still allowing her the protective buffer of space you'd give a fellow subway passenger, if you weren't an asshole.

"I don't want her to know that I'm upset." Laura sniffled, hiding her face in her hands in case Marie was looking in her direction, but of course the girls were oblivious.

Matt fished a napkin out of Kayla's miniature owl-shaped backpack and handed it to her. It smelled like jelly. Quietly, as simply and unemotionally as she could, she told Matt about how she'd met up with Callie and told her that she couldn't play any more tour dates but could be in the studio with them over the summer and would play shows in New York if they wanted. It had seemed like a reasonable compromise. She'd even offered that she might revisit touring when Marie was a little older. But Callie had said no.

"She'd said that it would be good to have my songs, but that if I wasn't going to go on tour it wouldn't make sense to have my voice on the tracks; it would set them up to disappoint people. I wanted to get mad at her, but I realized that she's right, actually. It would be weird for them to sound totally different on the album than they do live."

Matt blew air out of his mouth slowly, a genteel belch that also managed to convey solidarity and understanding.

"I want to believe—I want to pretend that this is something that will still be there for me when Marie is older, that I'll be able to just reenlist whenever I feel up to it. But I can tell that this is my chance to get back to doing what I'm good at, what I'm meant to do. And I'm not taking it because I'm scared."

"Scared of what?"

"That I'll like it. That I'll like it too much. That I'll forget about her, or that it will change the way things are between us, and we won't be able to get it back. She's the most important thing in my life; my life is hard, but it's also simple. How can a life have two most important things?"

Matt finished his beer and tossed it into the overflowing trash can next to the bench they were sitting on. "Well, I don't think you're being fair to yourself. I think you're making the right choice. It's what I would do, in your shoes. Look, life is long and your talent isn't going anywhere. Patti Smith took a thirteen-year maternity leave."

It was surprising that Matt seemed to have already thought this through. It was like he had spent time thinking about her. She felt obligated to push back against what he'd said, though; it was so optimistic and unrealistic.

"Patti Smith was already famous! She had made three great albums before she had her kids. I haven't done anything. I've accomplished nothing in my life so far."

It was a melodramatic thing to say, and Laura knew that she'd said it because she wanted to be contradicted. She was also aware that she was leaning on Matt for support the way that people did when they were in relationships, which was inappropriate; they were barely friends.

Instead of telling her how great she was and how much she'd done and citing keeping Marie alive and happy as an accomplishment, the way a female friend almost certainly would have, Matt started laughing at her.

"Seems like you set the bar pretty high for yourself. What would satisfy you, even? You want to raise a little kid and be a world-famous musician, knocking out the best songs of your life while also giving her everything she needs from you twenty-four hours a day?"

Laura smiled, in spite of how miserable she'd been feeling a minute ago. "Playing big venues, making lots of money, still tucking Marie in bed every night myself. Yeah, that's all. I don't know. Is that so unrealistic?"

Matt shrugged. "Maybe not for you. You seem like the kind of person who makes stuff happen, even though you get in your own way a lot. I'm the kind of person who is just satisfied to watch other people make stuff happen. For which I thank my lucky stars every day." He smiled at her. "I have to say, it's a trip to be around someone like you. I mean, I'm really enjoying it. I hope it doesn't ruin it that I just said that."

Laura couldn't resist the opportunity to insult herself again. "Someone as fucked up as me?"

This time, he took the bait; he would have been an idiot not to. "Someone as cool and smart and . . . uh, as beautiful. As you," he said quietly. They both looked to make sure the girls weren't looking at them, and then, as she'd known he was going to for a few minutes already, he furtively leaned over and kissed her.

Just once, no tongue. But it wasn't a friendly, reassuring back-pat of a kiss. It was a real kiss, and to the extent that Laura could stop herself from worrying immediately about what to do about it and how she might explain it to Marie if she had happened to be watching, Laura enjoyed it.

They sat back and made sure they had gotten away with it.

"Do you guys want to come over for dinner?" Matt asked after a minute. "We're going to order pizza and watch a movie."

"Are you sure it wouldn't make your life harder?" Laura said, watching the girls run as an excuse to avoid eye contact with Matt. She was afraid that if she looked at him she would start laughing and lose her nerve.

"It would make it easier," he said. It would make Laura's life easier, too, she thought. She sat and watched while he rounded the girls up to go.

———

Laura ordered the burger, and Matt ordered the mac and cheese, which were the things you were supposed to order at DuMont. It was the known fancy restaurant of their neighborhood, but Laura had never been there before. She had never actually been on a "date" in New York during the four years she'd lived there; this had occurred to her only as she was getting ready to go on this date with Matt. She had been on dates in college and high school, but they seemed to have taken place during a previous lifetime. What she'd done with Dylan had involved meeting at places, usually his apartment, but restaurants had never been involved. The babysitter had asked her when she'd be home and she'd been briefly flummoxed. It was possible that she would go back to Matt's after this, but it also seemed so gross to have to tacitly tell Caroline that she would be home at either ten or midnight, depending on whether she ended up getting laid. She'd said she would call to check in and left it at that.

The waiter left, and Laura tried to just relax and have a normal conversation without constantly monitoring the fluctuating levels of her attraction to Matt, and worse, the likelihood that he was doing the same thing. The date had been his idea, which was reassuring. She kept losing track of what they were talking about because she was staring at his face, the shape of his shoulders and the way he sipped his wine, the way he held his wineglass, evaluating the erotic potential in each feature, each gesture. The way he sipped was greedy in a way that could have seemed gross but wasn't; he had big, full lips, and at one point, briefly, she saw the tip of his tongue flick unintentionally against the rim of the glass. It had been so long since she'd had sex that the whole enterprise seemed kind of improbable and disgusting. But there was also the possibility that once presented with the opportunity she'd actually feel ravenous, insatiable, like when you go too long without eating and don't actually feel hunger anymore until you're presented with a plate of food. She forced herself to snap back to attention.

"Delaware," he was saying. "Like, the very most boring place in the world. Do you even have a stereotype in your mind about what people from Delaware are like?"

Laura thought about it. "Not into paying sales tax?"

Matt laughed, a little too long and hard, but still sincerely, and Laura felt her whole body relax. "Yeah, that's definitely part of our cultural identity. How about you?"

"Ohio, so all the dying-rust-belt-town clichés. Most of my parents' friends growing up worked for the Limited and Bath and

Body Works; their corporate headquarters employs, like, half of Columbus. They weren't farmers or steel mill workers, at least not in that generation." She shrugged. "I'm second-generation boring."

He widened his eyes. "Are you kidding? You're so far from boring. I think you're the most famous person I've ever hung out with. Definitely the most famous parent at Rainbow Tots."

"Not even! Abigail's mom was in an extra in *Eternal Sunshine*."

"Wow, like, a featured extra? Did she have a line?"

"I think she would be delighted to tell you all about it; she gave me like a loose thirty-minute set about it when we worked at the bake-sale table together."

Matt laughed again, and this time it didn't seem like a performance at all. "You're so funny, God. I can't tell you how long it's been since I've had any nonwork adult conversation, basically."

"So the bar is set really low, is what you're saying." They were both grinning stupidly. He was so receptive, so easy to parry with.

"You're vaulting over the bar so effortlessly. You are Olympic-level vaulting over it." He accidentally bumped her knee with his large one under the tiny tabletop, but then he let their knees rest against each other. Laura felt a jolt, then that completely bypassed the analytical-mode part of her brain. She drank the last sip of her fashionable juice glass of red wine and stood up. "Excuse me a sec? I'm just gonna call and check in with the sitter." She was going to be home at midnight.

9

One morning in the fall of 2007, Laura got up before anyone else and went into the kitchen. As usual, Matt had done the dishes, but he had, also as usual, left a few stray water glasses in the sink, plus the bowl that had contained the candy they'd shared while staying up too late watching TV. The dish drainer was full, stacked like a Jenga puzzle so that if Laura made one false move while unloading it, the plates would come clattering down and wake up everyone. She moved with finicky precision, lowering them gently one by one. When the drainer was empty she filled the kettle and set it to boil. She would grab it just before it whistled. Then she washed the dishes that Matt had left and started getting food out of the fridge for breakfast. Butter, eggs, bread, jam. If she got lucky, she would have a minute or two to herself at the kitchen table to drink coffee and stare at the wall, listening for the first sounds of stirring from the girls' bedroom. If she didn't get lucky, they would soon be upon her, all of them, leaving no inch of physical space in the kitchen or any other part of the apartment until they were tucked back in bed that night. She had not even cracked the first egg when she heard them, and then the day began.

The girls ran into the kitchen in their sleep T-shirts yelling at each other about something. There was still something toddlerish about their big heads and jutting bellies, but at five they were quickly becoming more like kids than babies. They could have conversations, and they required detailed explanations. They were, luckily, truly friends, and had handled the transition to living together as a welcome addition rather than a competition or a threatening intrusion. They called themselves sisters. Marie called Matt "Matt," but sometimes Kayla slipped and called Laura "Mom." Her mother had moved to California after Matt and Laura's wedding and now saw Kayla only a few times a year. She sometimes sent checks that Matt sometimes did not cash. How Matt felt about this was a mystery to Laura; even on the rare occasions when they were awake and the girls were not, their conversations were mostly about logistics. They were always too exhausted to talk about how anyone besides the girls was feeling.

"What are we doing today?" Kayla asked Laura. "It's Saturday, right? Can we go to the park? Can we go to the zoo?"

"First we have to eat breakfast, and then we can figure out what we're up to," said Laura. "Your aunt Callie might come by later. I'm going to see her play music tonight."

"Can we come?" Marie asked as they started to fork up their scrambled eggs.

"No, it's after bedtime. That's why Callie's coming this afternoon; she wants to see you guys. She hasn't seen you since the wedding."

Callie had been on tour for months, but it wasn't like she and Laura constantly hung out when she was in town, either. She was decent about staying in touch via email, though, especially when she had particularly good gossip; she shared the details of her conquests as though metrics like dick size and number of orgasms could still impress Laura, when the only thing that could spark true envy in Laura these days was affordable real estate near good public schools. Everything else was cordoned off in an area of her mind that had become derelict from neglect. Occasionally a random perennial in that mental vacant lot would bloom—a sense memory of her first time with Dylan, a pang of loss when Callie described the new album Laura wouldn't even have time to listen to, much less play on—but it was otherwise overgrown, unvisited.

She decided to take the girls to the zoo. Matt stayed behind, claiming that he needed to catch up on work, and because he would be on duty for the end of dinner and bedtime Laura cut him some slack. Their apartment was only two blocks from the edge of the park, but the park was enormous and the zoo was all the way on the other side of it, and it took them forever to get there. It was unseasonably humid and they were all sweaty and cranky by the time they arrived at the carousel near the zoo entrance, where there was a little stand that sold overpriced water bottles and ice pops. The girls agitated for both and Laura spent twenty dollars getting them all one of each, and they plopped down in the grass next to the carousel with lime-green FrozFruit dribbling down their arms. When the girls finished, they started playing a game with the ice pop sticks, poking them into each other's faces, then dodging at the last minute, which Laura put a stop to immediately.

"Absolutely not—someone is going to get hurt. Throw those sticks away," said Laura, but the girls were happy and laughing and occupied, and she had her phone out and was checking a text from Callie that said she'd be at least an hour later than she'd originally said, which would be fine, but probably meant she'd be even later than that. When she looked up, Marie was wailing and clutching her left eye.

"I'm sorry! I didn't mean to!" said Kayla.

"You did! You hurt me!" Marie shrieked. Other parents were turning around to stare. A Hasidic mother with two kids in a stroller and another three on foot had seen the whole thing, including Laura with her phone out, and gave her a look that somehow simultaneously conveyed sympathy and disdain. Laura sat Marie on her lap and examined her. There was no visible sign of injury, but she was clearly in pain. "We'll get you some ice, okay, baby?" Marie nodded and sniffled.

"Can we still go to the zoo?" Kayla quavered. "I said I was sorry!"

"If Marie still wants to, we can go," Laura said. "What do you think, Booboo? See the sea lions?"

Marie sniffled her assent.

"It's almost their feeding time," said Kayla to her sister, and helped her to her feet. They walked arm in arm in front of Laura toward the guard booth at the zoo entrance. Laura's heart was still pounding. Another crisis averted. It seemed like there was another one every day, and though this time she had been lucky, more lucky than she deserved, the constant almost-crises took their toll. Laura felt the material of her soul stretch a little bit thinner every time the girls were in harm's way. Sometimes it seemed like she was punished every time she even dared to think about anything else while in their presence.

Callie was late, but not much later than she'd said she would be. "Wow, this place looks like a real home!" she said as she walked into the apartment. "Stuff on the walls and everything!"

"Stuff all over the floor, stuff piled in every corner," said Laura, kicking the girls' mermaid castle out of the way as she led Callie through to the kitchen.

"You should see my apartment; it's so sad. I've been there for a year and it still looks like I just moved in. I just pack and unpack my suitcases." She walked around the room, admiring the view of the tall trees out the front windows.

It was, kid crap infestation aside, a nice apartment, Laura admitted to herself with some pride. She and Matt barely made enough to afford the rent, which made it necessary for Matt to do freelance film editing on top of his nine-to-five job and for Laura to spend a lot of time examining the family budget and transferring credit card balances. But it was worth it to be close to the girls' school, and the park, and to be able to look out the windows on a summer day and see well-kept nineteenth-century town houses on their block keeping the heat at bay with their thick dark walls and cool wide-planked wooden floors. If she could not actually live in one of these houses, it was nice to at least be able to see them from her window.

The girls obediently came and said hi to Callie, who gamely pretended to admire their mermaids and their identically French-braided hair. Then they traipsed off to their bedroom to throw things and shriek at each other while Callie and Laura sat at the kitchen table and drank tea. The area around Marie's injured eye looked pinkish still, Laura noted as they left, but she hadn't been complaining about it, so it didn't seem worth fussing over.

"I'm so glad you're coming out tonight! Is Matt coming, too?"

"He's staying here with the girls. But I'm bringing my friend Mara, I hope that's cool. She's a big fan of the band."

"That's totally cool. I hope she can hang out afterward, too."

"Maybe. Both of us have to get up early. She has a kid the girls' age."

"So she's old?"

"Not that old. I don't know, actually. I think she's, like, thirty-five?"

"That's old!"

Laura shrugged. Most of her friends were mom friends, and most moms were over thirty-five. It was still sometimes initially an uphill battle to win older people's trust and respect. They tended not to believe that Laura really understood the gravity of the situation, that life was fraught with pitfalls and consequences. They thought that because she still had elasticity in her under-eye-skin and a torso that had emerged relatively unscathed from the rigors of housing and feeding a baby, she wasn't really in the shit with them. But then they hung out with her a little bit and talked about sleep and viruses and the impossibility of getting men to proactively plan to accommodate other people's needs. Eventually, they always came around to the idea that Laura really was a mom, even though she could, in the right lighting, still pass for a member of the enemy class: unfettered women.

Matt came out of the bedroom, where he'd been either working or just dicking around on his laptop, and nodded a quick hi to Callie on his way to root around in the fridge.

"Honey, Callie's playing a show tonight. You saw it on the calendar, right?"

"Yeah, of course. Wait, are you going to it?"

"Why else would it be on the calendar?"

Matt stopped munching halfway through a string cheese, stumped. "I don't know, just so we'd know it was happening, I guess, in case we wanted to send good vibes?"

"Callie got me tickets. I'm bringing Mara. So you have the girls for dinner and bedtime."

"Shit, really? I mean, I can do it, I just also have to finish this project. Maybe we can get a sitter?"

"At five thirty on a Saturday? You're welcome to try."

"Okay, well, it's not ideal, but we'll manage. I'll get it done after they go to bed."

Laura knew that meant he would sleep in the next morning, which meant she shouldn't stay out late partying with the band—she hadn't really wanted to, but it was sad to have the choice taken out of her hands.

Matt left with his cheese. Callie rolled her eyes after him, but Laura hesitated to sell him out by complaining. She wanted Callie to admire her marriage like she'd admired the apartment. "He's actually so great at remembering stuff like that usually. I mean, if it weren't for him, I'd have to get a sitter every single time I wanted to leave the house."

"Yeah, and if it weren't for him, you'd only have one kid to take care of and it would be twice as easy for you to get away," Callie said lightly.

"Away to where, though? I want to be with them, most of the time."

"Well, you're very lucky then! You have exactly what you want." Callie smiled and sipped her tea. She didn't mean anything by it. She meant exactly what she said. She had no idea what she was talking about, thought Laura, and realized that she felt about Callie the same way the thirty-five-year-olds (unfairly) felt about her.

———————

Laura and Mara met up at a bar on Second Avenue, skipping the opening band so they could brace themselves for fun. The pregaming had been Mara's idea.

"I haven't been to a show where you couldn't sit down in years," she'd said when Laura had extended the invitation initially. "I'll need to ease into it."

Winning Mara over had felt to Laura like a triumph, almost like a romantic conquest. She'd seen her on the street for months, doing school drop-off, at the playground, wrangling her small child in the grocery store, and had admired her outfits and her forbidding, perpetually distracted facial expression. She'd tried the basic moves—small smiles of solidarity, "How old is she?"— and gotten nowhere, until eventually they'd found themselves at the same birthday party for one of Kayla and Marie's classmates. It was held in the backyard of a mind-meltingly enviable brownstone, with organic juice boxes for the children and chenin blanc for their chaperones, but no amount of social lubricant could make it unawkward for Laura, who kept trying and failing to join conversations between people who clearly all knew one another already. And anyway she had nothing to offer on the subject of Fire Island versus Martha's Vineyard. Mara stood by herself, near the wine, looking unapologetically bored. Laura had come up to her and poured herself another glass, then raised it to Mara in a toast.

"To the birthday boy, Caiden, or whatever," she'd said, and watched with excitement as a smile spread over Mara's face. Her teeth were slightly crooked; maybe she held her face so stoically to avoid showing them. They were cute, though.

"It's Theo," she told Laura. "Just kidding, I actually have no idea."

They had been friends ever since, but tonight was the first time they'd hung out without their children. It wasn't immediately a welcome change. Laura missed being able to gloss over any lull by taking an interest in the miniature social interactions running parallel to her own; without any distractions, they were forced to complete their sentences and follow their thoughts to conclusions. But after a couple of rounds the initial awkwardness faded, and by the time they decided it was time to walk over to the venue, Laura and Mara were both feeling almost carefree. The sun had almost set and the sky was still streaky, the air was a perfect temperature, just a little bit too warm. They were ready to stand in a dark room and be pounded all over by waves of music.

Inside the venue, Laura flashed the badge that Callie had given her and they were escorted up to a balcony that seemed to be suspended almost directly over the stage, so they felt like they were floating in the dark. The other people in this section had also all been deemed important for some reason; they were journalists here to review the show, or, like Laura, friends with the band. She spotted a guy who looked familiar and almost said hi before realizing that he was a semi-famous comedian, not an old acquaintance.

The feeling that Laura got as she watched Callie play her songs was so strange, a mix of pain and pleasure. Or maybe it was more like the kind of minor pain you can easily stand to inflict on yourself but that's intolerable when someone else does it. She stood there wallowing in it. She looked at the band and imagined herself in it, of course. She kept her jaw tightly clenched so that she wouldn't be tempted to mouth the words. All around her, other people were singing along.

The band had just come out for an encore when the phone in her pocket buzzed. She shouted, "I have to take this; it's Matt" to Mara quickly before pushing back through to the stairwell.

It was Marie, Matt explained. She'd woken up crying, complaining that her eye had an owie, and when he'd turned on the lights he'd seen that her cornea was red and her face was streaked with pink-tinged tears. He'd given her saline eyedrops and parked her in front of a Disney movie with a Popsicle, but the eye did look bad. Had something happened? Laura told him about the poke she'd sustained at the park. She had been so quick to dismiss it; the girls were so dramatic about every little bump, especially the ones they gave each other. And she'd been fine all afternoon. But maybe it was infected? At the very least, a visit to pediatric urgent care seemed like a good idea.

"In the morning, though, right?" she asked.

But she knew she would leave, was already regretting the drinks. There was no way she could go out with the band now and impress Mara by having such cool friends. Now that the possibility was being snatched from her, she badly wanted the consolation of getting drunk. It was supposed to be her reward for witnessing Callie onstage doing what Laura should have been doing. Her body was full of energy that had no place to go. She felt it course through her as a wave of rage.

"Why did you call me? Why couldn't you have just dealt with this on your own?" she asked Matt.

He exhaled slowly, and in the background she heard Marie crying. She sounded like she had as a much younger child, when she would regularly half wake from a nightmare and scream "Mama! Mama!" even though Laura was right there.

"Look, I'm sorry, baby. I know this sucks. You should stay out if you want to, okay?" said Matt, in his patient, reasonable voice that somehow only ever made her more upset.

"No, of course I won't. I'll come home. I'm coming home."

She went back out to the balcony to tell Mara that she was leaving and saw the look of disappointment flicker across her face.

"I totally understand," Mara yelled, mouth close to Laura's head so that she could hear her over the music. "Men can be so pathetic!"

Laura wanted to explain, or confess, or something, but it was too loud to have a detailed conversation about whose choices had created the family dynamic that pretty much required Laura's constant vigilance—Matt, who had passively allowed the dynamic to develop, or Laura, whose fear that things would fall apart without her had allowed Matt to avoid learning how to care for the children in their neediest moments. Long story short, Matt wasn't the only one who was pathetic.

As she made her way down the stairs to the exit, Laura passed the semi-famous comedian again, coming back from the bar with a drink in each hand. He gave her a nod of what seemed like recognition, and Laura realized that he'd made the same mistake she'd made earlier—he was pretending now that he knew who she was, because he assumed that they must have met and didn't want her to feel awkward. She was smiling to herself about it when she felt a tap on her shoulder.

When she turned, she saw that he had followed her and was now proffering one of the drinks, something cloudy and brown with a cherry. "I can't find the person I was bringing this to, and I thought you looked like you could use a drink," he said, with the confidence of a person whose pickup abilities have been bolstered for years by positive reinforcement. Laura did want another drink, though.

"I was actually on my way out," she said, reaching for it. "You're friends with Callie?"

"I know her, but Davey is my guy. He's been working with me on some projects," he said. "You and Callie go way back, right?"

"Wait, you actually know who I am?"

The comedian smirked, which wasn't exactly attractive, but his whole thing was about being a little bit more abrasive than your average person. He did an exaggerated pompous voice. "Do you know who *I* am?"

Laura was too tired and distracted to put energy into flirting, and was also trying to drink as quickly as possible so that she could more effectively mute her inner critic. "Honestly? I know your face. But I haven't watched a lot of TV lately that isn't for five-year-olds."

"That's right, you're the teen mom!"

She tried hard not to find this flattering. "Not exactly a teen."

166

"I've seen those shows, too. Not because I have kids—I mean, none that I know of. But I've done a lot of voice-over work. Do your kids watch *Dragon Dancers*?"

Laura nodded. Marie and Kayla were obsessed with those stupid dragons in tutus.

"I'm the pink one. Drogola."

"Whoa!"

"I know!" He was being satirically false modest, but Laura was genuinely impressed.

"That's a great performance," she told him.

There was a tiny moment of a crack in his bluster and Laura could tell he was genuinely gratified, but then he immediately reassumed his persona. "Speaking of performances, you used to be in this band, too, right? Why aren't you onstage?"

"It doesn't work like that. You can't just sometimes be in a band and sometimes not," she explained patiently, as though to a child, a dumber child than either of her actual children. The manhattan or whatever it was had been better and stronger than any of the other drinks she'd had that night; apparently, the comedian's fame gave him access to a better class of everything, even overpriced plastic-cup drinks. In her back pocket, her phone twitched. She pulled it out and read a text from Matt asking her to please pick up Popsicles if she saw any on her way home.

"Thanks for the drink," she said, putting the empty glass back into the comedian's hand.

"See you around, teen mom," he said, seemingly still under the impression that this was a funny thing to say.

Half an hour later she clattered through the door of her apartment, drunk and slightly nauseated by the smell of the cab she'd taken. Matt and Marie were sitting together on the couch, watching a DVD. Marie turned toward the sound of Laura coming in and she could see the red streak in her little eyeball from halfway across the room. "Oh my God!" she said, forgetting to try to seem calm for Marie's sake.

Matt shot her a look, less admonishing than confused, then registered that she was drunk. "Should we take her to urgent care?" he said in the hushed tone that they used to talk about the girls when they were right there. "I mean, should one of us? I'll stay with Kayla?"

"Mommy, where are the Popsicles?" Marie whined.

"Baby, I forgot, I'm so sorry. We can get Popsicles tomorrow." Exhaustion was threatening to envelop Laura. Today had lasted so long already. There had been so many different parts of it. Could there really be an entire new part of it still to go, at the pediatric urgent care clinic or the emergency room?

"But I want one now!"

"I don't think it's going to make a difference whether we go now or in the morning," she said quietly to Matt. "It looks bad, but I think it's just irritated. We should put a cold washcloth on it and try to get her to bed." She was pretending to be in control, making her voice calm and stern, but she was faking it; she wasn't some kind of eyeball doctor.

"Really? It's so red."

"Matt, it's not about to fall out of her head," Laura said, finally out of patience for everyone.

"My eye is going to fall out of my head?" Marie was now paying close attention. Matt looked at Laura with the cold, tight expression that meant he would, starting now, seethe silently for up to twenty-four hours, until she could weasel her way back into his good graces or until it simply became too inconvenient to hate her.

"No, it's not going to fall out, baby," said Laura to Marie. "It's just a scratch. I'm going to put a magic soothing cloth on it, okay? It's going to take the scratchiness away, and you can sit here with us till the end of the episode and then we'll all go to sleep."

"But I want a *Popsicle!*"

"You can have a lollipop."

"Does Kayla get one, too?"

"Not right now."

Marie snuggled under Matt's arm, satisfied that the negotiation had gone in her favor. Laura chanced another attempt at eye contact with Matt, but he was resolutely staring at the TV. On the screen, a dragon in a pink tutu floated down an inner tube on a lazy river.

"Come on in," the dragon said in a plummy, supercilious voice. "The water's delightful!"

PART III

10

The night that Marie threw her phone at her mom—impulsively, almost accidentally—was a new low. She had been waving her arms around and shouting and it left her hand and flew, much faster than she'd thought possible, straight into her mother's face, connecting with Laura's cheekbone with an audible *thwack* that made them both stop yelling. They stared at each other for the duration of a long silence that ended only when Laura put her hand up to her face and turned away from Marie, sitting down heavily on the couch.

"Mom? Are you okay?"

Laura didn't answer immediately, and Marie felt, irrationally, even angrier at her. The ball was now in Laura's court, because Marie's bad behavior had justified her anger. Before she'd thrown the phone, Marie had possessed the moral high ground, she thought. It was crazy that she wasn't allowed to go out, it was a Friday, she'd done her chores and homework, she would check in at whatever intervals her mom wanted, literally all of her friends were going to this show. She wasn't a little kid, she was fourteen years old. She had not mentioned that Tom would be there, of course. There was no reason to mention Tom to her mother.

In addition to anger, Marie also felt crushing guilt and the barest tip of a giant iceberg of sadness that was always lurking just below the surface. But the anger was much easier to feel, so she felt it first, and more, and then let it take over. The sadness about having hurt her mom—physically, this time, and not just emotionally, like always—was too big to touch. Her mind couldn't go there.

"Seriously, Mom, come on. Say something. Are you okay?"

Laura sighed heavily, then reached down and picked up Marie's phone. "No, not really. That hurt, Marie." She handed her back the phone with what seemed like effortful stoicism. Marie felt a hard something in her chest, an achy coldness.

"I just don't understand why I'm not allowed to go do something fun and harmless! I didn't mean to throw the phone. Honestly, I was not trying to hurt you."

Laura was still rubbing her cheek. It was shiny and red, probably going to bruise. "I know you weren't trying to, but you did. And 'harmless' is in the eye of the beholder."

Marie clutched her phone. "It's an all-ages show! I'm going to come home and go to bed at a reasonable hour. I get that you're concerned, but like . . . you need to trust me. I am way, way more mature than you think. I'm the most mature person I know."

Laura stopped looking like she was about to cry and started to laugh. "Okay, that doesn't make me feel better."

Marie saw the flaw in what she'd said and laughed, too, breaking the horrible tension. But then they stopped laughing and looked at each other for a long moment.

"Look, I'll check in every half hour," Marie finally ventured. "I will not be out past ten."

Laura's face clouded again. "Jesus, Marie, I said no! Why are you testing me like this?"

"I'm not testing you! I'm telling you, I'm going!"

They were right back in phone-throwing territory.

"You just threw something at me, and I'm supposed to reward you?"

"I said I was sorry!"

"Actually, you didn't!"

"Well, I am! I am really sorry. I feel really bad that I hurt you. I didn't mean to. But having me spend the night sulking in my room won't change what happened."

She walked over to the pegs near the front door that held a dangling, untidy mess of the family's coats and started pawing through, looking for the lightweight leather jacket of Laura's that she had adopted as her own as soon as it fit her.

Laura's eyes brightened dangerously. "You know what? I have a great idea. I'll come with you."

Marie stopped looking through the coats and turned to stare at her mother with agonized fear in her eyes. "You wouldn't."

Laura feigned ignorance. "Sure, why not! I was just going to sit around watching TV. Maybe Kayla wants to come, too, we should ask her."

"Why are you doing this to me?"

"Doing what? It'll be fun! It's been forever since we did something together as a family."

Kayla, perhaps hearing her name, came to the end of the hallway and squinted through her glasses at the scene in the living room, looking from Laura to Marie and trying to figure out who, if anyone, to throw her loyalty behind. "I'm not going anywhere. I'm sixty pages from the end of the fifth Darkwall Chronicles book. You guys have fun, though," she said absently, then headed back to the girls' bedroom.

Outside, an ambulance went by, which happened a dozen times a day, but this time they both noticed it. Probably without consciously meaning to, Laura touched her injured cheek.

"I'm leaving, and you can't stop me. I'll call you later. Bye," Marie said, and walked out the door.

Laura opened the door and ran after her a few paces, then stopped at the top of the stairs. "Are you going to be warm enough in that coat?" she called after her, but Marie was already at the bottom of the stairwell, almost out the door.

————————

A couple of years earlier, a few months before Marie turned twelve, she had woken up one morning feeling like she was about to die. Instead of dozily getting ready for school, elbowing Kayla at the bathroom sink and eating a sloppy bowl of cereal as she had every day up until this point in her life, she'd stayed pinned to the bed, unable to move. There was a weakness in her legs and arms and a tight feeling in her chest and stomach. Her throat clenched and her heart raced. She told her mom that she needed to stay home from school because she had a stomach bug, and spent the rest of the day in bed, occasionally trying to read or watch TV. But the characters in books and TV shows were all so annoying and everything they did was so pointless. Didn't they understand that we were all going to die?

The next day she got up and the crushing sadness was still there. Some instinct told her she would be better off making herself go to school than she would be lying in bed, and it turned out that she could distract herself from the weakness and icy clench and ache for short periods of time by forcing herself to go through the motions of being a person. But she worried, as she sat in class and ate her lunch and hung out with her friends on the playground after school, that everyone could somehow see how fake she was being. In every moment, she was trying to figure out how the real Marie would act, and then act that way. She could make herself smile, and even laugh. Sometimes she would even get caught up in the moment and *be* real Marie, but almost as soon as she realized this was happening, the replacement sad Marie would come back, and she would have to start pretending again.

The feeling had come and gone like that for a few days, and then it came and stayed. She knew that she had to tell her mom what was happening, but when she tried, she couldn't talk at first, only cry. Laura sat next to her on the couch, rubbing her back, trying not to show how much she was freaking out. Marie felt her trying, and that made everything even worse. When she was done crying, she didn't feel better. She told Laura that all she looked forward to, all she wanted to do, was sleep.

Laura took her to the doctor, who referred them to a psychiatrist. It seemed like he mostly saw much younger kids. His waiting room had a heartbreaking box of wooden toys next to the coffee table covered in *New Yorker*s and *New York* magazines. He prescribed an SSRI and a benzodiazepine for Marie to take as needed when she felt panicky. She had taken one the of the as-needed pills on the subway on the way home from the appointment, breaking it in half as instructed. Nothing changed immediately, but by the time they had reached Seventh Avenue and emerged from the subway she noticed a faint floating feeling and a loosening of the invisible turtleneck corseting her chest and neck. She took her mom's hand and they walked down the sidewalk together, a little bit cautiously and slowly, as though Marie were a toddler again and just learning how to walk for the first time.

"Your dad—your biological father, I mean—also struggled with depression," Laura told her as she tucked her into bed that night. "I'm sorry we haven't talked about that before. I feel like we should have been prepared for this, or that we should have prepared you."

Marie didn't want her mom to feel bad, too. She already felt bad enough for everyone. Laura looked like she wanted to say something else, but she didn't. She kissed Marie on the forehead and said she would stay till she fell asleep if she wanted, but Marie told her it was okay, she could go. Then she lay in the dark alone for hours, listening to her own breath, thinking about the endlessness of the universe, which they had learned about in school. At the center of all the endlessness, it now seemed, was Marie. Inside of her was black emptiness. Outside of her was something terrifying and large and inexplicable with no known limit. The next morning she woke up and there was blood on her sheets and she felt a little bit better; she had gotten her period. That was the beginning of her life as a woman.

———

Matt was working late all week, editing an ad for an agency that had the account for a national burger chain, watching gooey ooze seep from between the halves of a bun over and over again. He had told Laura a million times that he liked the soothing repetition of his work and the satisfaction of getting each puzzle piece in its perfect place, but she couldn't help but project her own thwarted-artiste shit onto him; wouldn't he rather be editing his own animated short films, the ones he'd worked on before he and his ex had Kayla? He always claimed that he genuinely did not. He liked doing assignments and getting paid and going home. His work was a game he was good at and his life happened elsewhere, though for years now he'd been working harder and longer than he wanted to. The reality of having two same-aged children who were going to go to college, which they'd once joked about, was now imminent and not at all funny.

The suburbs were an option, of course. Matt could commute, and Laura could teach music anywhere. But the thought of moving upstate or to the suburbs on the cusp of entering her forties was too sad to bear. It would be like definitively admitting defeat. Once she'd floated the idea to Callie, just to see what she'd say, expecting reassurances that would be comforting even if she knew they were lies.

But Callie hadn't even bothered to lie. "No, I would not come visit," she'd said. "You could visit me, but I don't have time to take the PATH out to bumfuck to see how innovatively Matt has renovated your split-level. I'm busy, and you need to be somewhere we can hang out all the time when I'm in town. You're not moving anywhere. You're not allowed to. End of discussion."

So as of tonight Laura still lived in her apartment. It needed a thorough cleaning but was hers, and Matt's, and Kayla's and Marie's. The line of light seeping out past the door of the girls' bedroom had disappeared around ten thirty and now Laura was alone, with nothing to do but wait for Marie to come home. She puttered around, picking up stuff off surfaces and neatening piles and putting stuff down onto other, more appropriate surfaces. She put away the pile of dishes in the dish rack and made everyone lunches for the next day, which the girls were supposed to do for themselves but rarely did. She scrubbed the kitchen countertop as she looked out the window at the curling leaves of the mulberry tree that grew in the backyard of their building, half listening to whatever was on WFMU as she tried to prevent herself from thinking about what, exactly, Marie was up to. At eleven thirty she sent her a text asking as nonconfrontationally as possible what her plans were.

"Hanging out at Anna's. Don't wait up," Marie responded almost immediately. This was grounds for getting in trouble—she'd promised to be home early—but Anna was a good kid, and Laura had no fight left in her.

"Okay, see you in the morning. Sweet dreams," she replied. She added a double pink heart emoji as an afterthought. Three dots briefly appeared, then receded. "Okay, fuck you, too," Laura said out loud. She still felt insulted when her daughter withheld these little displays of affection. Until recently they had still said "I love you" every time they said goodbye, unselfconsciously and honestly, if reflexively. When had they stopped?

On her way to her bedroom, Laura couldn't resist the temptation to peek in on Kayla; she craved the satisfaction of seeing at least one child safe and comfortable at home in her bed. Kayla was in bed, but awake, looking at her phone. She shifted around to glare at Marie. "Hi, knocking is a thing?"

"Sorry, honey. I just wanted to say good night."

Kayla could be oblivious, but Laura's sadness was too blatant to ignore.

"Marie's still mad at you?"

"I guess so. She's at Anna's."

"If I tried to pull something like that . . ." Kayla glowered at her, then trailed off as she saw the pain in Laura's expression and changed tactics. "You know, I never break any rules. I should get a special reward." She smiled to make it clear that she was joking.

Laura smiled. "Yes, that would be a good lesson to teach you about how life works."

Kayla rolled her eyes, but kindly. "Dad's not home yet, either?"

"Still at the office."

There was a small silence, and Laura thought about asking Kayla if she wanted some hot cocoa or something, but it didn't seem quite right for her to get her teenage stepdaughter out of bed just so she would temporarily feel less lonely. "Okay, honey, sorry to bug you. Sweet dreams."

"You too," said Kayla. She paused. "Want a hug?"

Laura accepted, feeling slightly pathetic.

Instead of going to bed, she padded back out into the darkened living room, remembering something that Callie had told her once, one of the times when she'd been trying hard to get her to write or play again. "You know those moments when you feel like you want to smoke a cigarette or run around the block?

There's something uncomfortable crawling around inside you and you just want to cough it up or extinguish it somehow?"

"Of course," Laura had said.

"What do you do in those moments?"

"Nothing? Wait for them to pass?"

"Wrong! That's when you're supposed to get out your guitar," Callie had said.

Maybe it was advice that she'd once given Callie, now dispensed back to her; they'd been friends for so long that this was always possible. Regardless, it wasn't bad advice. She opened the hall closet and got out her guitar, smelling the sour velvet of the case's lining before she even finished opening the latches. She took it to the couch and then sat, singing and playing softly so as not to wake Kayla. She played a lullaby that she'd once sang to the girls when they were little, which had nonsense words but a pretty tune, and a tear ran down her cheek and stung the abraded skin where Marie's phone had hit her.

———

Marie should have worn a warmer coat; it was an annoying realization, not only because she was cold but also because she hated it when her mother was right. In fairness, though, she hadn't anticipated that she would be spending half of this early-autumn night outside with Tom, in an overgrown corner of Prospect Park where people mostly went to have sex and do birdwatching. Tom had claimed that he wanted to show her the goats, but of course she'd already seen them. They were in a fenced-in hillside area, brought there to eat all the poison ivy out of this corner of the park in advance of a renovation that would displace the cruis-ing men and birdwatchers permanently. The goats were pretty interesting-looking—several different types, all different colors and with those eerie, marble-like eyes. Marie and Tom had taken a desultory glance at them and then sat down on a bench to make out. From the woods nearby they could hear some dudes having a guttural, grunting romantic endeavor, or maybe that was the goats.

Tom hadn't been that aggressive about making out with her, which was either because he was restraining himself or because he actually wasn't that into her and was interested in Marie only because of her connection to the Clips. But just the touch of his hand on Marie's was making her feel crazy; she wanted to grab it and pull it onto her thigh, up her thigh, past the waistband of her jeans. She shivered, sort of from the cold and sort of not. He didn't notice. He was talking about her dad again.

"So then they played that show at Brownies—no official recordings exist, but there are some bootlegs floating around online. And that's when they debuted 'Don't Let Me Come Over,' which has got to be my favorite Clips song, maybe my favorite of all the songs your dad recorded with them."

Marie nodded, pretending to listen as she studied the shape of Tom's face and the movement of his lips. She loved making out with him—it was the ultimate distraction, a great way of obliterating the tick of thoughts and worries that spun too fast through her brain at almost all other times. She was always on the hunt for that feeling, or maybe just the level of feeling that blotted out thought.

It was too bad that Tom was maybe gay in some deep unbeknownst-to-even-himself way. He was definitely gay for the memory of Marie's dead dad, she knew. But a lot of people were, especially boys. It had always been that way ever since she and her friends got old enough to be into things in general—some people were into *Star Wars*, or video games, or dancing or acting or writing. Some people were into music, and of those people, a very small but vocal subset were into her dad.

Not a lot of people knew he was her dad, of course. They didn't have the same last name, and even Marie had not known that the person her mom referred to as "your bio father" (whereas Matt was always, had always been "Matt") had been a tragic figure, famous to fans of her mom's friend Callie's band and to music nerds like Tom. Her mom had waited until she could reasonably be expected to understand not only the concept of death but also the more difficult concept of "semi-famous tragic figure" before springing that one on her.

Laura told Marie about Dylan a few months after her first depressive episode, after things had stabilized. She made up a sanitized, simplified version: "Your dad was a sad guy, but he was also very talented. At least, a lot of people thought so. I certainly thought so. I didn't know him very long. He was only twenty-five when he died. He had a stupid accident."

"Did I ever meet him?" Marie had asked. It had seemed like a reasonable question; she knew that a lot had happened in her life before she could remember things.

"No, baby, he never knew I was pregnant with you. He died before I even knew."

Then Laura had put an unfamiliar CD on the little kitchen boom box that they mostly used when they wanted to listen to sprightly, upbeat cooking music. They sat there without talking and listened to one of his songs together. It was hard for Marie to pick out any of the words through the fuzz and filters, but it had a nice tune. She didn't immediately want to hear it again or anything, though. She got the feeling, though she couldn't say why she felt this way, that her mom didn't really love the song, either. Maybe that was why she'd never played it before. Listening to it seemed to awaken something in her mother, though. She got distracted and seemed far away.

"Do you think this is a good song?" Marie had hazarded after a few minutes.

Laura shrugged. "Objectively, yes. It's not really my cup of tea, though."

The song had ended, and the next one had come on, but Marie reached over and hit stop on the boom box. "Can we listen to the *White Album*?"

"Sure, whatever you want. Do you want to talk about your bio father more? Ask me any questions?"

Marie had shrugged. "Not really. Maybe later. I don't think I have any questions right now."

Laura had looked into her face for a minute, and Marie had felt, as she now often did, that the price of her mom's love, the blood-warm ocean she swam in constantly, was this kind of heightened surveillance of her feelings. Maybe with two parents it would have been spread out a little more. Lately Laura was always checking to make sure she wasn't sad. Sad like her dad.

Marie was ashamed of being on medication for depression, but at least it was something about her that was special. No one had ever said this out loud to her face, but Marie knew that unless she could prove herself to be exceptional in some way within the next year or so, she was going to be pretty much fucked as far as college was concerned. Unlike Kayla, who had racked up prizes and awards basically since kindergarten, and who would surely get some kind of scholarship to study whatever boring STEM-related thing she wanted, Marie mostly coasted in school. She could sing and play guitar, of course, because her mom had taught her the same way she'd taught lessons to hundreds of other kids—but in a city full of kids who'd learned to play violin at age three, she didn't stand out as a prodigy. And while her mom wasn't discouraging, she also wasn't exactly pushing her onto the stage.

"I'm just glad you're doing something that makes you happy," she'd said once, when Marie had told her that she was probably going to place at least third in the freshman talent show. At the show, Marie had played cover songs on her guitar, but she hadn't picked very popular songs, and had come in fourth.

Marie tuned back into what Tom was talking about as he said, "So these rare recordings, plus a whole treasure trove of Dylan juvenilia, are owned by your grandmother, but she issued a statement after he died that she has no plans to release them."

"My grandmother?" Marie pictured her grandmother's messy house in Columbus, filled with the cousins she saw once a year on Christmas, who exchanged a ton of tacky plastic as-seen-on-TV gadgets and talked about Jesus in a way that made her mom and Matt visibly uncomfortable. Then she realized that wasn't the grandmother Tom was talking about.

"Oh, my bio dad's mother. I don't even know who that is. I guess that's weird."

"That is weird! Does she know you exist?"

"I think so. But my mom and I have talked about this stuff for, like, a cumulative forty-five minutes over the course of my entire life, you know? You definitely know more about my dad's family than I do."

"So you've never met her?"

"No, I've never met anyone in his family. It doesn't seem important. Look, can we talk about something else? Or, like, do something else?" She tried to look at him the way she had seen people do in movies and TV shows—flirtatiously, suggestively. She half closed her eyes and inclined her head in a direction that would have made it easy for him to lean down and start kissing her again. He ignored it.

"So this is kind of crazy, but what if you went to visit her and you asked if you could have the tapes? Like, as a kind of inheritance?"

Marie opened her eyes fully. "That's not kind of crazy, that's completely crazy. Where does she even live?"

"The internet thinks she lives in Massachusetts. We could drive there in, like, five hours."

"Let's just go right now, right? Road trip!"

Tom didn't catch her sarcasm, or refused to. "Well, no, but you could probably figure out how to call or email her. And then we could go visit. We could plan it together. It would be an adventure for us."

"Where would we sleep?" There was no way she would actually do this, but she liked thinking about it. She imagined a room in some kind of gross roadside motel, peeling back the rough comforter and climbing into a bed with Tom, and felt terrified and thrilled. It was like remembering a scene from a movie, not like imagining a possible thing that might happen in her life.

Tom shrugged. "I hadn't thought it through that far—in the car, I guess? Or at your grandmother's house, if she's nice."

Marie shook her head. During one of their many recent hushed, tense conversations about money, Matt had mentioned something about inheritance, and Laura had said that no amount of money was worth having to deal with "that awful woman." Marie was just now realizing that they had to have been talking about her grandmother.

"I don't know. Basically the only thing I know about her is that my mom doesn't like her." Marie pulled her hand away from Tom's grasp. "This whole idea is just too scary and weird, Tom."

He grabbed her hand back and started to rub the inside of her wrist with his pointer finger, lightly.

"A road trip is romantic, right?" He leaned in for a kiss.

They kissed for a long time. A goat bleated in the distance, but Marie barely heard it. When they stopped kissing, she was ready to agree to almost anything.

———

Laura woke up and knew, without checking, that Marie was home, safe in her bed. She must have barely breached the surface of consciousness at whatever point in the night that Marie had crept in the door, then dived back down into a deeper sleep. It must have been very late, but at least she had come home. Anyway, it wasn't worth picking another fight about, and she always wanted to keep Marie from feeling bad if at all possible.

She got out of bed and looked in the mirror over her dresser to see whether the damage from the thrown phone was still visible. Luckily it wasn't, though if you were looking for it you could see that the undereye circle on that side was slightly darker. Laura still looked incongruously young compared to most of her kids' friends' parents, but compared to all the versions of herself that had existed previously, she looked old. Not *old* old, but not young anymore. It wasn't about gray hair or wrinkles or anything that obvious, but more in the set of her jaw and the reflexive downward tilt of her mouth. Her default mode was skepticism and worry. When she'd been younger her default mode had been openness and inquisitiveness, and the light in her eyes had flashed at everyone indiscriminately. Now she wished she had saved some of that light, banked it somehow. Maybe there was a way to get it back? Some kind of soul rejuvenation that only the very, very rich knew about?

She left Matt to catch another few minutes of sleep, since he'd gotten home so late, and went to start getting ready for the day.

Laura usually walked the girls to the subway on her way to the school where she taught music. Though Marie sometimes complained about it, they all still enjoyed the ritual. Kayla and Marie walked slightly ahead of Laura, murmuring to each other occasionally with their phones in their hands, ready if they had to stop for any length of time at an intersection.

Though their building itself wasn't beautiful, their neighborhood was objectively perfect, with its brownstones and tall old trees, everything dark and staid and calm. The air itself seemed filled with the soothing, softening presence of money. Gentrification wasn't a messy work in progress here, as it was in all the other Brooklyn neighborhoods where Laura had lived prior to moving to Park Slope. The especially impressive brownstones had window boxes and tiny front gardens planted with marigolds and tufts of spiky grasses. Laura had thought she was inured to envy, after having felt it so often for so long. Today, though, she wished that she had the time and space to plant flowers. She thought of the planning and the annoying little tasks and micro-decisions required and soon she was exhausted by just the idea of the window boxes. Fourteen years ago, a version of Laura might have enjoyed the flowers' beauty. Now all she could see was the work it had taken to grow them and plant them and keep them alive. Nothing took care of itself.

She said goodbye to the girls at the entrance of the F train. Kayla gave her a desultory hug, but Marie stood off to the side, refusing to make eye contact, pretending to be entranced in her screen. After watching them descend the stairs, Laura walked the remaining block to the school where she worked. Today she was leaving right after her last group of students to have a drink with Callie in Manhattan, and the thought of this would sustain her through the day of mild irritations underscored by a baseline thrum of worry about Marie.

The job was fine. Or maybe it was pretty bad. It was a job. In a way, Laura missed teaching the baby music classes, even though the pay had been chancy and the owners of toy stores were often awful and there was a frankly evil pecking order among the established musicians, who tended to get territorial as they competed to lock in new students. At least then she'd been performing. That had made up for a lot of time spent cleaning drool off of shaker eggs after each class was over.

In search of something more stable, she had first found a job at a music summer camp, and through that gig she'd landed a full-time job at a public elementary school. The rise of standardized testing eliminated the budget for her position at first one and then another public school, and she'd found herself faced with the choice of working at either a charter or a private school. She'd decided to split the difference and do both part-time. The charter school's students were so disciplined they were almost animatronic, except when they could sense that they were in the presence of a teacher who would not enforce the ironclad rules, and then they were so unruly that Laura usually felt it was a victory if no instruments got broken and no one cried during class, herself included. At the private school, the students were nicer, though they were occasionally condescending. She sometimes couldn't shake the feeling that they thought of her as kind of a servant. It was still better than being cursed at by seven-year-olds, though. In 2013 she'd taken a full-time position at the Briar Academy, teaching music appreciation to first through fourth grades.

The fourth graders were definitely the worst, and she taught them last, ending her day on a low note. It was amazing how one "funny" boy student could tip an otherwise okay group into chaos just by making a fart noise with his kazoo. She sometimes tried to remember why she'd initially thought she would be good around large groups of kids; it had been early in Marie's life, when her love for her child had seemed to spill over into a love for kids in general. There were still kids she liked—students who had the same kind of enthusiasm for playing and singing that she'd had as a child, or even just interesting, quiet kids who she could tell liked listening to music on their own. But the brassy, bossy alpha types always turned the class's attention toward them, and then Laura had to fight to wrest it back. She was tired of these future CEOs and lawyers. She wished there was a way to oust them so that she could focus on the students like the gentle second grader who'd come to her last week complaining that her hands were too sore to play guitar anymore. She'd told the girl that her fingers would toughen up soon and to keep playing, the same advice she'd been given the first time this happened to her. Maybe her life would have been different if she'd given up. It might have been better, she'd caught herself thinking.

The class ended at last, and Laura had an itch to run out of the classroom as quickly as her students did. Instead, though, she spent a decorous moment gathering her things, putting the instruments back in their cubbies on the shelves, smoothing her hair and reapplying lipstick using her reflection in her phone's reversed camera as a mirror. She still always wanted to look good for Callie.

Laura took a seat at the bar they'd chosen as a mutually convenient meeting spot, ordered a glass of white wine and drank the first two sips like it was water. Though her back was to the door, she could tell when Callie walked in.

Even in their city full of professional-quality beauties, it was still rare to see anyone as beautiful as Callie. Everyone who saw her adjusted themselves in subtle ways; the bartender smoothed his hair back, and the college-aged women at the table nearest the door straightened their spines and pushed their collarbones forward as though showing off invisible necklaces. Callie rushed up to Laura, who stood up next to her barstool so that her friend could envelop her in a cool, perfumed hug. She was wearing a white shirtdress under a cropped black leather jacket, and there were little gold caps on the toes of her ankle boots. Laura wished she'd worn something other than her usual barely passable adult-wear outfit of black jeans, Converse sneakers, and button-down shirt, but it didn't matter. Whoever was with Callie was rendered at least temporarily beautiful or cool by association, and the bartender came around immediately to affirm this by putting misty glasses of ice water in front of each of them, topping off Laura's glass and leaving Callie with the wine menu, all without uttering a word.

"That looks good. One for me, too, please," Callie said, and was taking her first sip of wine within seconds. Laura had sat at the bar for five minutes before anyone had even given her a menu.

There was energy buzzing around Callie, mixing with her perfume and somehow promising fun, excitement, and money. Even after all these years of having the promise not quite deliver, Laura was still enthralled and enticed by it. They sat for a minute just sipping and smiling at each other, and then Callie reached out and touched the tender bruise under Laura's eye that no one else, even Matt, had noticed. "Did you take up kickboxing?"

"I probably should. Marie is kind of out of control."

"She punched you? What a little bitch!"

It stung Laura when anyone insulted Marie, though she of course thought of her daughter as a bitch all the time.

"Well, not quite. She threw her phone, not on purpose. But also not by accident, you know?"

"Did you punish her?"

"Should I have?"

"What would your mother have done?"

"Jesus, I don't even want to think about it. Called the cops, probably. I see my mother once a year for Christmas and talk to her on the phone once a month about the weather. If that's my relationship with Marie in twenty years I'll, like . . . kill myself?"

Callie smiled. "Fair enough! And of course I am the last person in the world who should be giving you parenting advice. I just hate seeing you get hurt. Emotionally or otherwise."

Laura shrugged and finished her glass of wine, which was seamlessly refilled.

"There's no way to avoid it. The whole endeavor is just one variety of heartbreak after the next."

Callie looked down at her own pretty shoes. "It seems like a distraction might be just what you need right now!"

"What did you have in mind?"

"I have a gig guest-curating a playlist for Google Play, like, a mixtape of sorts, and I want to put one of your songs on it. A new song, not one of the old ones."

Laura gave herself time to think by signaling to the bartender to top up her glass again, which this time she managed easily. Her gut reaction to any addition to her workload, mental or emotional or physical, was a resounding no. But Callie wasn't going to keep offering her third and fourth and fifth chances forever, and she *had* recently touched her guitar for the first time in years.

"You really don't have to do that. It is so nice of you to want to do a favor for me," she hedged.

Callie sighed. "I'm not doing this as a favor for you. I don't do favors, really, you know that. I got this assignment, I'm supposed to come up with stuff no one else could get, and I think you'd fit in perfectly with the other things I'm putting on there. I'm going for a sort of low-fi vibe, a little bit retro. It's due next week. I just thought I'd mention it."

"I have so much stuff I have to do between now and next week. Maybe if I had more time?"

It was rare for Callie to betray exasperation, but her patience seemed thinner than usual. There were bags under her eyes, too, Laura noticed, though she had taken pains to conceal them.

"You'll never have more time, Laura. You keep saying things will be different in the future, but it's never happening."

"Well, I still have hope!" Laura tried to say brightly, but there was an edge of desperation in her voice.

She signaled for the check but then didn't even feint toward it when it came. Callie could afford to pick it up. Callie had no idea what anything really cost.

───────

Walking back to the subway Laura felt numb, and not in a good way. Callie's offer made it seem like the universe was trying to tell her something, but for the moment at least she was determined to ignore it. The universe could go fuck itself.

She got a seat to herself on the F train when it came. Even better, the seat next to hers had a pen mark on it that looked like dirt, so no one sat down next to her. She spread out into the unaccustomed space, took out her phone, and prepared to lose herself completely in a stream of images of other people's happy lives.

Sunsets, succulents, babies, pets, and food usually soothed

her, but right now the magic wasn't working. She had an echo of the same thought she'd had about the window boxes that morning—someone had fanned out that avocado, planted those succulents, given birth to that adorable baby, and picked out the organic cotton onesie and then buttoned it up despite his thrashing. All of that labor, all for what? So that Laura would have something to immerse her tired brain in on the way home to her less picturesque life? She had the impulse to add her own photo to the top of the feed, and she scrolled through her camera roll looking for something to add, but there was nothing there that might make her life seem desirable to any imagined outside observer. She should have taken a selfie with Callie. That would have gotten a ton of likes, but it wasn't the kind of thing she would ever do. It would feel wrong, for the same reason accepting Callie's offer would seem wrong. She was determined to succeed or not based on her own merit, not her proximity to Callie's fame. Part of her knew this was dumb. If you really wanted to succeed, you'd use everything in your arsenal.

But what would "success" mean, then? What would constitute success for Laura? It was too late to replicate what Callie had, and anyway, that was a level of fame she wasn't even sure she wanted. Just being able to make music, and perform for people who liked it, would be enough, she thought. Not having to listen to flat scales played on the recorder by bored eight-year-olds anymore would be a bonus.

But she was too scared, or too busy, or too distracted, or just too tired, to do what was necessary to make her dreams come true. And also, if she devoted her entire mind and heart to making music, who would expend the mental energy required to keep Marie and Kayla safe and alive?

She found a photo of them that she'd taken a few weeks earlier, in a rare moment when they were both smiling about something, over a plate of french fries at the diner near their apartment. They were both such beautiful girls, and still so young; they hadn't forced their faces into the angles they used for their own selfies and were caught in natural expressions, unselfconscious, almost like they were still children. She tagged it #tbt, even though it wasn't Thursday, and used the last bit of signal before the train went under the East River to post it, so that it seemed like at least she had accomplished something today.

———

Marie and Tom's high school was tucked into a banal non-neighborhood behind Lincoln Center. They had two classes together, which were the high points of Marie's days. As a non-prodigy, she flew under the teachers' radar in most of her classes. She showed up and did her work, and she played in the jazz band, making up part of the sound that made it possible for the genius students' solos to sparkle in a competent setting. If you reliably did that, no one really cared what else you did.

They were allowed to go off campus, which still felt thrilling. You had to get back for your next class, so you couldn't go far, but just going to the unfamiliar stores on Broadway or even dipping into the park for a few minutes, watching rich old ladies walk their small dogs quickly past someone sleeping under a pile of trash bags, gave Marie a thrill of independence.

Today she went farther, skipping her afternoon classes and then, for something to do, getting a sandwich at a sad office-lunch place on Columbus and taking it to the park, where she sat on a bench next to twentysomething girls in ballet slippers and J.Crew print dresses. The sky above them was spectacular, full of perfectly shaped clouds that seemed to hover just above the tops of the changing trees. Marie ignored the leaves and the clouds and looked at her phone.

She'd already found the one interview Daisy had ever given about Dylan, from soon after he'd died. Daisy had been rude and aggressive with the reporter, and had tried to make her feel guilty about prying into Dylan's life. Marie could see why her mother had described Daisy as awful—but then, who wouldn't be angry at a reporter, in that situation? She tried to find anything more recent about Daisy, searching her name plus the town where Dylan had grown up, and she found almost nothing, except for an email address for info at the candle shop where the article had said she'd worked in 2003. She decided to hold off on writing until she could talk to Tom about what, exactly, she was supposed to be asking Daisy for.

When she got bored of sitting in the park, she went to go try on clothes at Urban Outfitters, trekking up Broadway till its giant sign loomed over her. They were still pushing nineties-throwback pretty hard, with some ye olde rave culture accents. She took an armful of dresses into the dressing room and watched herself carefully as she tried them on. She took photos of herself in the ones she found especially cute, but didn't post them anywhere in case her mom was snooping; she didn't want to get caught cutting class. She liked stripping off one outfit and putting on another and seeing herself as a potentially different person. Maybe a person who wore a shiny crushed-velvet baby-doll dress would be incapable of feeling sad or bored, or of being boring.

She didn't buy it, or any of the other ones. She left and headed back toward school to see if she could arrange to be there just as Tom was walking out, at which point they would naturally take the subway home together.

As she reached the intersection next to the school's imposing front stairs she saw him standing on the bottom stair, scanning the horizon, and thought with a ripple of gratification that he'd been waiting for her. But then he made eye contact with a senior boy she didn't know. Tom gave him one of those awkward macho half hugs and handed him something, then quickly crossed the street and kept walking, fast. It was almost as obvious as the deals they'd witnessed in the decrepit goat area of the park, where sometimes people would stand there counting out change aloud. She decided to try to catch up with Tom.

Marie hadn't done a lot of drugs, but she knew that she liked them. She also knew, because of her dad, that she should stay far away from anything addictive, even candy, probably, but there was plenty of time later in life to be virtuous and clean. Ever since she'd popped her first prescription benzos and felt the vise around her sternum loosen, she'd felt entitled to pursue other paths toward that same feeling. She never got fucked up, she just did enough to access a looser, more carefree version of herself. So far she'd done this only with small quantities of pills, her own and other people's, and with weed, which often made her feel bad in a different, novel way, and with quantities of beer and wine so tiny that her parents or whoever's parents would never think twice about their having gone missing. She wasn't stupid about any of this. She felt the same way about it as she did about school: basically, once you understood the system and how the rules worked, you could break whichever ones you wanted, within reason.

Tom turned and looked up just in time to make eye contact with Marie, who was still across the street. She waved and gave him an eyebrow raise to indicate that she understood what had just gone down. He raised a fingertip to his lips. He thought he was so cool, but he also sort of *was* cool. She crossed the street to meet him, and he greeted her by holding out his hand, which was almost as good as a kiss. Inside his hand was a little plastic bag full of brown twigs.

"Want to come over and eat mushrooms?" Obviously, she said yes.

———

Tom's parents weren't home, and his entire house was empty. He lived in the attic, the highest floor of his parents' mind-boggling brownstone on State Street in Brooklyn Heights. The ground floor had a kitchen and a den and the informal feel of a normal home—it was about the same size and shape as Marie's parents' entire apartment—but the parlor floor had high ceilings and large paintings on the walls and immaculate, light-colored furniture and carpets. That floor seemed intended only for display. Then the next floor was bedrooms, and the top floor was Tom's. It had slanted roofs, a worn-out but comfortable leather couch, a large TV, and an elaborate shelving system where Tom stored his record player and records and his books about music. It was about three times the size of the room Marie shared with Kayla, and it was immaculate. They sat on the couch, and he poured her a glass of red wine from a bottle he'd grabbed nonchalantly from a rack in the kitchen as they'd passed through it.

She didn't know what she'd expected, and of course she had other friends who lived in nice apartments, but for some reason knowing that Tom's family was superrich made him less appealing. It was easy to be cool if you could afford all of coolness's trappings without having to think too hard about how you'd get them. She drank all the wine that he poured for her almost immediately and then refilled her own glass as Tom shuffled through his records, deciding what to play. The doorbell rang downstairs.

It turned out that what Tom had planned was more of a party situation than a romantic thing with just the two of them. He'd invited his best friend, Jamie, and horribly, he'd also invited Sara K.

If Marie was unremarkable, except for the unwanted remarkableness of her mood disorder, Sara K. was the opposite. She was the shining star of their class, a true virtuoso who could pick up any instrument and play. She could sing, too, in a lilting, unobtrusive, but beautiful contralto that made it impossible to imagine casting anyone else as the lead in school musicals. And while all of that was undoubtedly nerdy, and could have made it impossible for Sara K. to be cool, she was also so attractive—in an interesting Olivia Munn way, not a straightforward-blond way—that she was rendered cool automatically. She was nice to everyone and got good grades, but it was also possible to imagine her daintily nibbling the brown twigs in the packet that

Tom had pocketed earlier. She could probably do that and still play a concerto without missing a note. And if Tom had invited her, that meant he liked her.

Marie tried to greet her with blasé equanimity, but Sara K. was genuinely, maddeningly nice. "Oh my God, I'm so glad another girl is here. It's usually such a sausage fest when Tom has people over. What did you say your name was?" She didn't even bother to introduce herself; it would have seemed silly, like Beyoncé saying, "Hi, nice to meet you, I'm Beyoncé."

Everyone had a glass of wine and it seemed like they were pretending to be adults, sipping from their glasses and talking about the nuances of the record they were listening to. Jamie and Tom sat on the couch, and Sara K. perched on the end of Tom's bed with one long leg tucked up under her and her other foot, in a striped cotton sock, tapping on the floor in time to the music. Marie would never have thought of sitting on the bed; it seemed much too intimate. Sara K. sat there in a way that made it seem like she'd done it before.

Marie had to do something to make it clear that she was the one who deserved Tom's attention, that she had a firmer claim to him. Her thoughts were already getting a little bit dulled by the wine. It was impossible to compete with Sara K. via any of the obvious metrics: hotness, talent, popularity. But Marie was Dylan's daughter, and probably the way to make Tom choose her over Sara K., who was now leafing through the stack of magazines on his bedside table, was to make it clear that she was her dad's true heir.

"So, about those mushrooms?" she interrupted loudly, in the middle of an unrelated conversation.

Tom looked up at her in surprise. "Yeah? Are you sure? I had thought you were chickening out."

"I'm sure! Bring on the drugs! I love drugs!" said Marie, trying to defuse the heaviness of the situation by acting like it was hilarious. She wasn't sure what mushrooms did, or were supposed to do.

Tom smiled at her. "You're drunk."

"I'm just buzzed. I'm just silly," she said, smiling at him in a way she hoped was winsome, or sexy, or sophisticated.

"What drugs are we talking about here?" Sara K. said. "On a Tuesday?"

" 'Got the club goin' up on a Tuesday,' " sang Jamie. He refilled his wineglass to the brim and put the empty bottle on the floor, then pulled his sunglasses down over his eyes.

———

In the immaculate subway-tiled bathroom one floor downstairs from Tom's attic bedroom, Marie puked and puked and puked. Then she felt fine—better than fine, actually. She felt better than she ever had in her life. She felt like she had been given some kind of Advil for the soul. Everything that had ever bothered her no longer did. She was excited to never refill her antidepressant prescription ever again. It was clear that she no longer needed any kind of drug except this one.

She made her way up the stairs again. The banister felt soft in her hand. Even the stairs themselves felt soft under her feet. She grinned at everyone as she reentered the room, and they smiled back at her. The room revolved around her, but slowly and gently, the way the record on Tom's turntable was twirling, making a low, raspy hum. The side had finished, but no one had flipped it over. She went over to do so and marveled at the grain of the black vinyl caressing her fingertips; it felt like the gentle lick of a cat's tongue. She lowered the needle with infinite care and gentleness, the way her mother had taught her to do when she was a little girl.

Her mother. Marie hadn't texted or called to say where she would be after school. It would be better to do that sooner rather than later. It would have been better to have called an hour ago. But now she didn't know where her phone was, and almost couldn't imagine the effort of finding it. She decided to rest for a while before she undertook that project, and maybe have another glass of wine. She poured one and sat down next to Sara K. on the bed. Sara K. hadn't eaten the mushrooms, and she was walking around a lot, creating a blurry streak wherever she moved. She looked like she was trying to find something, and then it seemed that she had found it: her shoes. She tied them on.

"Okay, well, I'll see you guys around. Try not to get in too much trouble," she said, seeming to be talking to Tom specifically, and then on her way out the door she touched his head and ruffled his hair with a gesture that seemed lovingly possessive. But it didn't matter, because Marie had won. Sara K. was leaving, and she was still here. Tom waited a moment after the door closed, and then came to sit down on the bed next to her. He looked up at Jamie.

"Hey, will you go downstairs and grab another bottle of wine?"

"Aren't your parents coming home soon? I don't want to run into them and have to, like, have a conversation right now." He giggled slightly and did a little half twirl.

"They're at some dinner or gala or something, they won't be home for hours yet. Don't worry about it. Make yourself at home down there, if you want. Like, watch some TV or something."

Jamie laughed again. "Ohhkay. See ya." Marie's reaction time was so slowed down that it took the click of the door closing behind Jamie for her to realize what had happened, what was about to happen. Involuntarily, she tensed up all over as Tom turned to her and leaned in for a kiss.

The edges of Tom's face blurred as it moved closer to hers. His body, too, was close, and for a second this was wonderful—cozy and warm, exciting but not in a heart-pounding, panic-inducing way. But then something in the way that he clutched at parts of her started to feel impersonal and claustrophobic. They still had on all their clothes and she was trying to kiss him, and in a way he was kissing her, too, sort of haphazardly, his mouth off to the side of her mouth.

He began pressing her down harder and harder into the bed. She tried to just roll with it, focusing on the parts of the experience that were enjoyable and trying to relax and become smaller, so that it wouldn't feel bad when he pressed down. But she was too fucked up to talk herself into thinking that this was fun. It was time to make him stop. She gave him a gentle shove and rolled out from under him, over to the side of the bed.

"Okay, that's enough for now."

To Tom's credit, he didn't protest. He even sort of apologized. "I'm really out of it," he said. "We should try this again when we're more sober."

He helped her find her shoes and even used her phone to get an Uber, which she would not have been capable of doing. The phone seemed so small, and the icons on it blurred under her fingertips. He waited with her downstairs till the car came, and opened its door for her, and kissed her gently, in the way that he should have kissed her on his bed.

The ride home wasn't good, but at least she didn't throw up in the car. She was hoping that somehow she would be able to sneak in, but it was still relatively early, and when she opened the door of the apartment (using keys, and deeply ingrained muscle memory), her mom and Matt and Kayla were sitting at the dinner table, eating taquitos from Trader Joe's.

———

Marie's drunkenness was so egregiously obvious that at first Laura wasn't sure whether to be angry or concerned. They made eye contact, and then Marie slurred something about having food poisoning and ran to the bathroom, slamming the door behind her. Matt turned to Laura as though expecting her to go do something, so she got up out of her seat but then just stood there, trying to figure out what she was supposed to do.

Marie was only fourteen. Laura had thought she had more time before this kind of thing would start to happen, more time to figure out how to be stern and parental but yet understanding and cool enough to keep lines of communication open. But all she could muster right now was anger, muted by exhaustion. The tipsiness from her drink with Callie had shaded quickly into a bone-achy tiredness—hence the half-assed dinner. Why was Marie doing this to her right now? Without saying anything to Matt, she eye-contact-pleaded with him to handle it, but he shook his head. Marie was her daughter; she was the first line of discipline. That had always been their deal.

Kayla cleared her throat. "Guys, there's no point in punishing or lecturing her now. She's probably not even going to remember it."

"Thanks for your input," said Laura sharply before she could stop herself.

"Hey," said Matt in a warning tone, quietly, but still.

It was a single syllable, but somehow it was all it took to make Laura feel completely enraged—not just at Marie, but at Matt and Kayla, too, at the whole stupid situation. How had she so fully lost control of what happened to these kids? Did no one in this household respect her at all?

She almost ran to the bathroom door, then pounded on it. "Marie? Let me in. You're in serious trouble. We have to talk about this."

From down the hall, she heard Matt and Kayla talking in murmurs, maybe discussing whether to intervene, and then the clink of silverware as they quietly cleared their places. They were so reasonable, so quiet. She suddenly felt the chasm in the middle of her family, the awkwardness of the combination of their households. How had she and Matt ever thought they and their wholly dissimilar daughters could all live together in harmony?

She pushed the door open. Marie was sitting next to the toilet, leaning her cheek on the toilet seat. Her cheeks were smeared with smudged eyeliner, and there was unflushed pink puke in the toilet. Laura was torn between the impulse to wet a washcloth and comfort her the way she had when she'd been little—the way she had even a year ago—and a warring impulse to shake her for being so irresponsible with her precious self. Above all she wanted someone she could blame, so that she could stop feeling guilty for having been out at a bar herself while Marie had been getting into trouble.

Instead she just stood there, waiting for Marie to look up. "Do we have to take you to the hospital?"

"I don't think so. I don't know. No. I mean, I'm conscious, I can talk," said Marie. "I'm really sorry, okay?"

She didn't sound sorry, though. She sounded like she was just saying whatever she thought would get Laura off her back.

"Sorry doesn't cut it, Marie. This is really unacceptable. I'm so worried about you, we all are. You can't do this kind of thing! You just can't!"

Marie looked up at her with tears in her eyes. "Do you even care how I feel right now? If you're so worried about me, maybe you could try to act more concerned than angry. Because I am already feeling really bad right now, okay?"

The effort of this whiny plea seemed to deplete her, and she slumped back to the side of the toilet, then said, "Oh, shit," and shakily leaned over it again to release another torrent of puke. Something about the color and smell awakened a sense memory in Laura. She knelt on the floor next to her daughter, rage draining from her and leaving something confusing in its place:

tenderness and nostalgia. She smoothed sweaty hair away from Marie's forehead and gently stroked her heaving back, flushed the toilet when she was done, and then let her slump in her lap and rest her head against Laura's chest. Without meaning to, she deeply inhaled the top of her daughter's head. She smelled like fruity teenager shampoo and booze sweat, but there was still some hint deep down of the smell that Laura had spent years huffing when Marie was a baby and a little girl; whatever it was that was unmistakably Marie and always had been, underneath whoever she was becoming. Filled with tenderness, she found herself taking a slight risk: opening herself up to Marie's disdain and shedding her scolding mom role for a second.

"I was throwing up red wine on the night I met your dad. Your bio-dad, not Matt."

"You've never told me that story," said Marie. She curled her shaky body into her mom's and prepared to listen, as if Laura were about to read to her from Dr. Seuss.

"Well, let me start by saying that I was twenty-two. Like, legally of drinking age. Okay?"

"Mom."

"Callie had taken me to see this band, and then we went to the after-party at their apartment. I had been living in New York for a week or something, I didn't know anyone, and I accidentally got way too drunk. I rushed outside to throw up in the gutter, and when I stood up he was there. Somehow it was cute and not disgusting."

"And then you guys lived happily ever after," said Marie. Laura looked down to see whether she was trying to be mean, but she seemed to think it was romantic.

"Well, you know, obviously not," said Laura.

"I do know, but you were happy for a minute, right? I mean, you were in love."

"I was in love. He was a special guy. He had a lot of problems, and he wasn't a very good boyfriend. But who knows? Maybe he would have become a good man. He might have even been a good dad to you." She could hear in her own voice that she didn't believe it.

"But probably not," said Marie.

"Well, who knows," said Laura. She was trying to spin the story into something edifying, or at least positive. "Maybe better than nothing, but definitely not better than Matt."

"You're a good mom," said Marie, as if intuiting that Laura wanted to hear it. "I mean, we've never been close, but you do a good job with, you know, the mom stuff."

"We've never been close?" Laura tried to keep the pain out of her voice, but her body had stiffened, and Marie, still slumped against her, must have felt it because she sat up and looked at Laura as she tried to explain.

"Don't be offended. It's just obvious, right? I mean close like how Matt and Kayla are close—how they always finish each other's sentences; they always win at Taboo when they're on the same team. I know you love me, because you worry about me all the time, and tell me what to do, but it's not like we text each other jokes or like the same music or have similar brains. Which is lucky! For you, I mean."

Marie was just drunk and rambling, but Laura couldn't help but feel lacerated by this little spiel. Not close? Not *close*? Did she not realize that for the first three years of her life, they'd slept in the same bed, breathing in the same rhythm, Marie's little legs kicking her in the stomach as she drifted from one dream to the next? Did she realize how, before that, they'd shared a *body*? You couldn't get much closer than that.

"I'm . . . I'm sorry you think we're not close," said Laura. She wanted to say it dispassionately, so that Marie wouldn't know how badly she'd upset her, but instead it ended up sounding mean and dismissive, like she thought Marie was mistaken about her own feelings. Marie sighed.

"I just think I might have had more in common with my dad. If he'd lived," said Marie.

That's so unfair, Laura thought. But she didn't say it. She wasn't going to engage with this bullshit. If her daughter wanted to dismiss the sacrifices she'd made and the love she'd poured into her to idolize a dead idiot whose mediocre songs would likely have been forgotten if he hadn't died, there was nothing she could do or say to change her mind. All she could do was defend herself from being hurt anymore by the little monster she'd ruined her life for in order to protect.

She put up a mental wall around everything Marie had just said and reinforced it with mental concrete. Callie had been right. She needed a distraction from the disaster of her life.

They got up off the bathroom floor after that, and Marie got into the shower. She assured Laura that she would not pass out and drown, but Laura still waited outside the bathroom till she heard the water turn off. She knocked on Marie and Kayla's door a few minutes later and came over to where Marie lay in bed. "Maybe you're right about having more in common with your dad," she said. "At least at this moment in your life. But I'm your mom, and I'm here, and I'll always be your mom."

"I'm gonna try and fall asleep, okay?" Marie sounded annoyed.

Laura left the girls' room and went into her own room. Matt patiently reiterated truisms about how teenagers are for a long time, but Laura couldn't seem to stop crying. She was still crying as she fell asleep, like a heartbroken child herself, like a baby crying it out alone in a crib.

11

The next morning, Kayla and Marie walked to the subway alone. Laura had left a note next to their packed lunches on the kitchen counter, saying that she'd had to leave for work early. Marie, who had been dreading a lecture, breathed a sigh of relief. Kayla looked at her with alarm.

"No, this is worse," she said. "She's letting it fester. She's still really angry with you. You're not going to get off easy. She's going to stay mad for a really long time."

Marie shrugged and opened the fridge to get some cold water from the pitcher there. She couldn't exactly remember what she had said to her mother in the bathroom when she'd gotten home but there was a strange numbness around her thoughts about it, as if her brain was trying to protect her from an extremely bad feeling that was still to come. Her stomach did not feel great. What had happened with Tom wasn't good, either. She still liked him, maybe, though probably that wasn't a correct way to feel. She tested out the memory of being in his bed to see if it felt exciting, the way imagining it had felt exciting, and found only the same curious nothingness. She imagined checking her serotonin levels the way you would check the level of a liquid in a deep, opaque container by dipping a stick in. She imagined that the stick would be wet only at the very bottom.

As they left their building and stepped onto the wide side-walk, Kayla put on her headphones. Marie reached over and pulled them off.

"Talk to me, please? I'm not feeling good."

Kayla blew air out between her lips. She looked pretty today, Marie distractedly noticed. She wasn't wearing makeup, she almost never did, but she'd brushed her giant tangle of hair and tied it up in a cute patterned scarf, and she was wearing new jeans with one of her typical oversize sweatshirts. For some reason, maybe her expression, she looked less like a little kid than she usually did.

"Oh, I'm sorry, are you suffering a consequence of your actions? Let's stop everything and tend to your needs, Marie. Let's just ruin everyone's lives until you start feeling good again."

"Wait, what?"

"Do you think it's easy, being the one they don't have to care about?"

"Of course they care about you. They just don't have to worry about you, because you're so . . ."

"So what? So boring? So not fucked up? You have no idea what's going on with me, Marie. No one does. I might as well not exist!"

Marie fumbled around inside herself trying to find the right feelings to have about what Kayla was saying. She was right, of course, but there was nothing Marie could do about it retro-actively. It wasn't her fault that she had always been her parents' most high-maintenance kid, and she resented being blamed for it.

But she also cared about Kayla, and recognized that being in her position right now sucked. She was just so tired, though. Caring about anyone besides herself seemed like it would take a kind of energy that she didn't have.

"Well, what do you want me to do?"

"I don't know. There's nothing to do. It's just a shitty situation. Luckily we don't have to live at home much longer. Luckily I have friends who actually notice how I'm feeling and are curious about what's going on with me, unlike my own sister."

"I'm curious!" said Marie.

"Bullshit," said Kayla.

They started walking again in silence.

"I do care about you," said Marie after a while. "I'm sorry I'm such a terrible sister."

"You're not even really my sister," said Kayla, very quietly. They were almost at the subway. It was too cold to be out in just a sweatshirt. Kayla's makeup-less lips were pale, and her hands were fists inside her baggy sleeves. Marie couldn't even muster enough energy to feel angry at her. It was true, they weren't related by blood. But of course Kayla was her sister. They had slept in the same room, sometimes in the same bed, since they were old enough to remember anything. She decided to let Kayla be mad. She deserved to be mad at Marie; everyone did. They all deserved a break from Marie. She wished that she could take a break from herself.

"I'm going to get a coffee before I get on the subway. I'll catch up with you later."

"If the train comes before you get to the platform, I'm taking it," said Kayla, trying to sound indifferent and not upset.

"That's fine. You totally should. I'll talk to you later. Love ya." She tried to say it casually, like it was something she said all the time, but erred on the side of inaudibility; at least, Kayla didn't show any signs of having heard her.

Marie walked to the bodega on the corner by the subway. When she'd been younger, she'd had a good relationship with the teenager who manned the counter in the early-morning shift, relieving a relative who'd been up all night selling cigarettes and Red Bulls and lottery tickets to the people who bought those things at two and three and four a.m. They'd bantered whenever she came in, and even broken the unspoken rule of bodega boundaries by introducing themselves and sharing some biographical information about each other. His name was Ashraf and he was from Yemen. And then one day he'd been gone, replaced by a similar-looking guy who didn't even thank Marie when she put her tea on the counter and handed across her dollar fifty. The new guy had earbuds in his ears and was always in the middle of a phone conversation. Marie had never gotten up the nerve to interrupt his phone call to ask where her friend—well, semi-friend—had gone. Maybe back to Yemen, or maybe he now worked a different shift. She had grown up with this kind of disappearance happening perpetually all around her, and most of the time she didn't even consciously notice it. The neighborhood where she'd lived as a small child was now unrecognizable; only a few storefronts, like Peter Pan Donuts and some of the Polish stores, were the same ones she'd walked past on Manhattan Avenue every day to go to day care. Glass towers rose near the waterfront wherever you looked. The run-down playground at the northernmost tip of Brooklyn, which had once been full of intriguing stray cats and canopied by 360-degree skies, was now nice but ordinary, and walled in by construction sites. People and buildings were whisked away as soon as you got to know them; there was almost no point in remembering that they'd ever been there at all.

She filled her paper cup with hot water and selected a tea bag from the little display of boxes in front of the coffee station, noting with satisfaction that there were exactly as many bags of her favorite kind, Devonshire English Breakfast, as there had been on Friday, when she'd last been here. No one else drank her tea here. This bodega was almost an extension of her home.

While she waited for the tea to steep, she turned to get money from the ATM. An idea was forming in her mind, still very vaguely, but the one certainty was that she would need money to make it work. She had an allowance that was supposed to be for clothes and shoes and school supplies, but she had managed to save it lately; she hadn't bought new fall clothes and shoes yet. She checked her balance: about $250. If she took a bus to Boston, a cab to where Daisy lived shouldn't be that expensive. She would just go for a day, not long enough to really worry anyone, and then come right home. She would see whether meeting her biological grandmother would help her somehow, and she would find stuff out about her dad that you couldn't find out from the internet or from her mother. And she would ask about the lost tapes, for Tom, because he'd like that and he'd like her more. Then she would come home, apologize to Kayla and her mother, and turn over a new leaf, somehow.

She finished up at the ATM and took her cup to the counter. The new cashier looked at her with his usual lack of interest as she handed over her change, but then surprised her by handing her a banana. "You need to eat," he said, and she wasn't sure at first whether he was talking to her or talking on his phone. But she was grateful for the banana as she waited for the subway. She hadn't managed to eat anything yet that day and hadn't realized that she was ravenous.

12

Laura had been sitting in a gray-walled recording studio in Midtown since before sunrise, alone with her guitar and a mic and a kind but vague stranger behind the soundboard who tentatively asked her now and then if she'd like to go again. She had a piece of paper where she was pretending to jot things down, but really she was just getting more and more frustrated with herself, occasionally checking her phone to see the increments of her rented time counting down. She had to be at school in just under three hours, and it would take at least thirty-five minutes to get there. There both was and wasn't still time to make today's endeavor worthwhile.

She'd wanted to book a session in the same recording studio where she'd visited Dylan fifteen years earlier, but that building and everything else on its block in Bushwick had been demolished, it turned out; on Google Earth, she saw the glass-and-steel condo lump that had risen in its place. It was too bad because she had been counting on memories of the heightened, desperate feeling she'd had in that room to help her get into the right mindset to produce a song. She needed access to that fever pitch; she had never managed to create anything without it, except for the nonsense jingles she'd made up for the baby classes out of loopy sleep-starved desperation.

Though, thinking about it more, she had wanted badly to write real songs during that part of her life. She remembered spending time with toddler Marie—those endless hours before a morning nap, or the similarly infinite spans in the late afternoon before bedtime—and feeling the stifled urge to release a song that was thrumming inside her, keeping her alert as she picked up and restacked blocks or reread a book about animal noises for the fourth consecutive time. Of course, if she'd been presented with a spare day in a recording studio in any of those moments, she'd likely have flailed around not knowing what to do with it, just like she was doing right now.

"I'm just going to play an old song to warm up," she told the engineer, who nodded at her wordlessly. He was probably counting down the minutes, too, looking forward to getting a sandwich or something, or to greeting whoever had booked the day's next session, someone who would likely be competent, or at least play music.

Fuck! She had to get it together and transmute the self-hatred and impotence she felt into something resembling creativity. She played the opening of her old song about Dylan, the plaintive one about wondering whether someone was your boyfriend, and without thinking too hard, began to make up new words to it, nonsense words at first. She sang angrily, loudly, the way she'd sung in the shower as a teenager, when she'd mistakenly thought that the noise of the water drowned her voice out. Gradually the song became a new song, though it had something in common with the old one. She repeated a chorus over and over again, some nonsense about someone not loving you the way you loved them.

She couldn't get any further than that. Still, it was something. She tried it again in a different key, and spent some time thinking about an arrangement with other instruments. At the end of her session, she sent a file of the song to Callie in an email titled "possible song in progress?" and then felt grateful that the rest of her day would keep her busy enough that she wouldn't be able to check email again for hours, waiting for Callie's response.

———

It occurred to Marie, as her bus pulled up out of the ugly warren of tunnels under Port Authority and began to make its lumbering way out of the city, that she had never left New York on her own before. She hadn't realized how easy it would be to just buy a ticket, wait in line, and escape. She would be in another city in just a few hours, a place she'd never even visited before. No one had stopped her to ask where her parents were. No one had even looked at her twice, or asked her for ID. She had the backpack she'd left home with that morning, full of useless schoolbooks. She wished she'd thought to pack a change of clothes, but she had her phone and charger and her ATM card. She could wear her underwear inside out tomorrow. She was filled with the sense of power and well-being that comes from deciding to do something on a whim and actually having the nerve to follow through.

The bus ride passed quickly, the blur of 1-95 interrupted only by a bad chicken sandwich at a rest stop in Connecticut. She had a window seat, and the bus didn't smell overwhelmingly of piss and disinfectant. The girl sitting next to her cleared her throat with an ominous crackling gargle every so often and blew her nose a lot, but she was at least apologetic about it, and with her headphones on, Marie barely noticed.

Figuring out where Daisy lived had been easy. The town was mentioned in Dylan's Wikipedia entry, and from there she'd just googled Daisy's full name and the name of the town and gotten both her workplace and home address. She also found an obit for Dylan's dad, who'd died of a fast-moving random cancer just a few years earlier. Her grandfather. It would have been nice to have met him, she supposed. She tried to feel angry at her mother for a moment, but instead just felt guilty. If Laura knew where Marie was, and where she was going, she would be so upset, even more upset than she'd been last night. Marie wasn't sure exactly what she'd said to hurt Laura so badly, but she sensed that something had fractured between them, maybe irreparably. If only she hadn't been so wasted, and if only she could just communicate effortlessly with her mother and make her understand how she felt—just to be able to share it with her, without alarming her or upsetting her. But that had always been impossible, and maybe always would be. She would text later to say that she was spending the night at a friend's house.

The car ride from the bus station to Daisy's house was longer and more expensive than she'd counted on; she hadn't factored in rush-hour surge pricing, but she still figured she would be able to afford the return trip and her bus ticket home. The driver didn't ask why she was taking a $100 ride to a random suburb, or try to talk to her at all. Somehow getting into a stranger's car seemed more fraught with peril in Boston than it did in New York. She had a moment on the highway when she'd realized that if the driver decided to kidnap and rape or murder her, there wasn't anything she would be able to do about it. But then she looked at the blue dot on Google Maps and saw that it was headed in the exact right direction. There was a small photo of a baby stuck on the guy's dashboard; he wasn't a murderer. And soon they were pulling into the driveway.

The house itself was beautiful, red like a barn-house toy she'd had as a child. She got out of the car and breathed crisp, piney fall air, a huge relief after the sanitized stuffiness of the vehicles she'd spent all day trapped in. The driver gave her a dispassionate wave and was gone before she had even made her way halfway up the stone path toward the front door.

Now she was stuck here. There was nothing to do but knock.

The sun was beginning to dip behind the tree line of the pine forest that surrounded the house, and there didn't seem to be many lights on inside. Briefly, Marie freaked herself out by imagining that maybe no one was home, and no one was coming home, but she did it in the same way that you purposely scare yourself when you're fumbling for keys that you know are definitely somewhere in your bag. Someone *was* in the house, she was almost certain, but that someone might be hoping she would go away. After a few minutes, this theory was proved correct: as Marie moved to knock again, a muffled voice came from the other side of the door.

"I'm not interested in discussing Dylan with his young fans, and since this is private property, you could be arrested for trespassing," the voice said calmly.

"Okay, that's fine. I'll leave. I'd just like to come in for a second and charge my phone," Marie said.

There was a long pause, and the sound of a dog scratching to be let out. Finally Daisy heaved a sigh and opened the door. The dog, a yellow Lab, bounded joyfully past Marie and into the yard, where she turned in circles a few times before relieving herself.

Marie couldn't help but compare Daisy to her other grandmother, who wore a lot of makeup and sweaters with ribbons and bells on them. Daisy was much more austere. She had white hair, cut in a bob, and was wearing loose jeans and leather L.L.Bean slippers. Marie tried to make out any family resemblance between her own face and Daisy's; if there was any, it was in her large eyes and furrowed forehead. Daisy didn't look like a happy person.

She was looking past Marie at the dog, whom she beckoned back inside with a commanding wave. Then she turned and gestured to Marie in a very similar way. "You can charge your phone, but then you're going right back to wherever it is you came from. I'm not running a tourist operation here. It's ghoulish and it doesn't do me any good."

"I'm sorry that you have to deal with people coming here," Marie said.

"You're sorry!"

"I'm different," she said, not knowing quite how to phrase it. She'd come up with a few different alternatives on the bus, but now that she was here, they all seemed melodramatic.

"Oh, everyone thinks they're different," said Daisy.

13

"You're not the first person to come here and try to convince me they're his child."

Daisy had poured herself and Marie both glasses of white wine from a large bottle, filling them both to the very top. It was flattering to be presumed to be an adult, and she wanted the wine, but something made Marie feel like she had to be honest with Daisy about everything in order to be believed about the crucial thing. "I'm only fourteen," she said, gesturing to the glass. It had gone through the dishwasher, she could tell, but still wasn't quite clean. The whole house was like that: a veneer of tidiness, but dust on everything, piles of unsorted mail, a musty dog-smell that was almost but not quite canceled out by the woodstove and the general freshness of the air outside.

"I'm sure you can handle a glass of wine if you're related to me," Daisy said with a grimace.

"I do have a high tolerance," Marie said, and took a sip. "So you believe me?"

Daisy scowled as she scrutinized Marie's face. "You're more plausible than the rest. And I met your mother once, I think. She was one of the ones who was seeing him around the time of his death. The one who was also in a band, with that beautiful friend of hers."

"Callie. Yeah. My mom's beautiful, too."

"She was pretty, but I didn't understand what he saw in her. She was a pushover. Too shy to be a singer. Not a match for him. They wouldn't have lasted."

"Well, probably no one's relationships that they have in their early twenties are meant to last, right?" Marie took a sip of her wine and pretended that this was hard-won knowledge, not something she'd assimilated from TV shows.

"I met Dylan's father when I was twenty-four. We were together for three decades. He stood by me through everything." Daisy's tone was deadened, not sentimental or wistful. "Now he's gone, too." Her glass was empty already, and she poured herself another; the bottle was still on the table. It wasn't the kind of wine Marie's parents drank; it tasted sugary, almost like a spoiled soda, but she gulped it down almost as fast as Daisy did. She was hungry, and the sugar in the wine was almost like eating food. She felt exhilarated. This was her grandmother! Marie felt like she was unraveling a mystery, though it wasn't clear what she was trying to solve. She'd known that Daisy existed, and that she was her father's mother. Was there something more to know? She struggled momentarily to remember why she'd come.

She'd thought her dead father, or what remained of his family, could be an alternative to her living mother. She knew her mother loved her but also wanted her to be a happy child still, and to stay that way forever, and it was already too late for that. She could tell that her sadness made Laura uncomfortable—it wasn't transient like Laura's own sadness, it was something bigger that she couldn't handle. It made Laura feel like she'd failed, and that was too horrible a thought to cope with. That after all the effort she'd put in, and everything she'd sacrificed, there was something wrong with Marie that she couldn't fix. And Marie, in turn, felt like she'd failed Laura, which made her feel even worse. It was impossible to talk about any of this, of course, so instead they fought about rules.

Whereas with Daisy she could start fresh. She might understand what it was like to be defective, brain-wise, in a way that couldn't be cured by a good night's sleep or a walk around the block.

"Tell me about our family," Marie said. "I want to know where I come from."

"I will, but first you should call your mother and tell her where you are, so that she doesn't worry about you," said Daisy. "Well, she'll still worry. But at least she'll know where you are."

14

After Laura got off the phone, she didn't tell Matt right away that Marie had run away from home. She cleared the table where he and Kayla had just finished eating dinner and put the dishes in the sink, then started washing them even though technically it was Kayla's turn to do this. Kayla did not point this out. She went into the living room where she spread out her notebooks on the coffee table and put on her giant pink headphones. Matt came up behind Laura and embraced her as she scrubbed a hardened ridge of dried-up lasagna noodle off a Pyrex pan, and she stiffened and nudged him away with her one raised shoulder. He took a step backward.

"I've told you a million times that I hate it when you do that," she hissed.

"Jesus, sorry that I wanted to hug you. What's going on?"

She turned off the water and wrung out the sponge, wiping the lip of the sink before resting it on the edge, where it balanced above the remainder of the dishes still floating there in a puddle of greasy, sudsy water. Looking at what remained to be done, Laura felt a wave of exhaustion. The dishes would dry, she would put them away, and then tomorrow her family would get them out and dirty them again, and on and on. Sometimes someone else would help, but most of the time Laura would be the one who moved the dishes from cabinet to table to sink and back. She sat down at the kitchen table and swept up a pile of crumbs with the edge of one hand, then just left them in a pile there, too defeated to stand up again and ferry them to the trash can.

"Marie took a bus to Boston this morning. She tracked down her biological father's mom, who I haven't talked to since Dylan's memorial service and who I'm pretty sure is not a stable person. I know she must not be a huge fan of mine. Anyway, she's there now, getting to know her 'dad's side of the family,' as she put it."

She caught the look of hurt in Matt's eyes before he quickly looked away. Even though Marie called him "Matt," it was understood that he was, for all practical purposes, Marie's father. Matt was what "dad" had meant to Marie since she'd been able to form memories. It was ridiculous that she could bring herself to use that word to refer to anyone else.

"I guess it's to be expected, right? You remember what being her age was like—I would have done anything to annoy my parents. She's just doing what she's supposed to be doing. And at least we know where she is, and that she's safe."

"We don't know that!" Laura exploded. "I have no idea what this woman is like!"

They both reflexively glanced over at Kayla, but she still had her head bent, bopping in time to whatever was playing through her headphones.

"Did she say when she was coming back?"

"I told her to come back tomorrow, that we'd pay for the train—I gave her my credit card info. She told me she'd think about it. I was so upset that I hung up on her. She'll *think about it?* What does she think, that she's going to go live there?"

"She can spend a couple of days, if she wants to. Let her get bored and miss her friends. She'll come around if you don't freak out and try to force the situation." He took a step toward her as though to hug her again, but she moved away, still unwilling to let him comfort her in any way.

"We're supposed to reward her for running away from home by being nice about it?"

Matt shrugged. "I'm just saying, every time you crack down on her, it pushes her further away. You know that it does."

Laura shook her head at Matt, past trying to communicate with him if he kept refusing to get as enraged as she was, or at least to meet her halfway. He was probably right about not pressuring Marie to come home, but who was he to tell her how to discipline her own child? Just because Kayla would never pull something like this didn't mean that Matt had some kind of parenting expertise that Laura didn't. It just meant that Kayla was a self-sustaining little jade plant of a teenager. Kayla's hardiness had as much to do with Matt as Marie's sadness and rebelliousness had to do with Laura. She wanted Matt to understand all this, but she was too tired to explain it all, and besides, what was the point? She felt a deep need for oblivion: a glass of wine, a cooking show, something to dull the terror that she felt every time she thought about Marie, miles away, sleeping in a strange bed in the home of a stranger who probably wanted to teach her how to hate Laura even more than she did already.

15

Daisy and Marie ate a sad limp stir-fry that Daisy dumped out of a frozen bag into a skillet, and drank more wine. Marie slowed down to focus on eating—though the food wasn't tasty, she was starving—and soon found her equilibrium returning. Daisy, though, got drunker and drunker, continuing to refill her own glass long after Marie had cleared the table and politely started washing the dishes. Daisy talked the whole time. She asked Marie a few questions about herself but used them mostly to springboard to complaints about her own family and life. Dylan's childhood seemed to have been her happiest time, and she looked past Marie with a dreamy expression as she told a story for almost half an hour about the first time a school music teacher had singled him out for a solo in the school band.

Marie tried to think of questions for Daisy, but she still wasn't sure what she wanted to know about Dylan, or why she wanted to know it.

"Do you think Dylan would have liked me?" she finally asked, as Daisy seemed to be running out of steam. There was only about an inch of wine left in the big bottle.

Daisy squinted at Marie and almost smiled. "I'm not sure," she said. "I don't know you well enough. I don't think he would have liked being a father—he wasn't ready to be one. Not at all."

"My mother wasn't ready to be a mother, but she did it anyway."

"Yes, and I think that's quite odd. I don't understand her decision. Didn't she also have a band? She probably thought she'd get some money out of it because Dylan was doing so well with his band."

"I really don't think so. That's not what she's like."

"So then why did she do it? Was she just disorganized and waited too long? That's been known to happen. I don't imagine she'd have told you that, though. She probably told you something about having been so in love, and feeling an obligation to honor his life in some way."

Marie shrugged. That *was* what her mother had told her, of course. She had never questioned it; it had seemed like the truth. Daisy was an asshole for trying to make her question Laura's motives. On the other hand, just because she was an asshole didn't mean that she was wrong. Maybe Marie's life—the baseline fact of her existence—*was* nothing but a long-con cash grab. It was the darkest thing she'd ever imagined about herself, but her odd day had left her in a mood where anything seemed possible. She thought of Laura's voice on the phone—resigned, tightly controlled, obviously trying not to yell. What if all her overprotectiveness, which had seemed like a form of love, had just been about protecting an investment?

No, there was no way. Marie hated her mother but she also loved her, and knew that Laura loved her, too. Their life together before Matt and Kayla, which she barely remembered, had been hard. Laura talked to her sometimes about their tiny first Brooklyn apartment, her fights with the landlord over rent and heat and bugs. No one made those kinds of sacrifices or feigned that kind of affection, long term, in the hopes of getting a cut of some royalties.

She finished loading the dishwasher, squeezed the water out of the dingy sponge and put it on the corner of the sink. "Well, I guess, if it's okay, I'll need to figure out a place to sleep?"

Daisy shook herself out of her slumped-over position at the table. "Of course. You can sleep in your dad's bedroom."

16

Laura had considered canceling her studio time the next morning, but Matt had convinced her not to do anything differently; she couldn't spend the day clutching her phone, waiting for Marie to call. Callie hadn't replied to the email; maybe what Laura had thought was a spark had been a dud. As she tried it over and over and made it sound somehow worse every time, it certainly seemed that way.

As she fumbled through her song one last time, she became aware that the band that had studio time booked next had arrived a few minutes early; she could hear them milling around in the cold cement hallway outside. This distraction was the last straw; she quit aimlessly strumming and started packing up her little pile of gear, turning off switches, generally aiming to leave the place nicer than she'd found it, unlike whoever had left an open bag of Cape Cod salt-and-vinegar chips on the console before her. Their stale, almost bodily odor mixed with the warm electrical smells of the room in an almost pleasant way, but she had still been mommishly offended. When she was satisfied that everything was tidy, she opened the door and let the band in.

They were kids, four boys, probably ten years younger than Laura. They mumbled hey and walked past her with their heads down, studiously rushing to maximize their time. The tallest one looked her in the eye as he passed. "Thanks for the extra ten minutes," he said.

"No problem; I wasn't getting anything done anyway," she admitted. She realized she sounded pathetic, but he laughed. "We've all been there. We're probably about to be there, but you gotta give it a shot."

There was a sharp line where his haircut ended and the skin of his neck began. On a man her own age, this kind of attention to grooming would read as suspicious, narcissistic, or overcompensatory. He was still looking at her, squinting in what seemed almost like recognition.

"Hey, this is so random, but did you play a show in Philly with the Clips like ten or eleven years ago?"

She was so shocked that she almost dropped the cord she was too deliberately bundling up. "Yeah, that was me. You've got a great memory."

"Oh, it made a huge impression. I mean, I was sixteen; it was one of the best shows I'd ever seen. You were incredible. Do you still play with them?"

"No, I . . ." She couldn't figure out how to explain the lost decade of her life quickly to a stranger. "It was just that one time."

"Well, if you ever want to sit in with us, it would be a total honor. I'm Leo, by the way."

She put down the cord so they could awkwardly shake hands. He was still making eye contact. Laura decided to pretend to Leo and to herself that this was the kind of encounter she had all the time, instead of only the second time she'd been recognized and admired in more than a decade.

"Hey, what are you doing right now? We didn't have anything we were really itching to play. We could just, like, jam?" He rolled his eyes as he said it to make sure she knew that he wasn't the kind of person who said "jam" in earnest (but was also still sincere about wanting to jam).

"I've got to go. I have a . . . thing," she said, for some reason not wanting to mention that the thing was work, or that the work was teaching middle schoolers.

"Okay, well, let me give you my number. We can do it some other time. Or not, but just so you know, it's, like, an option." Leo seemed weirdly flustered. It was bizarre to Laura to be the person in this situation who was making someone else nervous. She studied him more closely as he took her proffered phone and typed his number into it, then sent a text from it saying, "Hi Leo, it's Laura 😂." He looked up at her shyly as he did this.

The likeliest explanation for his behavior was that he just moved through the world like this—seducing everyone a little bit as his default mode. He probably got a lot of free coffee. She remembered going through phases, pre-Marie, of doing the same kind of thing—deciding to approach ordinary situations in an extra-charming way, just for fun, for variety. When she'd done this, she'd thought of it as "being Callie."

When he handed her the phone back, she tried to turn on that Callie mode, smiling with a "we have a mutual joke or secret" look in her eyes. She let her hand brush his during the phone handoff, and he actually blushed—it was working! She still had whatever measure of "it" she'd ever had access to. It was nice to know this, but also bittersweet to realize how meaningless this power was, and also how finite her access to it was. She was thirty-seven; how many more hand-brushes would there be?

On the curb outside the building she waited for an Uber, and when it came, she tried to keep her streak going with the driver, letting an extra hint of breathiness enter her voice as she made some meaningless comment about the weather. The driver made a noncommittal noise and returned to his phone.

She pulled her phone out, too, and looked at the text "she'd" sent Leo, then added another line. "Nice meeting u," she typed, then spelled out "you," then deleted the whole thing, settled on just a waving hand, but then couldn't decide whether to render her skin tone as white or tan or stick with default yellow. She finally picked one at random and then put her phone away and stared out the window, feeling her heart beat, thinking about a song.

———

Marie woke up early and tried to fall back asleep, but it wasn't working. She didn't want to be awake, but her heart was racing; something in her dreams had been chasing her through a maze, and she didn't remember the details, but she had not managed to escape. She rolled over and burrowed more deeply into the stale-smelling bed, trying to dive back down into unconsciousness. Her mouth was sticky and dry and there was pain in her body, not anywhere specifically but everywhere slightly. This was always the first sign of slipping back into depression: not wanting to get out of bed in the morning, not wanting to be awake but not being able to sleep, either.

Marie felt a surge of anger. She hadn't done anything to deserve a mood collapse. She'd taken her medicine, she'd talked to her therapist, she'd sat with her uncomfortable feelings instead of shoving them back down. It was so unfair that this curtain of blackness could just descend without warning and force her to slog through it. Was this just how her life was going to be forever, no matter how hard she tried to keep her brain healthy?

Maybe if she just started doing things, had some coffee, the black mood would lift, not worsen. Maybe she could will herself to feel better; maybe that would work this time. She pulled back the covers and forced herself to get out of bed and look around at the room, which she hadn't really seen last night, when she'd drunkenly fallen asleep in her clothes, facedown on her dad's old bed.

It was a teenager's room, but from another era. There was a Discman on the desk and a stack of CDs next to it, and the posters on the walls celebrated bands she'd barely heard of: Fugazi, Operation Ivy. She opened the shades and looked out on the expanse of the yard and the woods beyond. Snow had fallen overnight and turned everything pristine white. She tried to force herself to appreciate its beauty—sometimes this worked, fixating on details and making herself admire them so that her brain would stop chanting at itself about how bad she felt.

There were small black birds jumping around in the snow. The sky was bright gray. She had no boots and her jacket wasn't waterproof. Would she be able to leave as easily as she'd arrived, with snow on the roads? Part of her wanted to leave as soon as possible, but the process of getting a car to come pick her up and take her to the bus station, then getting a bus ticket, seemed unbearably daunting and exhausting. She felt weak and sick. Maybe she wasn't depressed, only ill? But she had no physical symptoms except a lack of appetite and a desire to lie down and drift into blankness.

The house was cold, echoey and empty-feeling. The dog was curled up on a rug in front of the woodstove, still asleep, and it seemed that Daisy was, too. It wasn't yet seven. The kitchen was more obviously dirty in the blank-white snow light; the bottle of wine on the table had fruit flies in the dregs at the bottom. Marie felt an overwhelming urge to get out of there. She wanted to text Kayla but wasn't getting a signal inside the house. There were coats and boots piled by the door, more than could plausibly be Daisy's, and Marie thought about how they must have belonged to her dead father and his dead father. She pulled on the first jacket that seemed like it might fit, a faded-red Patagonia parka, slipped her feet into Daisy's boots, and opened the door as quietly as she could.

The snow was perfect and untouched for as far as she could see; there weren't even animal tracks disturbing it, and the air stabbed at her lungs as though she'd plunged into cold water. She crunched to the edge of the yard and then saw what looked like the beginning of a trail leading into the woods; someone had cleared the brambles and pushed logs aside, at some point. Though it was now overgrown it was far from impassable. She imagined herself being led into the woods. The warmth of sleep still clung to her and made the air seem warmer than it was, but she was still aware that it was chilly. She took out her phone to see if her weather app had been able to refresh, so that she could see how cold it actually was, but her phone blinked off as soon as she pulled it out of her pocket. Well, that was how cold it was, then. So much for texting Kayla.

She heard a distant rushing sound that could have been a road or a river. Whichever it was, she decided to walk toward it, just to have a goal in mind. She wasn't worried about getting lost; she knew she would be able to retrace her footsteps in the snow, which would be a great plan until it started snowing again. The trail got less well defined and eventually she had to admit that it had stopped really being a trail at all. But then the rushing became louder, and she found herself walking along the edge of a stream. It was frozen at the edges but still moving in its center, and that led her to the edge of a frozen pond that stretched so far into the distance that the falling snow obscured its other shore.

It was beautiful, she told herself. There was so much beauty in the world, but she didn't get any satisfaction from any of it; it entered her through her eyes and did nothing to fill the infinite hollowness that had opened up within her. She was tired of walking, and so she sat down in the snow, feeling the cold and wet seep through her thin pants into the skin of her thighs and calves. She took out her phone again and noticed that her body heat had managed to revive it. With a reflexive flick she tapped the button that pulled up her most recent conversation with Kayla.

"I'm sad," she typed, a non sequitur under the last thing she'd texted, which had been about her homework assignments. Kayla responded immediately, asking where she was and when she was coming home, but her phone blinked off again before she could type anything back. She lay back and let fat flakes settle on her cheeks and trickle into her eyes. Dimly, the way you know information in a dream, she knew that she should be panicking, but somehow there was no panicky energy left in her. She closed her eyes and felt her body sink deeper into the packed crust of snow.

17

The perfect song that Laura had written as a teenager was coming back to her. Something about what she'd experienced with Leo—that flush, that wave of crush-feeling—had cracked the safe where her talent had been sitting and moldering away all these years. She was struggling to write quickly enough to keep up with her thoughts.

It was her lunch break, but she hadn't eaten; instead, she was sitting in the burnt-coffee-smelling glorified closet that passed for a teachers' lounge, scribbling in a college-ruled notebook she'd taken from the lost and found. Someone had previously used it to take notes in math class. She couldn't tell whether she was remembering the words she'd forgotten long ago or making up new ones, but it didn't matter. She summoned up a mental image of Leo, to linger in the moment that had felt so exaggeratedly good: the moment of being admired, being seen. The line of fresh-cut hair at the nape of his neck, and the idea of how it might feel under her hand. The feeling she'd been waiting to feel for so long was finally back, like it had never left; she knew this was a real song, and she could already imagine singing it over and over again.

She was so engrossed that it took her a minute to realize that her phone was vibrating, and she almost silenced it without even checking to see who it was, but habit overruled her tiny irresponsible impulse, and when she saw it was Kayla, she answered.

"Hi, honey, is everything okay? I'm in the middle of something and can't really talk."

"No, it's not okay, Laura, would I be *calling* you if everything was okay? I'm worried about Marie."

"I am, too, Kay, but we just have to wait. She'll come home when she's ready. I'm sure it won't be long."

"I think she's in trouble. She texted me a few minutes ago, and now she's not responding to my texts or calls. I have a bad feeling. She was weird when she left the other morning. What if she's getting depressed again, like, really depressed? What if she tries to hurt herself?"

"I think she's just acting out, pushing us away—I don't know what there is to do except wait for her to snap out of this."

Kayla was silent for a minute and then said, "I don't think so. I'm just telling you that I think she's not okay right now. Just call whoever she's with and see what's going on there, please—you have this woman's number, right?"

"I'll call her right now and let you know what I find out. Deal?"

She could hear the relief in Kayla's voice. "Deal. Please call back as soon as you can."

Laura looked at the time as she searched her texts with Marie to find Daisy's number. There wasn't enough time left in her lunch period to get any more work done. What if that spark was gone again the next time she tried to access it? Well, then it was gone. She couldn't worry about that now. She just had to have faith that it wasn't a fluke.

Daisy, when she answered the phone, sounded as if she'd just woken up. Laura could hear shifting around, footsteps, a dog barking, and then a silence on the other end of the line as she asked to speak to Marie.

"Seems like she went out for a walk . . . took my coat, that's good, it's much warmer than the cheap one she was wearing when she came here."

The sting of the insult about the coat barely registered. Laura reeled at the news that Marie was just *wandering around*.

"Seems like? Do you know when she left? Did she say when she was coming back?"

"No, I've been, I've . . . I'm not feeling well this morning. Tell you what, though, I'll have her call you as soon as she's back. It probably won't take her long to get tired of tramping around in the snow. It's freezing."

"Daisy, I'm concerned. Why did you just let her walk out the door? She has no idea what she's doing."

"Now this is my fault? No, I don't think so. It is not my fault that you can't control your own daughter, you dumb bunny," said Daisy.

Laura took a deep breath; getting upset would not help. Panicking would not help. She had to try to get Daisy on her side; the important thing was making sure Marie was okay. Beneath Daisy's defensiveness there was guilt, Marie could tell; she knew she was in the wrong, and was trying to shift the blame so she wouldn't have to feel it.

"You're right. You're so right, Daisy. But I know you know how it feels to worry about your child and to know you can't protect them. Right now it would just make me feel so much better if you would go outside and see if you can find her. Maybe she's right nearby and we can both breathe a sigh of relief together. Okay?"

Daisy was silent, but Laura could hear rustling. "I'm putting on my coat," she finally said grudgingly, then hung up the phone. Laura sat in the teachers' lounge silently for a minute, hoping she would call back immediately, but when a call did come, it was Kayla.

"She's not sure where Marie is," Laura admitted. "And it's snowing there—I think you were right to worry."

"Come pick me up and let's drive up there right now."

Laura looked down at the math notebook, but only for a second. The music had left her mind completely; she was already figuring out the logistics, rehearsing the excuses she would make at the front desk and telling the student teacher who'd cover her class which busywork exercises to assign. "I'm on my way to you. Maybe your sister will call us back before we even get to the car."

"Probably," said Kayla, but Laura could hear in her voice that she was pretending to have confidence that she didn't feel, and that brave effort on Kayla's part was what finally pierced her with real terror.

All the fear she'd felt up until this point in Marie's life, she realized, had been tempered by a deep-seated belief that everything would actually be okay, that nothing truly bad could or would happen to her own family. But that wasn't true now; it had never been true. The compulsive loops of worry had been a shield, but they hadn't worked. She almost ran out of the building. She left the notebook behind.

18

Matt was waiting for them at the garage with a bag packed with basic clothes, toothbrushes, and contact lens solution, as she'd requested. He also had a backpack of his own stuff with him. Laura stared at the bag and at Matt.

"You're coming?"

"Why wouldn't I? You don't know what you'll have to deal with when we get there, I can help with the driving, and I already took the day off work."

"What about tomorrow?"

"I'll figure it out."

They stared at each other for a moment and Laura became aware of how rarely she really looked at Matt. His face was just as it always had been, his friendly, softly lined, stubble-pocked face that could have desperately used a good scrub with an exfoliating cleanser and a dose of moisturizer, neither of which he would ever use. She thought very fleetingly of that morning and Leo. It already seemed like an extremely long time ago.

Matt's dark eyes were opaque to her, even as she searched in them for something to latch on to, something he could be to her in this moment besides an extra driver. It would be nice to have an extra driver. But they really couldn't afford for him to miss two days of work in a row; he was paid by the hour. Laura had paid sick leave. And she really didn't want his help—it would come with a tax, she knew, of his interference, his judgment, his witnessing her fear.

"Honey, it would be nice to have one of us here to hold down the fort. And we need you to go to work tomorrow."

"We can handle my missing one day, Laura. It's not going to mean that Kayla has to go to community college."

"I'm right here," said Kayla, who was leaning up against the car, not looking up from her phone.

"Well, Kay, explain to your mom that you think I should come get Marie with you guys. I'm her father?" he said, letting upspeak sneak into his voice as it always did when he was nervous or unsettled.

"You are," said Laura, "but I have to handle this on my own. You can have everything all nice for us when we get back. Fold the laundry. Get groceries. We'll keep you posted about everything that happens."

"I'm staying out of this," said Kayla, but when Laura booped the car's doors unlocked, she got into the passenger's seat. "We'll probably be back really soon, right? I could probably not even have to miss a full day of school?"

"You don't have to come with me, either, if you don't want to," said Laura, "but it was your idea."

"Oh no, I'm coming. Bye, Dad! Love you!" She closed the door and sat in the turned-off car, looking at her phone.

Laura moved toward Matt to hug him, but his body did not respond to the hug. This wasn't good, but she didn't have time to care. Trying to parse her feelings for Matt, which had until recently been the cozy, non-worrying equivalent of a big, bland meal, was a layer of complication her brain couldn't process at this time.

"Please do let me know as soon as you've spoken to her."

"Of course," said Laura. "Please try not to worry."

"About her or you?" he said quietly as she got into the car, and she pretended not to have heard him.

———

They'd barely gotten outside the city when Daisy called. Kayla answered the phone, which was excruciating for Laura; she had to wait a maddening minute trying to parse the possible meaning of Kayla's *mm-hmm*s. When Kayla hung up before Laura got a chance to talk to Daisy, Laura was so upset that she almost inadvertently swerved into the SUV in the next lane.

"Why didn't you let me talk to her?"

"Because you're driving? You said it's illegal to talk on the phone and drive and no one should ever do it."

"Your sister is *missing*! What did she say?" She was pulling over, preparing to call Daisy back.

"She said she looked around in the yard but didn't find her, that her tracks in the snow led into the woods, but that she's not worried because the path in the woods leads into town, and she's probably at the Dunkin' Donuts or something."

"So is Daisy going to the Dunkin' Donuts?"

Kayla rolled her eyes and handed the phone over. They were parked on the shoulder, slightly too close to a bend in the highway for comfort, but Laura ignored her claustrophobia as she waited for Daisy to pick up the phone again. She was letting it ring for a ridiculous amount of time considering that she'd just put it down. Finally, she picked up.

"I'm going to go look there now," she said, anticipating Laura's question. She sounded drunk.

"Are you sure you should be driving?"

"What's that supposed to mean?"

Laura felt a convulsion of rage pass through her. Now she knew that she couldn't ask Daisy to keep looking for her daughter. If Daisy fell in the woods or crashed her car, it would be Laura's fault. Maybe it was time to get the cops involved, though they probably wouldn't do anything; Marie had been missing for only a few hours, and she was likely, as Daisy suggested, just hanging out somewhere indoors and safe with a dead phone.

Except, what if she wasn't? Laura had a visceral flash of Marie's face during her first depressive episode: the horror of looking into her daughter's eyes and seeing the glazed blankness there. She remembered what it had been like to realize that she was talking to someone who didn't just not want to be talking to her but who didn't want to be, period.

Marie had been fine for so long now; Laura had almost forgotten that she hadn't always been. The latest iteration of teenage-rebel Marie had been alarming but full of spunk. She hadn't seemed like someone who would hurt herself, but Laura also knew that those moods could change on a dime. Maybe the drugs she'd taken the other night had set off some chemical reaction. She thought about calling the doctor who'd prescribed Lexapro and Abilify for Marie, but it didn't seem like there was time for anything now except to keep driving, as quickly as possible, to try to get to Daisy's before nightfall. If Marie hadn't come back home or made contact with Kayla or Laura by then, that would be the time to call the doctors and cops and freak out. Right now she was still probably just overreacting. Right now she could still imagine that everything would turn out to be fine.

———

It was still light out by the time they arrived, but barely; dusk was gathering at the edges of the woods, and it was already hard to see the tracks that Marie's borrowed boots had made in the snow. "There are two paths; the one into town veers off to the right about ten feet into the woods," Daisy said from the yard. She was holding her dog's leash as he strained at the end of it. She didn't seem drunk, just tired and wary and unfriendly. Laura wanted to punch her in the face.

Instead she willed herself to make eye contact, to ask her civilly if they could take the dog. "She's not going to help you track the girl, she's not trained like that," Daisy said, but she still handed over the leash.

The dog bounded forward down the path, obscuring the tracks as she rushed through the snow, heading straight in, away from the town path. Kayla and Laura followed after her without another word to Daisy.

The dog seemed thrilled to be outside, and Laura wondered how often Daisy took her on long walks; she was a young dog, not the one she'd met the last time she'd visited this house. It didn't seem quite real that she'd been there before; she never thought about this place, though it was such an important one, in a way. It was where Marie's father had been a child and an unhappy teenager, and where Marie herself had likely been conceived. No wonder Marie had felt some kind of pull toward it.

Laura shouldn't have left this part of her daughter's existence shrouded in secrecy just because it was inconvenient for her to acknowledge it. She had done so much wrong. She had done her best. She silently promised that she would do everything so well, would put her entire heart and soul into making things okay for Marie and Kayla, if only Marie would be around the next corner, walking toward them wholly unharmed after a day of peaceful wandering. Laura would stop being distracted from her children by her pointless, fruitless hobby of dicking around with music, if that sacrifice was what the universe required in order to make Marie turn out to be okay.

The woods' silence was broken only by their footsteps, trees creaking in the wind and the dog's snuffles. "Are you thinking about how this is your fault?" Kayla asked.

"It is my fault," said Laura. "Who else's fault would it be?"

"I don't know, mine?"

"How would it be yours?"

Kayla shrugged, and Laura dropped her pace slightly in order to walk next to her; she had been rushing ahead, letting the dog pull her forward in a half run. "I should have known something was up with her. I should have told you she was gone sooner." She was trying to keep her face expressionless and cool, but tears were streaking down her baby-fat cheeks.

Laura stopped, though she wanted to keep rushing forward. She put her arms around Kayla. "It's not about whose fault it is. It's not about fault. And it's going to be fine. We'll find her and it'll be fine."

She let Kayla burrow into her shoulder and sniff tears and snot onto the waterproof fabric of her coat. It had been forever since either of the girls had cried on her shoulder; it reminded her of when they used to cry daily about some tiny disappointment or delay. A snatched toy or a sad cartoon could dissolve them. And then at some point they'd learned to control their tears, or keep them to themselves. She had forgotten this feeling: a child's full weight leaning on you, depending on you, needing to collapse into your body for comfort. She loved Kayla, of course, but suddenly she craved having Marie in her arms like this. The other night in the bathroom, as Marie had bitched about their lack of closeness—why had Laura not just gone to her and enfolded her and let her be a child again for a moment? She wouldn't have let me, Laura thought, and almost started crying along with Kayla but bit back her tears and steeled herself. The dog was going crazy at the end of her leash; they started walking again, redoubling their pace. Through the trees, she could see that there was a pond up ahead.

19

They carried Marie into the living room and put her on the couch while they waited for the paramedics to come, Laura crouching over her while Kayla sat on the floor nearby, googling on her phone what to do about frostbite and hypothermia. Daisy leaned against the kitchen island, staring into space and swaying slightly; she *was* drunk, Laura realized. Marie's eyes were shut, but she was breathing regularly. Her hands, though, were so cold that it terrified Laura. They felt like the hands of a doll or a mannequin: dead hands. She held them pressed between her own warm hands, willing the warmth to pass between them. If Kayla hadn't been there, she probably would have been crying or screaming at Daisy. But as it was, she felt an obligation to seem like she was in control of the situation. "She'll be okay," she murmured, and Kayla widened her eyes at her. Kayla liked to be the one who decided how much to worry.

"She was out there for a long time. I don't know why the ambulance isn't here yet."

"I should have gone out and looked for her sooner. I meant to, after you called," Daisy called weakly from the kitchen. When no one bothered to respond to her, she shuffled off down the hallway that led to the bedrooms.

"Go sleep it off, you witch," Kayla muttered, and Laura couldn't summon the energy to chastise her. But a few minutes later Daisy returned with a pile of blankets and heating pads. They all busied themselves draping them over Marie's prone body on the couch, working together in silence except when Kayla asked Daisy a question about the settings on the heating pad. They were still rearranging and draping the pile of quilts and afghans when they heard the siren, followed immediately by a sharp rap at the door.

"Oh, come in, Phil," said Daisy. She knew the paramedics, of course. The town was tiny. They were an older man and a much younger, almost teenage-looking woman, and they took Marie's vitals while they asked a series of questions about how long she'd been outdoors, medications she'd been on, whether she had a history of drugs or narcolepsy. While they were doing this Marie opened her eyes.

"I'm fine, just lil' tired," she said, slurring. "I got lost. Mom's here now." She looked at Laura and partially smiled, then closed her eyes again.

The young woman paramedic examined Marie's fingers, then let Laura resume holding her hands as she scrutinized Marie's feet. Her expression was professional and dispassionate, and Laura could tell immediately from the speed of her movements that she wasn't very concerned. Laura allowed herself to feel just slightly relieved. The paramedic looked up and addressed all of the women.

"You all are doing the exact right things already, and luckily she doesn't have severe frostbite, just what we call 'frostnip.' If you keep gently rewarming her she should be able to avoid any lasting damage, though the fingertips and toes may blister. Don't go dunking her in a hot bath anytime soon, just keep warming her up gradually. Offer her hot liquids when she's more awake. I don't think she needs to come in, Phil, do you?"

Phil shook his head. "Normal breathing, normal body temperature, I think all they'd do at the hospital is a psych eval." He turned to Laura. "Which, if you're thinking that's a good idea, we should go ahead and take her."

Laura impulsively shook her head. "No, we're good. Thank you so much."

Phil and his younger counterpart looked at each other. "Okay, then. Careful out there," he said. "It's going to keep being chilly like this, and it's risky if you're not used to the temps or don't have the right clothes."

"Thanks so much, Phil. What a relief! Tea or coffee for you two?" said Daisy, but they were already halfway out the door.

There was an awkward silence after they all listened to the ambulance drive away. Laura had been sure they were in for a long night in the ER, mysteries and pain and stress. Of course, the essential problem—that Marie seemed to have tried to kill herself—was still with them, but without any imminent and solvable crisis, it was hard to maintain their panicked momentum. And Marie was sitting up now, wincing as she moved her stiff hands, looking more alert.

"How did you guys get here?"

"We drove, dumbass," Kayla said, then started crying uncontrollably. Wordlessly, Marie stretched out her arms, and her sister fell into them. Marie shivered as Kayla hugged her, Kayla's back heaving with sobs. "We thought you were dead, you complete asshole," she said almost unintelligibly.

"I am a complete asshole," said Marie.

"Both of you stop it," said Laura. She left them sitting on the couch together and went into the kitchen, where Daisy was pouring brandy into a mug of tea.

"Is that for Marie? I read that you're not supposed to give someone alcohol when someone has hypothermia, because it's dehydrating," she told her.

"It's for me," Daisy said. "Would you like a cup?"

Laura shrugged and let Daisy decide for her, then accepted the hot mug as it was pressed into her hands and took a large gulp.

She and Daisy sat opposite each other at the kitchen table, its scuffed surface a testament to hundreds of family meals. Now Daisy ate there alone. She had no one. The alcohol was threatening to dissolve the dissociation that was keeping Laura from collapsing. She looked up from her mug and accidentally caught Daisy's eye, and saw something other than blankness and meanness there. Daisy understood what she had just been through, and would likely go through again, she realized with a thudding horror. Dylan had put Daisy through what Marie had just put Laura through, probably more than once. And then he had finally made her worst fears real. Laura had been so young the last time they'd met, and yet not a mother herself. She'd had no idea how to empathize with Daisy's loss. Also, Daisy was an asshole. But she was Marie's grandmother, and she understood.

"I'm sorry that I was so rude to you earlier," Laura said, hesitating to see how Daisy was receiving her meager offering. "I know that what Marie did wasn't your fault."

Daisy shrugged and continued firmly patted the dog's head, seeming to draw comfort from the animal. "It is, in a way. Genetics." They sat in a tense but amicable silence for a while, the dog's tail-thumping the only sound. From the other room, the girls' chatter filtered in, unintelligible but light and almost cheerful-sounding.

"She might try again, but you can't live your life around protecting her, you know. You can't save her by sacrificing yourself. If that worked . . ." She left the sentence hanging. "It doesn't work," she concluded.

"But what am I supposed to do?"

"You have to live your life," Daisy said, sounding resolute if tipsy. "At least let them see you trying to live. Maybe that helps. I don't know."

Marie appeared in the doorway. She seemed to want to step through but was hesitant to approach her mother, to interrupt. She had the shamefaced look of a child in trouble. Laura opened her arms and let Marie come to her, and she got to hold her as she had longed to do. For the moment, it was the only thing that mattered.

20

Marie woke up that first morning back at home in her own bed and looked up at Kayla's bunk above hers and only felt mild dread of the day that was coming, not crippling full-body horror. Maybe the fog was lifting. She got up and went to the kitchen and started the coffee and made herself toast. It was a Saturday, so she didn't have to worry about missing more school. She took her cup and plate into the living room and sat on the couch, munching and absently looking at her phone and waiting for the rest of the household to wake up. It was the first time she'd been up early in a while. She was still not doing okay, but she could feel herself on the escalator, toward the bottom, gradually moving toward the light.

Tom had texted her. She took the opportunity to block him.

Kayla and Matt emerged a few minutes later, blearily helping themselves to the coffee she'd made. She could tell they were giving her space, letting her be the first to initiate conversation. Was she really that scary? She felt Kayla look at her and then look away. They settled into different morning routines without really talking to each other. Matt lay down on the floor to do his physical therapy stretches for his bad knee.

"Where's Mom?"

"Sleeping in, I guess. She was really exhausted." Matt grunted as he crossed one leg over the other, supine on the floor. "How are you feeling this morning, okay or . . ."

"I'm fine, I'm going to be fine. I want to see Mom."

"She'll be up soon."

"Who's going to make us breakfast, you?"

Matt sat up. "Is that a challenge? I'm going to make a great breakfast. Your mom isn't the only one who can fry an egg around here."

"You know that she is, though," said Kayla.

"I'm going to wake her up," Marie said. She walked down the hallway to her parents' bedroom. When she and Kayla were little, they had waited as long as possible before rushing into her mom's bed on weekend mornings, but had always delighted in waking her.

"Shh, Mommy's sleeping," Matt would say, but they'd known that Laura was just pretending to be asleep. She looked the same now as she had then, one arm flung over her head, eyes squinting shut in a way that genuine sleepers' eyes never are.

"Mom, are you up? Can I talk to you?"

Laura stirred and pretended (Marie could tell) to wake up. She sat and tugged her T-shirt down over an exposed slice of her stomach. It occurred to Marie that her mom was beautiful; without makeup, with her dark hair a mess and circles under her eyes, she looked young and glamorously disheveled, like she'd been out late partying. She didn't have any set expression on her face, and for a minute she looked somehow not mommish. Marie had the discomfiting feeling that she was seeing her mother as she really was, as people who were not her daughter saw her. She winced when Laura turned to look at her and something about her expression—a patient brow furrowing, a barely perceptible tightening at the corners of her mouth—transformed her back into a mom. And this was a relief to Marie, as well as something like a disappointment.

Laura reached out her arms and wordlessly invited Marie to come lie down next to her. They snuggled back into the pillows and looked out the window at the leafless trees. The sky was winter-white. They were inside and warm, for the moment. Marie snuggled up to her mother's side, and Laura ran her hand through her daughter's hair, stopping at a snarl and patiently unknotting.

"You should comb your hair more often."

"Like I don't know that."

"You know, you're right. Comb it whenever you feel like it," said Laura, and instead of sarcasm Laura heard something else in her voice: acceptance, a peaceful kind of giving up. Maybe the crisis had shifted the rules around, and now Laura wasn't going to bother micromanaging Marie anymore because it didn't work and because it wasn't worth it.

Or maybe Laura just had something else on her mind. On their way home from Daisy's house she'd seen her mother receive a text that had made her face light up with a completely foreign variety of smile, and then just as quickly the smile had disappeared. When she'd asked about it, Laura had said that she was going to play a show soon and that Marie and Kayla should come if it wasn't on a school night, she would have to check.

"I'm busy then," Kayla said, even though she didn't know the date yet. "I have an important book I'm going to be reading that night."

Laura had shrugged. "Suit yourself." Marie hadn't said anything. She knew she would be there. She wanted to be there.

21

Laura called in sick to work, which she almost never did, so that she could prepare for her show. She didn't actually have to be at the venue until 9:00 p.m., a time of day that usually found her at home, tidying and prepping for the next day of her family's life or sitting on the couch with her bra off, halfheartedly trying to watch TV and check in on the day's news. She needed to save her energy for that moment. Somehow Laura knew that if she made herself do any of her ordinary activities—teaching, commuting, taking either of the girls anywhere after school, shopping, cooking, making dinner—she would be depleting some essential resource that she needed full reserves of in order to perform. So she lay in bed until everyone was out the door in the morning, then got up, showered, and forced herself out the front door without even breakfast or coffee. If she had stayed a minute longer in the apartment she would have begun taking the clean dishes out of the dish drainer and replacing them in the cupboards and picking up any of the stray articles of clothing scattered around the living room and moving them to the laundry hamper, and then she'd be doing the laundry because why not, and the whole point of her day off would be defeated.

Instead, she bought herself breakfast and forced herself to open the notebook where she'd started writing the new lyrics to her old song. She sat in the bad-good diner on Seventh Avenue, fried egg congealing on her plate, and tried to summon the words to create the feeling that she wanted people who heard this song to experience. It was hard because it was a feeling that she herself hadn't experienced in years. She had to remember Dylan in order to call up a flash of it, and then she had to edit out everything that tainted her memory of him. With her eyes closed she channeled their sweaty courtship in his fetid East Village apartment, remembering how it had felt to pine so hard for someone who was in the same room as you were—to want someone so badly it was like missing them while they were right there. There had been something animal and beyond logic about how she'd known, the first time they'd made eye contact, that she needed to fuck him. She would have run miles, committed crimes. The best pop songs were about that feeling, and the very best of them contained a word or a phrase or a tune that made the people who heard them feel it, too, in a homeopathic-level distillation that wouldn't destroy their lives in the way that experiencing that feeling for real would.

Feelings really could destroy your life, she knew. Lust, love, whatever you wanted to call what she was trying to evoke—it wasn't something she expected ever to feel again.

On the other hand, she was only thirty-seven years old. It was a fifty-degree late-winter day, just warm enough to make the ground and trees release a hit of wet spring. And Leo was just walking into the diner, coming over to her table. He was wearing a denim jacket over a ripped gray sweatshirt, and he smelled like he'd just woken up and come to meet her without showering or shaving. He smelled like sleeping in a warm bed. He was, very clearly, not a real adult; a real adult would have showered. He slid into the booth across from her.

He glanced over at the waitress. "Ready to go? I'm just going to get coffee first. I'm kind of hungover."

"You can finish mine, she just poured me a refill," Laura said, and tried to hand him the cup. But her hand collided with the side of his as he reached for it and the liquid sloshed out onto the saucer. Laura recoiled as though she'd been splashed, but she hadn't. Instead, she'd been zapped; skin-to-skin contact with Leo traveled up her arm and erased her brain. She couldn't prevent herself from looking into his face to see whether he'd also felt it. He met her gaze with frank, wide-open equanimity, a blank look that could have meant anything. Then he widened his eyes almost imperceptibly and gently bit his lower lip like "guilty."

Spending the rest of the day alone with Leo and then the evening onstage with his band was a patently terrible idea. Part of Laura wanted to run out of the diner, back to her apartment, and spend the rest of the day reorganizing the pantry and creating lesson plans for the rest of the spring. But she'd already posted on Facebook about the show. She'd invited Callie. She'd even invited Marie. She didn't want to disappoint her, though of course she inevitably would, in one way or another.

Leo's gaze dropped to the notebook and she hastily pushed it into her bag.

"I'm going to see the song soon enough. Is it almost done?"

"I think so, yeah."

"Then let's go to the studio and start trying to get it down!"

They walked by her apartment on the way to the train. There was a moment when she could have peeled off, bolted up the stairs, not even explained. It would have been weird, but she could have done it. But instead she kept walking, and in her head the song played on a loop, stuck there as if she'd heard it on the radio instead of made it up herself.

Acknowledgments

Thank you to my stalwart writing group: Anya Yurchyshyn, Lukas Volger, Bennett Madison, and Lauren Waterman. Thank you to mom thread, Meaghan O'Connell and Jessica Stanley. This book would not exist without you.

Thank you, Julie Buntin and Heidi Julavits, for giving me the chance to become a writing teacher.

Thank you to Atsuko and Satoru and to Sari Botton, for your welcoming hospitality and writing space in Kingston.

I'm very grateful to the entire team at Avid Reader for taking a chance on *Perfect Tunes* and working so hard on this book's behalf. I'm especially grateful to Jofie Ferrari-Adler and Julianna Haubner for their vision and guidance and patience during the editorial process.

Thank you to my family: Kate and Rob Gould, Ben Gould and Alex Willard, Alexander and Tatyana Gessen, and all of my aunts, uncles, cousins, and in-laws for supporting me and putting up with me.

Thank you to Ruth Curry, my best friend.

Thank you to Raphael (Raffi) and Ilya, for being the absolute best thing that has ever happened to me even if you do make it much harder to write books, and to Keith for making everything possible.

Thank you most of all to Donasia "Asia" Credle, for your friendship and for taking such good care of my children, and to Rebecca Winkel, for introducing me to Asia and for continually teaching me what it means to be a mother under any and all circumstances.

About the Author

EMILY GOULD is the author of the novels *Friendship* and *Perfect Tunes* and the essay collection *And the Heart Says Whatever*. With Ruth Curry, she runs Emily Books, which publishes books by women as an imprint of Coffee House Press. She has written extensively for the *New York Times*, *New York*, *The New Yorker*, *Bookforum*, *The Cut*, *Elle*, *Poetry*, the *London Review of Books*, *The Guardian*, *Slate*, *Jezebel*, *n + 1*, and *The Economist*. She lives in New York City with her family.